Bed Rest

Bed Rest

Rita Kashner

PIATKUS

For Howard

This edition first published in
Great Britain in 1987 by
Judy Piatkus (Publishers) Ltd of
5 Windmill Street, London W1
by arrangement with
Macmillan Publishing Co., Inc., New York 10022

British Library Cataloguing in Publication Data

Kashner, Rita
    Bed rest.
    I. Title
    813'.54[F]   PS3561.A6968

    ISBN 0-86188-561-9

Printed and bound in Great Britain by
Biddles Ltd, Guildford and King's Lynn

Acknowledgments

My thanks to the following people for their assistance to me in writing this book. Any lapses in *Bed Rest* are due to my not knowing what questions to ask, and not to the answers they gave me.

Susan Obel, endlessly patient, provided general background and technical information about the process of voice training.

My father, Ludwig Danziger, and Marvin Lifson shared with me their experience in the field of construction and in the perilous business of bidding a job.

Elisabeth Scharlatt edited this manuscript with care and love. Her perspective has been invaluable and her support unwavering.

Bed Rest

1.

I don't think, after all, that the Wednesday morning in April when it rained and I caught the cold was the beginning of it. It is a starting place, though. Start with that Wednesday. Start with me on the train, watching the Crestwood station recede and saying my Wednesday-morning litany over in my mind, orderly and watchful.

It was longer, the litany, because of the rain—because I had to check over in my mind that they were protected from the rain as well as from everything else. One at a time. *Randy*. All right; she had been picked up by the junior high car pool, would be returned home at 3:00 in the same station wagon. She had her lunch —I'd put it in her canvas bookbag myself. Was the sandwich in? Yes, I could see it lying across the top of the juice can and the apple. She had her raincoat. Had I checked to be sure the key was in its hiding place for her? Yes. Burners off in the kitchen so the house would still be there when she returned? Check; I could see myself touching all the knobs to be sure. Okay, Randy checked out. *Michael* . . . had I called to remind the school secretary he was eating lunch in school? Yes. Sandwich in the bag, bag in his knapsack? Yes, he'd fussed about the way I'd put it in. "I hate squished tuna fish," he'd said. "You always put it in so it squishes." Methodically he'd rearranged his lunchbag so the Fritos and the juice cans made a wall around the upright sandwich. I'd

3

had my head under the faucet, washing my hair in the kitchen sink while he finished breakfast and got his things together, but through the hiss of the water I'd heard the coins jingle as he dropped them into the bag. Richard's rule was that the kids could have only one sweet a day, not before 3:00, but Michael really hated to eat in school and it was our tacit agreement that on Wednesdays he'd take the money from the change jar and I'd let it go by. Where was I? Michael. Lunch. Check. Rain poncho? Check. Marion prepared to pick him up at 3:15 if it was raining? Check. Randy would be home by then to let him in. Anything special he'd been supposed to bring to school? No. Tomorrow he'd need the brown shirt and Randy's brown tights for his fox costume. Nothing today. Michael checked out. Now, had I locked the door? Yes, I could see myself switching the briefcase to my other hand so I could turn the key. Car locked at the station, money in the meter? Yes. Yes. All ends tied.

The impulse, as always, was to start all over with Randy and run it through again, but I forbade myself to do it. I closed my eyes sternly and took a long breath, held it, let it out slowly, pushing out the last of it, willing my shoulders down and the muscles of my stomach relaxed. When I opened my eyes, the Botanical Gardens station sign was gliding past and I was ready to look at the music.

It was a pleasure just to pull it out of the briefcase. I'd taken a tremendous chance, buying that briefcase. Not because of the expenditure—it had been drastically reduced at Lord & Taylor's because it was a little scuffed. And not because it wasn't the right thing—it was. The leather and the size of it and the squared-off handles said Real Work. I even liked it that it was scuffed; it made it seem established and matter-of-fact. It made me seem real. But that was the risk: what if I bought it, carried it for a semester or two, and then didn't become anything?

Richard didn't see it as a risk. "So you don't use it after this semester," he'd said. "You'll put it away and in a couple of years Randy will use it." Easy, like that. Hand it over to Randy. Hand it all over. He meant to take the pressure off me. I know that.

4

But as I walked upstairs that night to put the briefcase in my closet, I thought about Gideon. Let myself think about him. Pulled the encounter in the car out from where I'd buried it and gave it a proper airing, for the first time since it had happened.

Almost a week ago, it had been. The chorus was into final rehearsals at St. John's now, with the professionals, and as Gideon and I drove into the city we were talking about the strains of singing the Erb piece, where in spots the only notation was the basic key and each member of the chorus had to improvise for ten measures. Everyone hated the piece; three of the members, in fact, had handed in their music and refused to do the concert at all. I hadn't, because it was so important to me to be singing, but I hated the Erb, too. Especially the improvisation. "It makes me so uneasy," I told Gideon. "I never know how far to go. I stretch this far—" I put out a hand to show him "—and then I hear myself stepping on the others, so I back off. I can't wait for that section to be over." He covered my hand with his. "Freedom is terrifying," he said. "To everyone. You never know how far to go. It isn't just you—didn't you know that?" He curled his fingers around mine a little, so now he was holding my hand. A companionable gesture? In that case, it would have been an affront to pull it away. I didn't move. We kept on talking about the music and when we came to a light, he took his hand away to shift. Then he shifted back and took my hand again. So it was more than a friendly gesture, but now I couldn't make an issue of it. When he had to shift again, I reached for something in the folder to show him and then casually put my hand in my lap. He didn't seem to notice. He drove with both hands on the wheel.

The rehearsal was endless and full of tension. We didn't get out until 11:00. It was raining lightly as we walked to the car. "What's Richard going to say, you walking in at eleven-thirty?" he asked. "Richard will be asleep," I told him. He opened the door for me, and when he got in on his side I started to say something about the chorus director but he talked right through my words. "Sit still," he said. "I'm going to kiss you."

When I thought about the kiss, standing there at my open

5

closet door, it played back all over my body. Probing, it was, delicate and knowing. Not the groping, needy first kisses of the boys I'd known before I was married. Not any of the various assured kisses of marriage. It was civil. Leisurely. Sensuous. All that in a kiss. It had been a carefully delivered message. Only now, at the door of my closet, I was decoding it. "It's a problem I have with you," he'd said then. "How far to go. You have to help me a little. Cue me. Where are you?" "*Da capo*," I'd said, "to bar one. And staying there. We can't do this." He'd started the engine, turned on the windshield wipers. Before he put the car into gear, he'd touched my neck with the backs of two fingers. "We can, you know," he'd said. "And nicely. Quietly. But I won't come at you with it. You'll have to tell me, if you're ready."

Never, I'd thought. I'll never be ready for that kind of trouble. And for a week I'd imposed radio silence on my thoughts. But somehow when Richard said that about Randy and the briefcase, it felt good to remember it. Just to remember it. Now every time I looked at the briefcase, I thought of it a little.

The book was a collection of pieces for sightsinging, for a class in ear training I was taking at Mannes School of Music. The one I was worried about was a *bel canto* piece of Cherubini's, full of twists and turns and double dots. I'd meant to tackle it during the week, but I'd had to present an issue for consensus at the League of Women Voters' meeting and Michael had been home with a cold and it hadn't left much time for homework. The course didn't count for anything because I was only an extension student, but I was thinking about switching over to the diploma program and, more than that, I didn't want Mrs. Wilton to be disappointed in me. She taught with such passion, and she had hopes for me. That counted. I put my mind to the music.

When I got off the train I was following the Cherubini in my mind, trying to untangle the tricky timing in a beast of a passage. I had my umbrella up and I was doing that defensive minuet you do in the city when everyone's umbrella is up and you don't

6

want to be the maimed or the maimer, so I walked right through a big puddle without even seeing it. Just the kind of thing I yell at the kids for doing. I was wearing sandals, too, and my feet got soaked. Then the uptown bus was late, and I'd opened my raincoat to shelter the briefcase, so by the time I got to Mannes I was chilled. I saw myself reflected in the glass front door, hunched and besieged-looking. But then, past my reflection I saw the lights on inside and heard the stray sounds of practicing. I pushed the bedraggled image away and went in where it was warm.

Mrs. Wilton called on me first thing, and she did pick on the Cherubini. I only had to show her that the notes were correct, but it was such a pleasure to have the melody to fly with after the Erb that I really opened up. I got the timing right, too. But then as I went to sit down, I saw the faces. Surprise. Pleasure. Indifference. Scorn, in Enders's smile? Right, scorn for a posturing housewife pushing a pleasant voice past its bounds. Jesus, why did I expose myself? Fourth soprano from the right in the Philharmonia Chorale is plenty far enough, I thought. Now my face was hot and my toes were cold.

I walked out of the class with Mrs. Wilton at 1:00. We were talking about the possibility of my switching from extension status to the diploma program when she broke off and stopped a large man with dark, curly hair and very red cheeks as he walked out of a practice room. "Vincent," she said, "hold up a minute. This is Mrs. Clahr. She's a very good student of mine. I want you to hear what she does with a Cherubini *bel canto* piece."

"Now?" he asked. "My dear Rosie, civilized people are dining at this hour. I am on the point of starvation, and while I have no illusions about dining, I must certainly eat before I can attend to anything—even the voice of Mrs. Clahr. But you will lunch with me, ladies? And we shall discuss," he bowed floridly to me, "your career."

He meant it, too—about the eating and the discussion, both. He ordered meatballs and a salad and wine, and ate it all, with a basketful of bread. I ordered a chicken breast and pushed it

7

around on my plate while he grilled me and I tried to find the right tone for my answers. I went through worldly, demure, and earnest professional before I settled for bleak. It *was* pretty bleak. Five semesters of serious voice training in college. Three years of solo singing, until the age of twenty-one. Married now, two kids, twelve and seven. Yes, an occasional solo in the twelve years since I was twenty-one—PTA shows and such. Church. But I had been singing seriously in the Philharmonia Chorale for two years now.

"Lecrief? I know him. A good man," he said, chasing a meatball with his fork. He held it suspended, leveled an eye at me, and said, "And what do you do in Lecrief's chorus? You submerge? You—" he drew a long, low horizontal line in the air with the meatball "—blend in?"

I smiled. He had me. "Now I do," I said. "I've learned: a good chorus can't afford any solo voices."

"And Brescia tells you, a strong voice can't afford choral singing," he said. "It's the personality, you understand. Either you command the bow or you row in formation below; you can't do both. Rosie," he turned to her, "she can sing? Such a reed, so thin, and such a lady. She has a voice?"

"I don't even know that I *want* to train my voice," I said. "I just want to study for a degree. Teach, or something. Make a life in music."

"Yes," said Mrs. Wilton. "She can sing."

So I sang for him. He led us back to Mannes, to his studio, and I sang the Cherubini and sight-read some other exercises. I tried one of the Schubert *lieder*, but he made me stop. He was all business now, and after the first few minutes I wasn't nervous. It was like being with my college voice teacher. Mrs. Wilton left after the second exercise, and we went on for a long time. Finally he sat looking at me and drumming his fingers on the piano bench. "It's possible," he said. "The instrument is neglected and ill-used, but it's possible. You'll come to me once a week for now, and we'll see."

"What's possible?" I asked. "I'm almost thirty-three years old."

"The voice doesn't fully mature until forty," he told me. "And particularly if you've had training and solo work before, this is a good time for development. That's for the instrument. As for the rest—I cannot tell you what is possible. You will tell me, eventually."

When I left the building I had an application for the diploma program, course-choice forms, and a folder of music for solo voice zipped into the middle section of the briefcase. I didn't look at it at all on the way home, but I didn't take my hand off the briefcase either.

It was still raining hard when I walked into the house. I saw the boots and books piled up in the front hall—three pairs of boots, three bookbags—and I heard the television. I slammed the door and yelled hello. Randy came out of the family room. She had a Yodel in her hand, and she was trailing crumbs. "Hey, look what you're doing," I said. "Pick them up, and please don't walk around with food." She bent to pick up the little wads of chocolate and white cream, squashing one with her sneaker on the way down. But there was something dejected in the way she was holding her shoulders, so I didn't say anything, just scraped it off the floor with a fingernail and followed her into the kitchen.

"How was your day?" I asked.

"Okay."

I played the "okay" over in my head a couple of times for intonation: Okay, a day like any other? Okay, something bad but she didn't want to tell me? Someone put her down? Bad day in the junior high personality scrimmage? "Really okay?" I asked her. "How was your science test?"

"Easy. Rebecca wants to know whether I can play. I told her I'd call when you got home. Can I?"

"*May* you. How about homework?"

"Half an hour of French is all."

"Piano?"

"I'll practice after dinner."

"Why were you watching television if you had homework?"

"I dunno. It isn't much homework. Can I play?"

I knew why she'd been watching TV. She was lonely, coming into the empty house. "Okay," I said.

She headed for the phone. "Who's with Michael?" I asked.

"Evan."

"What are they doing?"

"*I* don't know. They're up there with the door closed. Making a hydrogen bomb, probably."

I stood at the bottom of the stairs and called Michael, forcing my voice. My throat was scratchy and I could feel the glands' under my jawbone. The rain, I thought. Michael came hurtling down the stairs. "I needed my fox costume," he shouted. He stood at the landing, Evan at his heels, and wrinkled his forehead at me. "I borrowed a dime from Mrs. Quintero and called you and you weren't home and they all tried on their costumes and got fitted but me. Where *were* you?"

"Michael, you know where I was. I was in New York, at my class. And it was Thursday you were supposed to have it. Tomorrow, not today."

"They did it today." His eyes were brimming and his voice was full, but he wasn't going to cry with Evan there. "So tough for you," he said. "The costume mothers said you'd have to fit it yourself. Come on, Evan." Evan, grinning, turned to go back up. Michael stood and looked at me for a minute. "It needs a tail," he said. "You have to make me a tail. By Friday."

I was standing at the sink getting the chicken ready for the oven and trying to remember what kind of a tail a fox has when I became aware of the headache. I took an aspirin and when the chicken was cooking and I had the table set, I went up and changed into a bathrobe and warm slippers. Rebecca walked in as I was coming back down with Michael's animal book in my hand. "Hi, Mrs. Clahr," she said. "You sick?"

"Yes," I said. "I think maybe I am. Or getting there."

It was because of the headache and the sore throat that I didn't say anything to Richard at dinner about Vincent Brescia. He asked me how my day had been, not remembering that it was

10

my Mannes day. Usually I reminded him and told them all much more than they wanted to hear. It was the only day in the week when I really had something to tell at dinner. But it hurt by then to talk, so I just said, "Okay. Wet." Then as soon as I had Randy settled at the piano and Michael in bed, I went to bed myself.

2.

I woke up hearing Richard explaining something. But it was dark. We were in bed. I listened for a minute: nonsense syllables. He was talking in his sleep. I tried to make it out, but only until I woke up enough to feel my throat. It was raw and screaming and the glands in it were painful. I felt my head. Hot, I thought. I got up for an aspirin and then, since I was up, went downstairs for juice. Even the juice hurt going down. And the whole upper part of my body ached. I thought about what I'd have to cancel: a morning meeting to arrange the program for the League luncheon; a junior high car pool. Oh, and sick or not, I had to make Michael's tail.

Richard was snoring when I got back into bed. I touched his arm. He was sleeping in his shirt again. For Father's Day last year I'd bought him two pairs of batiste pajamas from Spain, pale gray and white. But he slept in his underwear, or in his shirt. He only put on the pajamas when he wanted to make love—Saturday nights, usually. He rolled over. "You were snoring," I said. "Richard, I'm sick."

"Be fine," he said. He was asleep.

Just before daylight I dreamed I was sitting on a piano bench with Vincent Brescia. He was playing the Erb piece, the part before the improvisations. And he was kissing me. "We can do it quietly," he was saying. "You can improvise a solo." I was crying, trying to tell him that I wasn't ready for a solo, that I hated the Erb, that he had to stop and let me go, that I had to get home. Besides, Mrs. Wilton was watching and I was uncomfortable about the kissing. I didn't want her to be disappointed in me. Then I ran and ran for the train. I was still running when I woke up, and my pillow was wet. I was crying straight through my dream into the morning light.

There was so much talking I had to do that morning. Explain to Richard and Randy and Michael that I was sick, twice to Michael. Confer with Caroline, my co-chairperson, about the program for the League luncheon. Change my junior high car pool day to Friday. Arrange for Michael to eat lunch at Evan's. By the time they all left the house, my throat felt scraped raw through into my ears. I fixed some orange juice and took it upstairs with the paper. The bed was a mess. I pulled it roughly into order and rolled in. I fell asleep clutching the first section of the paper and ticking off in my head, car pool switched, Evan's for lunch, sandwich is in the bag, bag is in her knapsack. . . .

The phone kept waking me up. It did have an off switch, from the time when Richard had the back injury, but I was afraid to turn it off. What if one of the kids fell off the climbing bars in gym or got sick and needed to come home? So I explained to Michael's class mother and to Leone Taub, the League chairperson, and to my friend Laura that I was running a fever. "Tell you what," Laura said. "I'm making macaroni and meat sauce for dinner. If Leonard can struggle through it, so can your crew. Send Randy over for it after school. And don't say I never did anything for you—you owe me lunch at Windows on the World."

"Lutèce," I said. "Laura, you have no class," and fell back asleep.

I was awake and drinking orange juice when Gideon called. "Going to rehearsal tonight?" he asked. I had forgotten; there were only two more rehearsals before the performance.

13

"I can't sing," I said. "I'm sick; there's an inferno in my throat. Gideon, guess what."

"What?" he asked. "You shouldn't be talking."

"I have to tell you," I said. I did; I had to. "I may be going into the diploma program at Mannes. I may be taking voice lessons." I told him about Brescia and what he had said about the possibilities. "I'm scared, Gideon," I said. Why did I say that? I hadn't even thought about it before I said it.

"Of course you're scared," he told me. "It's always scary—starting out, not knowing how far you can go." The words hung in the air for a minute. "Rest your voice," he said finally. "And see a doctor, for Christ's sake. Get well, I'll miss you tonight."

"I'll miss being there," I said. "Even with that horrible Erb, I love the chorus."

He laughed a little. "All right," he said. "Then the *chorus* will miss you. I'll call you tomorrow. When's a good time?"

"They all pile out at eight-thirty," I told him, "and Michael doesn't come home for lunch until twelve-fifteen." Why did I put it like that?

"Tomorrow morning, then," he said. "Between eight-thirty-one and twelve-twelve. Be well."

I thought about the kiss, lying there. I tried to imagine making love with Gideon, but I couldn't get past where we'd go and what would I do about the kids. I tried to put all that aside and enjoy the fantasy, but I couldn't, with all those loose ends. I had hit on the idea of a chorus trip—an overnight trip—when I drifted off again.

I pulled up out of a deep, spiraling silence. "Mommy! Ma? Mom-my. *Mom!*" It was Michael, standing by the side of the bed in his wet poncho, conjuring me in a harsh whisper. I heard Randy's voice at a distance. "I told you not to wake her up!"

"I didn't! She was up, right Mom?"

"She was not. And you dripped all the way up on the carpet."

"I did not."

"Did so. And left mud marks in the hall."

14

"I took my boots off. Ma?"

"*Before* you took your boots off. And they're just lying there in the hall, making a puddle."

I sat up. There was a noise in my ears like the high hum of the car radio. Everything was muffled. "Michael, did Mrs. Delaney pick you up?"

"Yup. But she came late because she thought you were coming. Me and Robby helped the crossing lady until she came."

"Out in the rain?"

"I had my poncho. Ma? Where's my tail?"

Jesus. The tail. "I'll tell you what you do, honey. Go up in the attic to the closet. You know where the summer things are hanging? In a box on the floor is a brown fuzzy hat. Bring it to me. And my sewing box."

"It stinks in that closet."

"You want a tail, Michael? Do it."

"Okay." He went out, holding his nose. "But I'll get all stunk up. Don't blame me if I'm a stinky-stunk skunk." He was in high spirits.

Randy came in. "I told him not to wake you up, Mommy. I couldn't stop him. Are you okay?"

"I'll live. How about you? How was your day?"

"Okay. I did lousy in gym. Last picked for the team, as usual. But Mindy Kosoff sat with me at lunch. She's not so stuck up anymore, since Tracy moved away."

My reluctant Christian had made it through another day in the arena with the lions. I wanted to transfuse her with some elemental comfort. It was easy once. Remember when you were an infant and you'd surprise us both out of our naps, yourself and me, in the early evening before Daddy came home, and I'd take you into bed with me and lay you down in the crook of my arm and you'd nurse? Both of us half awake in the heat, you in diapers, me in underpants. Milk would leak out of one breast while you worked at the other, and trickle down toward your face. It was all you needed, then. Everything you needed. I had it all. He'd come in sometimes and find us asleep there, you marking your place on my nipple with your open mouth, me curled around you like half a parenthesis. Sated, both of us. He would close the parenthesis on the other side, laying his Palm Beach sleeve across your toes to touch my hip and smelling of the outside world.

But I didn't touch her. I felt as if I was sending out waves of contagion. "Better not hang around in here, honey. You'll catch this thing." You had my immunities at birth, a good system. If I could have given them all to you. If you had them now. "Call Mrs. Delaney, would you, and tell her thanks for picking the kids up? No, never mind. I'll do it." Better call her myself so she'll hear that I'm sick. It's the only excuse for missing car pool, besides a death in the family or car trouble. Please, Mrs. Reynolds, may I be excused from gym? I have cramps. The one thing they can't argue with . . . if you report pain, they have to believe you. I never had cramps a day in my life, but they owed me the days off, for pain. I took them in cold calculation, spaced them out to save my skin. One for the overhead ladders and the palsy and the liquid terror of that pilgrimage from hole to gaping hole. One for the ropes, hands burning, for dangling helpless midway up. One for the sawhorses and the leaden leaps. I used to dream she'd strip me to see whether I was really bleeding. Die, Mrs. Reynolds, I have an excuse.

I made Michael leave the hat and the sewing box at my door. I got up, then, to go to the bathroom, and brought all the stuff into bed. The hat was dark brown fake fur, a fuzzy dome. We'd all worn them. My hair was long then, and I'd pile it up into the hat. When I got into the library I'd take the hat off and shake my hair loose. Sometimes it would snare one, he'd follow me with his eyes, all that black shining hair. Then I'd bring my hand up to pull a strand off my face, the hand with the engagement ring. Sorry, this one is taken. Bitch. Tease. I wanted to catch them for a minute first before I shook them off. The hat would sit on the shelf of the carrel, the snow beading on it and turning transparent, running off into puddles. Thawed, stifled, I'd read Dewey and think of Richard. Oh love when we're married. And watch under my lids

16

when they'd pass: khaki legs, desert boots. Tumble my hair down over my shoulders. Bitch. Hot bitch. Tumble to me, boys, I'm taken.

Every spring when we brought order back to the attic under Richard's baton, he'd spot the box and ask the question: "How about that hat? Why don't you get rid of it?" For years I thought I might wear it, but then it began to look alien to me. Not just outdated—tacky. I'd worn fake fur? But still I protected it. "It's not bothering anyone, Richard. Leave it." But now it was the hat or me; I had to come up with a tail.

Actually, the inside of the hat was a skin. Maybe it wasn't fake fur, maybe it was lamb's wool or something. Anyway, it cut pretty easily. I cut a six-inch-wide strip and sewed it into a long tube, but when I was about to taper the end it didn't look right. I looked around for the animal book. Downstairs, I remembered. In the kitchen. I called Michael, but he didn't answer. It was murder to raise my voice, but the thought of moving was worse. I tried once more, calling Randy. She came running in from her room.

"Go down and get Michael's animal book," I told her, "and a wire hanger and the wire clippers from Daddy's workbench." When she brought me the book I saw what was missing: the fox in the picture had a little white edge to the tip of his tail, curving up the underside. "You know those pieces of white fur you have?" I asked her. "Bring me one, honey."

"But those are mine," she protested. "You gave them to me."

Right. I had. They were the collar and cuffs off an old sweater. "Just one piece, Rand. You'll get it back," I promised. "Right after the performance."

"No I won't. Michael will lose the tail or someone will swipe it." She was probably right, but I was ruthless with the weakness of the fever and the need to deliver up a passable fox tail. "Randy, I'm not feeling well enough to argue with you. Just bring it to me, okay?"

She returned with it, sullen. "You could use cotton."

"Cotton would clump. It would look like a bunny tail. I'll make Michael guard it with his life. Okay, babe?"

17

"Do I have a choice?"

No, she didn't. "Of course. You could deny your poor, sick mother on her bed of pain. Make me go out in the storm with a bow and arrow, hunting ermine." She surrendered: a grin. I'd made her yield up the fur and a smile besides. Relentless, unyielding bitch mother. Take it all.

The fur was the right touch. With the wire from the hanger inside it, the tail curved up just like Br'er Fox's. I laid it on the night table. My head was pounding and I was shaking. I lay down, thinking of my dream about Brescia. Oh please, I thought, don't throw me in the briar patch. I fell asleep grinning.

I woke in a panic, reaching for the tails of the horrors as they receded: hands, handles, zippers catching soft flesh, thorns—no, briars—bleeding, wires. Falling. Jesus, it hurt even to move my eyes, even to breathe. I was dizzy. Everything was distant, except the pain in my throat.

"—hear me? *Daddy's* on the phone." It was Michael, hand flat on his head in exasperation. Just like Richard. "Okay," I said. I reached for the phone, knocked it over. The receiver dangled near the floor. When I bent to get it, I knocked the sewing box off the night table. I watched the spools and bobbins hit the floor and run for cover. "Shit," I said. "Hello?"

"Beth? What the hell is going on there?"

"Hi, honey. Nothing. Chaos."

"Why are you whispering? Listen, I'm running. Meet the seven o'clock, okay?"

"Richard, I'm *sick*. I can't go out."

"You still sick? What's the matter?"

"Fever. Throat. Ears. Head."

"Okay, don't worry. I'll get home on my own. What are you doing about dinner?"

Dinner. Hop to the moon. "Richard, I can't."

"Okay, no sweat. We'll manage. Just throw something together. I'll see you soon." He hung up.

"You're supposed to take care of me," I said into the dead phone. "You promised."

Michael was looking at me with interest. "Did Daddy yell at you? How come you're crying?"

"Michael, Daddy doesn't yell, you know that. I'm feeling crummy, that's all. Get Randy, honey."

"RANDEE," he yelled. "MOMMY'S SICK. SHE'S CRYING. GET UP HERE."

She came thundering up, eyes wide. I smiled at her, pulled the smile from the innermost core of the world, grafted it with monumental effort onto my face. "Listen, honey, Daddy will be home at seven-thirty or so. How'd you like to order a pizza?" Every word had to be propelled by sheer force through the flames.

"Pizza? Can we? Daddy said so?"

"Daddy says pizza is crap," Michael put in.

"If Daddy doesn't want pizza," I said, "he can throw something together. You guys will have pizza. Can you order?"

"Sure," said Randy. "Where's the money? Do I give the guy a tip?"

I pointed at the dresser, where my pocketbook was. The briefcase was there, too. She brought the pocketbook. I gave her a ten and scribbled a note on my grocery pad: "Tell him to deliver at 7:40. Give the kid who delivers it a 50-cent tip. Set the table—paper plates and cups. Juice, no soda. Can you make a salad?"

"Don't worry about a thing, Mom," she said. I wasn't. I just wanted to discharge my responsibility and head back into oblivion. They raced downstairs, Michael shouting, "I want a Sicilian, tell him a Sicilian," and Randy saying, "Michael, I'm in charge of this."

Richard turned on the light when he came in. It hurt my eyes. "What's going on?" he said. "The guy delivered a pizza, and now Laura calls and says she told you to send Randy over for dinner. I told her we didn't need it because we already had this pizza."

19

I closed my eyes. When I opened them, Richard was still there. I rolled over and pulled out the grocery pad again. "Laura," I wrote, "I plead fever. Fell asleep and forgot all about your casserole. Will you send it home with Randy anyhow? Richard will be relieved not to have to eat pizza, and it'll take care of them tomorrow night, too. You're an angel. See you at Lutèce." I handed it to Richard. "Send Randy with it right now," I said.

"She's eating," he said. "Pizza. And Hawaiian Punch. It's too late for a real dinner. I'll send her later."

"Now, Richard," I said. "Before Laura gets any more insulted." He looked at me. "Please," I said. He yelled for Randy, sent her out, came back, kissed me. He whistled, piercing my ears, laid his cheek against my head. He smelled of smoke, from the train.

"Hey," he said. "You're burning up. Did you call the doctor?" I shook my head. He went out, came back shaking down the thermometer. He stuck it under my tongue. "Poor baby," he said. "You should have told me." I did, Richard, I told you three times. Be fine, you said. Have a good day. Throw something together, you told me. Tears ran sideways down my face, into my ears. Cheap shot, Beth, I thought, and wiped them away before he saw. He was dialing the phone. "Is this the service? Richard Clahr calling. Tell Dr. Lippzer my wife is very ill—937-0188. I want to hear from him within fifteen minutes, please. What? Wait a minute." He pulled the thermometer out of my mouth. "A hundred and two point five," he said. "And—a cough?"

"Sore throat," I said. "Ears."

"And a sore throat and ear pain. Fifteen minutes, tell him. . . . You'll find him." He looked at me. "Turkeys," he said. "Watch them screw it up."

But it was only a few minutes later when the phone rang. "Hello, Monroe," Richard said. Man-to-man hearty. "Listen, I think you'd better look at Beth. You got the message? A hundred and two point five and a bad throat. No, tonight, Monroe. . . . I know when your office hours are, but if you get her on the antibiotics now she'll *be better* by then. We need her around here, you know. Well, that's your department, but at least look at her

20

and make the decision. Yeah, eleven Berkely. Off Oak, to the left. What are you *doing*?" That was to me, in his regular voice. I was crawling around on the rug, picking up spools and bobbins and stacking them in the sewing box.

I handed it to Richard. "Put it away," I whispered. "Please. And wipe around in the bathroom?" I put the pitcher and the glass on a book and wiped the night table with a Kleenex. Richard stood there, holding the sewing box. "It's not a League luncheon, it's just Monroe. He's going to look at your throat; he isn't going to inspect the house."

Grimly I headed for the bathroom. While I brushed my teeth I was working out a battle plan: Windex the mirror and sink, wipe up the floor with the dirty facecloth, stick the hair drier in the cabinet. I was throwing the facecloth into the hamper when I heard the bell ring. I yanked the shower curtain closed and made for the bedroom while Richard and Monroe were sparring at the door. Richard's shirt was on the bookcase. I shoved it under the quilt on his side of the bed and sat up against the pillows. Ready, doctor.

They came upstairs. First thing, Monroe headed for the bathroom to wash his hands. See, Richard? He had a jacket and tie on. His fingernails were rounded and immaculate. He was calm, just aloof enough to convey his displeasure at being called out. "All right, Beth, let's see," he said. This had better be good, he meant.

Monroe knows every inch of my body, but he has a policy of looking at only one part at a time. Checking the breasts, cover the stomach. Palpating the stomach, reveal not thy breasts nor thy loins. Doing a pelvic, drape the knees so the top half won't know what the other half's up to. And call in the nurse, an impartial witness: did I rape this woman, whose feet were in my stirrups last Monday morning and whose knees supported a sheet beyond which neither of us could see? Never, doctor. You never. And I swear, your honor, he never fondled her neither. Uses a latex glove, he does.

"—don't see anything bacterial in there. You have a pretty raw

21

throat, but it doesn't look like a strep. We'll see what·shows up on the culture; you can call me tomorrow and check. Meanwhile, aspirin and lots of juice. Use the vaporizer—got a hot air one? Use that. And gargle, Beth, every hour or two. Lozenges for the throat. Complete rest. I wouldn't get up at all, at least for the next twenty-four hours or so, except to go to the bathroom. Bed rest."

"Monroe," I said. "Will this hurt my voice?"

"Your voice?"

"Yes, for singing."

"You sing? Choir or something? No, I don't see why it should. Don't strain it, that's all. Don't use it at all if you don't have to. Turn the phone off—you still got that gizmo on it? And don't sing until you're healed. You won't feel like singing, anyway, for a few days."

I didn't feel like doing anything at all, but I did. I had to arrange for my bed rest.

I wrote a note for Richard:

Put Michael's tail in a bag for tomorrow. Don't let him leave without it.

Pack lunch for him. Randy'll tell you what goes into it. Tomorrow AM, call school (number's on the emergency list in green ink)— tell them he'll be eating lunch there.

Call Marion (937-2473), tell her I'm sick, ask her to drive the kids tomorrow if it rains.

Call Minna Freihof (937-7092) and tell her tomorrow's my day for junior high car pool. Ask her to drive for me—tell her I'll take her day next week.

Ask Randy if her homework's finished. Tell her to wash her hair, pack her lunch.

Tell the kids if they need me tomorrow to get me through Laura. I'll have the phone turned off.

Please bring me—the aspirin
                     the throat lozenges (medicine cabinet, 2nd shelf, left side)
                     a glass of juice
                     new NEW YORK magazine

Thanks, honey.

The kids stood at the door to say good night. I broadcast a smile. " 'Night, troops," I whispered.

"Hope you feel better," Randy said.

"I will," I mouthed. "Don't worry."

Michael stood there a minute, chewing on his pajama sleeve. Then he made a megaphone with his hands. "Good night," he bellowed. "Sleep tight. Don't let the bedbugs bite. Go to bed, rest your head, hope that you don't wake up dead."

3.

I'm sure it wasn't the next day that it started either, because I spent it swimming in and out of deep sleeps. In fact, the last thing I remember of the day is Gideon's call.

When Richard was leaving in the morning, he came up with a container of orange juice and some cups. "Remind the kids about the phone," I whispered. "I'm turning it off. Are they set?"

"Yes, they're all set. Everyone's got lunch and rides and I called all your dames. Rest, will you? You have a day off. Enjoy it."

But I didn't turn it off, because I remembered about Gideon. He said he'd call. I said I'd be here.

The phone rang at 8:40. I grinned to myself. Didn't waste much time, did he?

It was Leone Taub. "Beth, how are you?" she opened.

"Sick," I said.

"Well you *sound* sick, I must say. What's wrong?"

"Virus. I'll live, but I can't talk."

"Well, as long as it isn't serious. Speaking of serious, you heard about Jessie Handler, I guess."

"Heard what?"

"You mean you didn't know she was going in?"

"Going in? She said something about a checkup—"

24

"It's not good, Beth." That meant cancer, not good. It was the local code for doomed.

"Oh, Jesus," I said. Don't tell me any more, my voice said. Not another word.

"Right. Look, I won't trouble you now. I called to ask you if you'd consider a nomination to next year's League board. We think you'd be a real addition. Will you think about it and call me when you're feeling better?"

"Of course," I said. "Thanks, Leone."

That was it, my just deserts. I'd worked hard enough for it. Normally, even with the throat, I'd have chatted for a while and worked an acceptance into the conversation, but I wanted to get Leone off the phone. I wanted the line free so Gideon could call. Do anything, Br'er Fox, but puh-leeze don't throw me into that briar patch.

Gideon called at 9:30. I let the phone ring one and a half times. "Hi," he said. "How are you?"

"I'm genuinely sick," I told him. "The doctor says so. I'm having an honest-to-God day off, in bed with the aspirin and a gallon of orange juice."

"You shouldn't be using your voice," he said. "For Christ's sake, Beth, don't strain it now. You're just getting started."

Just getting started. Was I? Hearing him say it made it sound like a possibility. I loved it, that he saw me that way. Just getting started.

"I'm going to turn off the phone," I said, "and wallow."

"After this call?" A smile in his voice. A softness. *You've been waiting for me.*

"Yes. I've got things straightened away now, and I've notified the world, so I can check out for a day." *No I haven't.*

"I won't keep you talking. Just wanted to see how you were and to tell you the Erb is no fun without you."

"It's no fun under any circumstances," I said. "Hey, maybe I'll miss the concert and I'll never have to improvise that passage again."

"Yes you will, Beth. If not that passage, others. It's all opening up for you . . . you've got to go with it." There was a silence. It was my turn, but I couldn't fit anything into it. He picked it up after a three-beat rest. "And I hope you won't miss the concert. I was looking forward to the evening. I like the drive with you. I like being with you. Is that okay?"

"Of course."

"So get well. Turn off your phone and sleep. I'll catch you next week."

I did. I turned off the phone, and I slept.

By Sunday the fever was gone, but my throat was still raw and I had intermittent earaches. Everything sounded muffled, and there was a constant feeling of pressure on my ears. I kept swallowing to clear them, but it didn't work and I felt disoriented. I couldn't seem to connect with anything anyone said.

Richard said he'd take the kids to the movies in the afternoon. When they were getting ready to leave, Michael burst in, his voice escalating with every word. "Can't I have a soda in the movies?"

"What does Daddy say?"

"He says no soda." His voice skated near breaking. "He says it's junk. Can't I even have a *orange* soda?"

"What Daddy says goes. But maybe if you're a good sport about the soda and you don't fight with Randy in the car, you can get some popcorn. The soda always spills anyway. Have you got a jacket?"

"I'm boiling. I don't need a jacket. Tell Daddy I have to get popcorn. DAD!"

"Mike? Let's *go!*" Richard yelled up the stairs. Michael stood there at the night table, jiggling so he shook the bed. Without turning his head he yelled, "C'mere!" One hand picked at his jeans and when we heard Richard running up the stairs, it closed protectively over his crotch.

"Do you want to go to this movie or n—"

"Tell him," he hissed, pulling impatiently at himself.

"Michael?" Richard was in the doorway. "Wh—"

26

"I'm *going*. But she says—"

"*Who* says?"

"*Mommy* says I—"

It was funny how, even though my head was blocked, every word they said pounded against my eardrums. I didn't hear it so much as feel it. "I told him maybe you'd get him popcorn at the movies if he didn't fight with Randy in the car," I said, closing my fingers gently around Michael's kneading hand and pulling it away from his pants. Richard opened his mouth, exasperated. "Won't you be late for the movies?" I asked him.

"Damn right we will. Let's go, Michael." He walked out.

Michael took two or three steps after him, eyes still on me, then turned and raced from the room. "But can I?" he yelled on his way down the stairs.

"What?"

"Have popcorn. Mommy said." The door slammed.

After they went out, I realized they'd gone without their jackets. I could have called to them in the driveway but I didn't. I looked at the clock. 1:30. Two o'clock movie, out at four. I had three hours.

I hadn't been out of bed, really, since Thursday night. I looked around the room. The sewing box and the wire cutters were on the chair. The floor in front of the bed was covered with Michael's Lego pieces. Looked like half a building and a truck and lots of spare parts. His spelling book and his collection of colored pencils were on the dresser. Dirty juice glasses and three days' *New York Times* on the night table. I got out of bed and started to straighten up. I thought about dumping the Lego stuff into the box and putting it in Michael's room, but I didn't want to break up his building, so I gathered up all the unused pieces and put them away, but left the building and the truck. I stacked up the newspapers and balanced the dirty glasses and the juice container on them. I carried the pile downstairs. When I saw the condition of the family room and the kitchen, I just put it all down on the counter. Let George do it, whoever George might be. Richard. I got a frozen yogurt out of the freezer and carried it upstairs.

27

Coming back into the room, I felt as though I'd come through a cluttered, threatening neighborhood and returned home. That was the beginning of it, I guess. That and the fact that I felt grubby, so I decided to change the linens. I stripped the bed down to the mattress covers—I won't do the whole thing, I thought, just change the sheets and pillowcases. The room is pale blue, with accents in apricot, and we have sheets in blue and in apricot and in a mixed floral, but I pushed them aside and rooted around in the back of the linen closet until I found the old yellow ones. They were wrinkled a little, but I put them on the bed with a sense of pleasure and a strange excitement.

I'd forgotten how smooth sheets could be. These were so old, so laundered, that they were really showing wear, but they felt different from all those deep-color, wrinkle-free decorator bed linens from Bloomie's. I'd forgotten. The top sheet had creases in it from being ironed and folded. Really, we didn't need a top sheet under the quilt, but I wanted it against my body. I shook the last of the four pillows into its pillowcase and stood holding it, running a finger over the embroidered scallops.

We'd put them on the bed together, the week before the wedding. Made the bed and left it, so it would be ready when we came back from the honeymoon. We grinned at each other, shaking the new yellow blanket out over the sheet, but we didn't say anything. I remember I showed him how to make hospital corners, feeling very competent.

Did he ever know it, that all those weeks later, after I cried and told him in elliptical sentences with so much left out that I wasn't with him when he came, that he had to wait, somehow he had to wait and bring me along—did he know that there was a night when I went through hope to anger to resignation, and when I waited until he was breathing evenly where he'd rolled over and I moved away, way over to my side of the bed, sliding on the yellow sheets in my slippery nightgown and resorted to it, yielding deliberately and grimly to the old fantasy and, with the deepest cynicism of twenty-one years, took into my own hands again my own pleasure? The thing I thought I'd never have to do again

28

after we were married? That I lay rigid, not to shake the mattress, defiant and despairing, and stole my own finish?

He couldn't have known. Because all Richard knew about me was what I told him. Messages by satellite. Reports from planet me. And when I finally accepted that, I stopped trying to tell him. Because what was the point? He was supposed to know what I wanted, needed, without my having to spell it out. That was what loving was supposed to be. The way Mama loved me.

So he couldn't have known. Or it would be different now.

I heaved the quilt back onto the bed, smoothed it out, brought the top sheet out over it and folded it down. Then I took every thing off the night table, wiped it down, and put it all back. Phone. Kleenex. Aspirin. Magazines. I went and got the briefcase, put it on the floor near the bed.

It was 2:05. I sat in the chair and ate the yogurt slowly. It had melted a little, and it felt good going down. Then I showered, a long, steamy soak, and scrubbed my face and cleaned my ears and brushed my teeth. And powdered my body. Johnson's Baby Powder. I chose the old white nightgown because it was soft.

I propped two of the pillows up and sat back against them, pulling the sheet and the quilt over my legs. It was quiet. I was clean and everything touching me was clean and soft. I sat quite still, feeling all over my body the softness and the even weight of the quilt and the silence.

I must have been five or six, that summer evening. I had a new nightgown, puckery white cotton. I'd been bathed and powdered and fresh calamine lotion had been applied to the mosquito bite on my arm. The bed had been moved under the side window, in the cross-breeze, and she'd heard my evening prayers and pulled the sheet up over me. I was alone in the room, adrift from the wall. It was still light out. I lay unmoving, the nightgown was perfectly straight under me and the sheet was smooth, unrumpled over me. I could have scratched at the mosquito bite. I could have leaned up on an elbow and found the players to go with the melodies I heard out there—Ringoleevio. There goes one, see his light? Did not. Did too. You liar, you never said Mother May I. But I lay there, smelling the newness of the nightgown and myself all powdered, and knowing that if I didn't move, didn't wrinkle the sheet or bunch up the nightgown, the magic would hold. I would be safe. I was. Safe.

I fell asleep halfway between sitting and lying, having meant to take the music out of the briefcase and begin.

4.

So that must have been the beginning.

I was much better the next day, only my ears were still clogged.
When the kids left for school I changed the radio in the kitchen
from Richard's news station to WNCN, as I did every morning.
It was a Telemann concerto, and I heard it as though through a
helmet. I fiddled with the tuning, but the only effect was that
the bass thudded against my eardrums. I turned it off.

George had not done it. Nor anyone else. The whole downstairs was a shambles. The morning had been a shambles, in fact,
with Randy having to make her lunch at the last minute and
Michael frantic because he couldn't find his math test.

"You have to sign it. I have to bring it back signed."

For Your Eyes Only. Sign And Return To File. "Michael, you
can tell Mrs. Quintero you couldn't find it. Did you look on
Daddy's desk? Anyway, how come you didn't just have Daddy
sign it?"

"She said have your mother sign it. And you were sleeping all
the time, so I waited."

"Michael, when she says that she means mother or father.
Daddy wants to see your work just as much as I do."

He moaned, a preliminary. He was twisting the bottom of his

31

football shirt between his two hands. "You have to sign it," he said. "*You* do."

8:25. If it went on any longer, he'd be late and I'd have to drive him to school. I wasn't ready for that. "Tell you what," I said. "I'm going to send a note. I'll explain to Mrs. Quintero. Won't that be okay? And while you're at school I'll look for the test. Okay, honey?"

"Mm-mm," he said. E-flat, C. Tears held in his jaw made the melody.

I wrote it on the paper he and Randy had given me for Christmas. It was a pad. Every piece said MICHAEL'S MOM RANDY'S MOM in continuous print around the border. Pastel hues. This one was lavender.

"Dear Mrs. Quintero," I wrote. "Michael is very concerned because he can't find his math paper for me to sign. I've been sick, and I'm afraid it's under the debris here somewhere. May he have an extension? He did try."

"What does it say?" he asked me. I always forget he can't read script. He had one hand on his fly. Oh, Michael, I won't let Mrs. Quintero take them away. He was sniffing in a businesslike way; the scene was over, he was just getting himself back in order. I read it to him.

"Okay?"

"I guess."

I grinned at him. "I kin read readin', Miz Rabbit, I jest cain't read writin'," I said.

"What?"

"Nothing. Go on, honey. You'll be late."

I found the paper two hours later when I checked his jeans pockets before throwing them into the washer. There were two inscriptions on it. One, in Mrs. Quintero's Palmer script said, "Michael, you must check your work." I wondered if she knew he couldn't read it. The other said "SINE HEAR." It was followed by a multicolored dotted line and autographed "MICHAEL THE GREAT."

32

I was just loading the dishwasher—my dirty juice glasses were right there on the counter, on top of the newspapers where I'd left them—when the phone rang.

"Beth? Caroline. How are you?"

"Much better, thanks. I played it for all it was worth, but it was only worth three days. I'm up to my neck in solid waste here. How are you?"

"I'm in a League flap is how I am. Elizabeth Holtzman turned us down, so we're without a speaker for the luncheon. Got any suggestions?"

"Why don't we cancel? No one would have to find a baby-sitter, Phyllis wouldn't feel compelled to make those godawful pecan surprises of hers, and everyone would wind up two pounds to the good and fifteen dollars richer. Liz Holtzman wasn't going to tell us anything we didn't all agree with anyhow. Whaddaya say?"

She laughed. I liked Caroline. She didn't take the League as seriously as some people. We'd agreed, often, that contrary to the beliefs of some of its more earnest members, the League didn't single-handedly keep the federal, state and local governments on course, but that it did keep us all off the streets and relatively well informed. It was because she had this perspective that I'd agreed to co-chair the luncheon with her.

"Right," she said. "I'll just call Leone and tell her we refuse to be surprised by one more pecan. She'll see our point."

"Get the sense of it," I amended. League lingo.

"Right. Get the sense of it. And you know and I know that Leone would crucify me right there on her agenda board. So who'll we get?"

We talked about the possibilities for a while, but all we could come up with was a debate on the Westchester sheriff's office. "Caroline?" I said. "No kidding, if we have to push this hard to come up with a topic, maybe we should forget it. What if we had a luncheon in the fall? Or not at all, this year?"

There was a little silence. "You're not serious," she said. "We have to have the luncheon."

"Why?"

"*Why?* Beth, the fever has poached your brain. If you think I'm going to preside over the only nonluncheon the League has ever had, you're nuts. Now *think*. Who'll we get?"

"I am thinking. I think we're pushing a dinosaur down a jet runway. I think maybe we should stop and try the flying machines."

"Why? Because Elizabeth Holtzman is busy on the nineteenth?"

"No. Because the speaker is an excuse to proceed with the luncheon and the luncheon is a relic. It isn't relevant to anyone's life, really. It isn't to mine. Now that I think of it, I have better things to do. Listen, Caroline, did you hear about Jessie Handler?"

"Grace told me. Isn't it horrible?"

"Caroline, Jessie Handler could die." When I said it out loud I knew it was true. Jessie could die. I was angry, suddenly. "All those consensus meetings. All those presentations of issues that didn't change a thing. All those *luncheons*, Caroline. She could have been making something happen. She could have been traveling around the world, or painting, or anything. She could have been having a love affair. *Something*, so when it came to get her, she could say, 'Screw you; I lived.' She might die, Caroline, and what pleasure will it give her to think that for fifteen years she went to a League luncheon every June nineteenth?"

Another silence. When she did speak, her voice was tight. "You're upset," she said. You've turned out to be inadequate and a little flaky, she meant. "I'll look into it myself and get back to you. Okay?" Last chance. If I let it go, forty-three women would know by dinnertime that I'd backed out for no reason and left Caroline holding the bag. There'd be no trouble reaching consensus on *that*.

"No, you're right," I said. "I'm upset about Jessie. And still a bit shaky myself." (Remember, Mrs. Reynolds? I've been sick.) "I'll see whether Richard's connection with Victor Gotbaum is still alive. He could come and tell us about the union negotiations with the city and their fiscal impact."

34

"Beth, what a terrific idea! Hey, wouldn't that set Mrs. Huxley on her ear? And Ce-cile Arp. All those Lady Bountiful types." She giggled. I was back in the game. Close squeak though—so far but no farther. All right.

By the time I sent Michael back to school after lunch, I really was shaky. My legs felt fragile under me. I thought I'd wait one more day before I tried to face the supermarket. I headed upstairs, thinking I'd tackle the kids' rooms, but while I was leaning against Randy's doorway surveying the scene in there, the phone rang. I picked it up in my room. It was Laura.

"You back among the living?"

"Sitting up and taking nourishment," I said. "And taking in wash. And picking up five days' worth of garbage. I'm ready to leave home."

"Want to come over here? I'll give you a cup of coffee and a limited amount of sympathy."

I sat down on the bed. "No," I said. "This is my lot in life. And actually, I'm not doing any more today. Maybe I'll take a nap before I leave home. I'm suddenly very tired." I was. I ran my hand along the pillow. The conversation wound on for a while, taking me with it. It's like that, talking to Laura. It's like getting on the rides at Playland. Once you give the man the ticket, you're on for the whole ride. I thanked her for the casserole. She let me know Richard had offended her by refusing it. I took the blame. We got onto the subject of Jessie Handler. Laura knew all the details, and she told me every last one. She always seems to be the second one to know, after the surgeon. And she always finds a way to insert herself into the immediate family. "John told me it was a radical mastectomy, and they just don't know. She's terrified of the chemotherapy."

"You called John?" John is Jessie's husband. Laura doesn't know him at all, really. She only knows Jessie from working with her on the crafts fair.

"Yes, well I fixed dinner for them and I called to see when I could drop it off." She does that. Hears of an illness or a crisis

35

and shows up with dinner, offers to get the groceries, and take the kids. People all over the neighborhood who hardly know Laura have been astonished to find themselves in her debt.

She went on about the chemotherapy. I undressed as much as I could with one hand on the phone, holding it away from me so the words would run together, so I wouldn't have to hear. Finally she heaved a pitying sigh and before she could pick up speed again, I begged off. "I think I'll grab a nap before the kids get home," I said. "Think the skies'll fall in if I do that?"

"They'll arrest you for impersonating a Person," she said. "You're just a mommy, and don't you forget it. Get to the back of the bus, and on the way, pick up the gum wrappers. Sleep tight."

I had to pull the phone through my sleeve because I'd gotten all tangled up. I left my clothes in a heap on the floor and sank into the bed. I was running a hand over my breasts, thinking of Jessie, when I fell into a deep and silent sleep.

I woke up the minute Randy came upstairs, although she came up pretty quietly. In fact she stood at the door a minute, peering at me, before she came into the room. She looked pale and scared. "Randy?" I said. "What time is it?"

"I dunno. Three-fifteen, I guess. Why didn't you answer the door?"

"I didn't hear. You were ringing the bell?"

"I rang it and rang it, and then I got scared because your car was in the driveway but you weren't answering the door."

"You let yourself in?"

"No. I went to get Mrs. Delaney. She came across and let me in with her key to the front door." Oh God. Pat Delaney again. "Is she here?"

"She's waiting downstairs to see if everything's okay. I was afraid to come in alone."

"Okay. Just tell her to wait a minute." I sat up and swung a leg out of bed. Randy looked at me, wearing nothing but underpants in the middle of the afternoon. I turned away and pulled on my jeans and shirt.

I found her in the hallway. Thank God I'd cleaned that part of the house before I gave up. "Thanks, Pat," I said. "I'm alive. Just got tired suddenly and fell asleep." We chatted a while about how these colds linger on, and she left.

Randy was in her room with the stereo on. She was lying on the rug, feet up on the bed, and reading. "You'll ruin your eyes," I said. "Randy?"

"Yeah?"

"Why were you scared to come in alone?"

She shrugged. "Just was. I didn't know where you were."

When she was tiny, her crying was the factory whistle in my day. Three-hour segments I had to live in, fringed on either side with listening. Enough time to hem the curtains, if I wasn't interrupted. Enough time to run a couple of loads of wash, or shower and wash my hair, or eat lunch and read the paper. I ate a lot, then. I was always feeding myself a little treat. We'd get together and sit in someone's kitchen with two babies sleeping, and we'd drink coffee and eat each other's homemade coffeecake. We were all eating too much cake and telling each other too much about our pasts.

But one day she cried, on and off, all day. It wasn't enough to nurse her and bathe her and put her in, clean and full, for a nap. There was something else she wanted from me. She was usurping my three hours. I panicked, but I tried, nicely, walking with her and burping her. I tried feeding her a little more, but she only got angry. I tried changing the diaper. Every time I put her down in the crib, she cried harder and I was more and more panicked. And angry, angrier than I'd been since I was a child. The last time I walked out of the room, there was a silence. I stood outside the closed door and waited, thinking I would heat up a piece of the lasagne for lunch and start the new Alistair MacLean book. Then the crying started again, in full force, without the little preliminary mews. Terrified and enraged, I screamed through the door, "What? What do you *want?*" The crying turned to screaming, so we were both screaming. I opened the door. On the floor was the plastic roly-poly clown someone had given her, lying on a pink receiving blanket. I'd been down on the floor with her in the morning, pushing the clown to see whether she'd follow the colors as it moved, and the sound of the bells inside it. I picked it up and threw it viciously across the room. It hit the toy chest and rocked wildly on the floor, knocking against the chest and jangling. She was quiet now. "What is it you want from me?" I screamed, but I knew. She wanted it all.

When she began to cry again, scream after scream, each on the heels of the last, choking a little between cries, I picked her up, hot and flushed in her yellow kimono. I walked carefully to the rocking chair and sat down, steadying the chair with a shaking hand. I smoothed her hair back and fumbled to release a breast from the nursing bra so we could be comforted. I felt my breasts fill up, that hardening rush, and I willed my body still and untensed. She was still crying, little reminiscent sobs, as she sucked. Like a person. We rocked there until our breathing became regular and even and we had stopped crying. I sang then, "Toora loora loora." She fell asleep with one hand spread out on my breast, open and proprietary. Long after she fell asleep, I rocked to comfort us. "Okay," I said. "It's okay, Miranda. It's okay, love. Mommy's here." And when I closed my eyes I saw shadows. Forms. A void, terror. I saw myself unable to reach any of it, or stop my pain, or hold onto the source of my comfort. I felt myself alone and hungry into eternity. Miranda, is that how it is until I come to you?

"I fell asleep," I said. "I guess I haven't got my strength back yet. I'm sorry I scared you."

"It's okay," she said, frowning up at the book. She turned a page.

I went in and knelt down on the rug next to her, leaned over

38

to kiss her cheek. There were little blackheads around her nose, and as I leaned across her my breast grazed hers—new little mounds under the T-shirt. "I love you, Rand," I said.

"Love you too, Mom," she said, dismissing me.

5.

Making the bed for the second time that day, I thought of calling Jessie. I even picked up the phone, but just then Michael rang the doorbell, leaning on it and shouting "Ma-a-a!," so I hung up in relief and went to let him in.

I didn't think of it again until the next morning. I had switched the radio to WNCN. It was Stern playing Tchaikovsky's violin concerto, Rostropovich conducting, and I suddenly realized I was hearing it clearly. No pressure on my ears, no background hum, just the music going cleanly into my head. I thought with pleasure about being well, and then I remembered Jessie. Before I could lose my nerve, I dialed her house. Someone answered. I said, "Jessie?"

"This is the nurse," the woman said. "Mrs. Handler is resting now. May I ask who's calling?"

I told her my name. "How is she?" I asked. "Can she talk on the phone yet?"

"Oh, certainly. She's just fine. I'll have her call you back."

"No," I said quickly. "I'll call her," and I hung up before she could pin me down.

I was full of energy that day. I dug into the kids' rooms, ruthlessly clearing out the debris and stashing things away in Michael's room. It wasn't so easy with Randy's; she knows where she wants things, and every tattered, pencil-written note is sacrosanct, so I just stripped her bed and remade it and piled everything I picked up—books, pens, records, night brace, junk mail—on her bed. At least I was able to run the vacuum over the rug.

I stripped our bed, too, although the sheets had been on it for only a day. This time I did pull off the mattress covers. The night before, I'd been shifting around trying to get comfortable, and it had seemed to me there were ridges under me. Now I saw what it was. The mattress covers were old, and the quilting had opened up and the filling had moved around. Time for new ones, I thought, and I threw the sheets into the wash, made a grocery list, and headed out.

The phone was ringing when I came back in carrying a bag of groceries in each arm and my keycase in my teeth. I lowered the groceries onto the counter and let the keys fall out of my mouth, snatching the phone off the hook.

"You've been out, so you must be better." It was Gideon.

"I've had a miraculous recovery," I told him. "From death's door to the supermarket in five days."

"We'll be at St. John's Thursday night. I'll offer up thanks then. I've been praying you'd be well enough to go to rehearsal. See that? I have influence in high places."

"Well while you were at it, why didn't you pray me onto the stage of the Met instead of into Gristede's?"

"One step at a time. You'll get there. How's it going? Have you made application for the program?"

"No. The stuff is just where it was last Wednesday. I haven't touched it. In fact, I've been avoiding even thinking about it. I haven't even discussed it with Richard, and you have to send a check in with the application. Not to mention money for the voice lessons."

"Will he object?"

"No, of course not." I wasn't sure, but I didn't want to say it to Gideon.

"So do it, Beth. When do you go to Mannes?"

"Wednesdays. Tomorrow."

"Fill it out. Bring it with you. Where's the school?"

"East Seventy-fourth, between Lex and Third."

"Want to meet me for lunch? I'll launch your career with champagne." He'd been very breezy, but now his voice went soft and teasing. "It would be my pleasure."

"No, Gideon. Thank you. I can't. I have class before lunch and I have to talk to Brescia right after lunch, even if I don't take the lesson."

"A quick lunch. Just lunch, Beth. I'll meet you up there somewhere. One hour and a split of champagne."

"No. And anyway, I have to have my wits about me with him. Champagne would do me in."

"Why? Is he after you?"

"Me? As a woman, you mean? Don't be silly."

"It's not silly." There was a little pause. "You don't know what you are."

"Well I know what he is. He's an overweight, self-indulgent, ego-ridden tenor. You should see him, Gideon; he's not real. He's the caricature of an Italian opera singer." I chattered, describing Brescia's shape and mimicking his accent. Gideon broke in:

"All right, I yield on lunch. I see I've made you uncomfortable. I'm sorry. I said I wouldn't push it. But when I pick you up on Thursday, you'd better tell me you're enrolled in that program or I'll leave you on the Major Deegan and let you walk."

I hesitated. "I don't know if I'll go Thursday night. My voice might not be ready. I don't want to strain it."

"Okay. Check with the doctor. Who do you use?"

"Lippzer."

"Monroe? He's a lousy tennis player."

"Well, he's good at close range."

He roared, a short, deep burst of laughter. I really did like his laugh. "Okay. Him I'm not worried about, even at close range. So let him check you out. I'll call Thursday to see what he says. You'll be in?"

"I guess so. In and out."

"I'll catch you."

42

I was just hanging up when Michael came in, carrying the bag from Lord & Taylor.

"What's this? Is it for me? You left the door open and the trunk of the car is open and there's groceries in there. Who was on the phone?"

"It's mattress covers, not for you. The phone was ringing when I came in. That's why everything is open."

"Oh. Who was on the phone? Was it Evan? Him and me want to have lunch together. Can he come here? Was that him?"

"No it wasn't. It was Aunt Dot. Sure, he can come if he wants to. Want SpaghettiOs?"

"Yeah. I'll tell him."

The boys ate in about six minutes, swallowing SpaghettiOs, drinking a quart of apple juice and yelling riddles from Dixie riddle cups at each other, all at once. Then they ran out, to be the first ones on the school playground after lunch.

I was hot and sticky and hungry, and the Mannes thing was on my mind. When the last of the groceries were put away and the kitchen was straight again, I put some cottage cheese on a plate with a sliced apple and poured a glass of iced tea. I put it all on a tray and took it upstairs, balancing it in one arm and dragging the Lord & Taylor bag up in the other hand.

I put the new mattress covers on the mattresses, dug out the other set of old yellow sheets, and made the bed. Those sheets were split at the corners, but the elastic held them on. When the bed was made and the corner of the quilt was folded down, I put the lunch tray on Richard's side, along with the briefcase. Then I took a fast shower and, clean and powdered, in fresh underpants, I slid carefully into the bed. I propped up the pillows, sat up against them, pulled the sheet and the quilt up over my legs. I slid my legs cautiously out and back together. No wrinkles under me. I pulled the sheet taut over my legs again. No wrinkles over me. I set the alarm on the night table for 2:30. It was 1:05. I had an hour and a half.

43

6.

I ate lunch slowly, with the course application form propped up on the tray in front of me. I fixed my eyes on it, but I thought about Gideon. I thought of him saying we could "do it nicely. Quietly." How did he know? From experience? Lots of experience? I knew his wife, Fran, from town government meetings. She was pretty, in a blond, preppy way. Dressed very well, in sporty clothes. Played tournament tennis. My impression of her was that she was fair, amiable, level. In all our conversations, driving to the city to rehearsals and back, standing around during breaks while Lecrief worked out the phrasing, Gideon had never mentioned her.

We had talked about Richard, though, now that I thought about it. Months ago, in the car on the way to the city for the first rehearsal of the season, I'd said something about a business dinner we'd gone to at the new Rye Town Hilton.

"What *is* Richard's business?" he'd asked and peculiarly enough that was the moment when I understood, knew, that he wanted me. I heard it in his voice for the first time then, when he asked about Richard, the male scratching for position in the henyard. Checking out the competition.

"He's in construction. Chief estimator with Russo Associates."

"Sal Russo's firm? Richard's in partnership with him?"

"Not yet. He's thinking of buying the stock this year, though."

44

I'd spread a wifely wing over absent Richard, blocking this in-quisitive cock. Richard's whole life centered around bringing in enough contracts to force Russo to allow him to buy that stock. His whole life.

"That's one rough business. And Russo's a tough guy. I know something about him."

"Oh?"

"I've done a couple of deals with him. It was okay for me—he needed *us*—but I'd hate to be . . . well he's no pussycat, that's all."

"Deals?" in a soft voice, padding my crass curiosity. Unseemly interest, Beth? Well, but he's pecking around in my yard, isn't he?

"That's what I do. I put money and opportunities together. Land deals, mostly."

"You work alone?"

"I pay a few people to keep me company and share the aggra-vation." Oh. So we both knew all we needed to. You may scratch at will.

The page came into focus. "Professional experience," I saw. "Pres-ent business address."

I closed my eyes. I would be in my room, in a hotel in some city. On the overnight chorus trip. We would have sung trium-phantly and toasted ourselves backstage afterward, and now I would be ready for bed, in my hotel room. Wait. I couldn't be wearing any of my nightgowns. Two were white cotton and the one that had been glamorous was worn and tired. So it would be a new one, light blue, maybe, and Grecian. Demure but inviting. Wait. What if you could see through it? There'd have to be a peignoir, too. But why would I have it? Maybe I bought it for the trip. No. I didn't do that. Maybe it was a gift. Okay, a gift. I am alone in my room. A light knock on the door. I'm surprised. "Yes?" I ask. "Gideon," he says. I open the door. I look a question at him. "It looks very bad if I'm standing here at your hotel-room door, talking to you in your dishabille," he says. "Let me in quick or we'll be a scandal." He comes in and closes the door. I step

45

back. "It's all right," he says. "No one at all was in the corridor. No one in the world knows I'm here." He doesn't move. He has a split of champagne in one hand, two glasses in the other. "Don't be afraid. I won't attack you," he says softly. He's smiling, a knowing, tender smile. "I know you won't," I say, "but you can't be here." "I am," he says. "I'll go, if that's what you want, but first I owe you a drink. Remember, I said I'd launch your career." He moves over to the dresser, opens the champagne, pours two glasses. He brings one to me where I'm standing. Should we be sitting? Where? Is there a couch in the room? No. And not on the bed, certainly. So we're standing. That's better, anyway, because I move away a little. He lifts his glass. "To you," he says, "starting out." He snags my eyes with his. "To improvising," he says, "and not knowing how far it might go." He drinks and he waits for me to drink, and he puts his glass down and takes mine and puts it down. I am in his arms, he's kissing me, lightly exploring with his tongue. He unties the peignoir. It falls away. Now I can feel him, through the nightgown. What's he wearing? Not a dressing gown—he came through the hall and he'll have to leave again looking respectable. Regular clothes, then. He's dressed and I'm wearing only the nightgown. He dips down to kiss the hollow in my shoulder, the side of my neck. I feel my loins open up and my nipples harden. He knows it. "Beth," he says, "tell me now that you want me to go away." He has his hands in my hair; he makes me look at him. I don't say anything. He takes my hand, opens it, kisses the palm. I run a finger along his cheekbone. He leaves me, bolts the door, turns off the light, comes back. We're on the bed now. Is he still dressed? No. Just briefs. Where did he undress? Never mind. I still have the nightgown on, and he hasn't moved to take it off. He's moving his hand down my back gently, up, over my breasts. I feel it through the nightgown. I'm going under, I try one last time. "Gideon," I whisper. "We can't. It's wrong." He raises up on an elbow, looks at me. "It's right for me," he says. "You are. Nothing's ever been so right." Fade. No briefs now, no nightgown. Just a sheet under us. And he is in me, moving, reading

46

my beat and moving with it. "Ah," I say. "Ah. Gideon." The rest of it I don't say. Fade.

It came into focus again. "Name of person responsible for tuition payment," it said. "Jesus," I said. I put the tray aside and, resting the application form on the briefcase, filled it out. That part was easy. The course-choice forms were harder. I went through the bulletin, page by page, checking off courses that I wanted. I wanted almost all of them. Some I wasn't ready for and some were way out of my field, but that didn't narrow it down enough. I was almost thirty-three, and I had to decide: where was it leading? Performance? Or midwifery, passing music on to others to perform or appreciate? I went back through the bulletin, putting an A next to courses in voice, musicianship, and so on. A for active. So next to the others I put a P, for passive. I opened the bulletin to the inside of the front cover, and on the blank page there I wrote:

> Ask Mrs. Wilton:
>   Goals of "P"?—what jobs? which courses best?
>   Reasonable goal of "A"?
>   how long?
>   which courses?
>   Combine the two? How? To what end?
>   Half-time program?

Sweat was running down my ribs, and the sheet was damp under me. My heart was racing, shaking the pen in my hand. I folded the application up, put it inside the bulletin and returned it to the briefcase. Nothing further I could do anyway, until I saw Mrs. Wilton. Yes. One thing I could do. The last line of the application said "$50 registration fee, payable upon application. Nonrefundable." I could ask Richard for the $50.

It was 2:25. I shut the alarm off before it could ring, got up, made the bed, and was dressed and in the kitchen when Randy came in.

47

At dinner I reminded the kids that Wednesday was my day to go to the city. Richard looked up from his meat loaf. "How's it been going at Mannes?" he asked.

"Okay," I said. Only that.

7.

The train clicked along in a ragtime beat, lurching sideways in syncopation to the forward thrust. Key in hiding place, I ticked off. Checked the burners . . .

I saw myself standing at the doorway of an artist's apartment, one hand lightly resting on the stage-set door. I was dressed, fetchingly, in a spectacularly modest gown. The face of the tenor was turned toward me, as was the entire hushed audience at La Scala. "*Mi chiamano Mimi . . .*" I began. I just brushed the words, saving the full swell for "*Il primo bacio*" and the poignant overtones for the refrain in the dying scene. Control, control. The power to lift my voice over the notes, touching down easily and lightly on them. I was just approaching the shimmering end of the aria when the voice came bawling out of the tinny microphone: "Hunnerd and twenny-fif Street, this station stop, hunnerd and twenny-fif. Remember to take your belongings, and watch your step getting out."

Shocked, I looked out at the station sign. 125th Street. Key, I thought frantically. Burners. Now what? Michael. But I wasn't concentrating; I wasn't *knowing* it was all in order, because under the checklist ran a new, a jarring thought. Travel. I'd have to travel, wouldn't I, to sing. I couldn't expect to start out in New

York. And then, if I was really good, I'd have to go where the roles were. Randy's twelve, I thought. Michael is seven. In three years, maybe, I'd be ready. Randy'd be fifteen. High school. Michael would be ten. Fifteen and ten: wrong time to leave them. What's the right time? Eighteen and thirteen? I'll be thirty-nine. Nineteen and fourteen? The voice is fully mature at forty.

"Tickets, please. Ticket, miss?" I'd been holding it, rubbing at the corner of it. I held it out, arranging my face automatically in pleasant lines, and I realized I'd been clenching my teeth so hard my jaw was sore. I unclenched them, consciously stilled the muscles in my face and shoulders and stomach. Breathed out. Michael . . . sandwich in the bag, bag in the knapsack, school secretary knows he's eating in school . . .

I caught Mrs. Wilton before she went into the classroom. "Could we have lunch today?" I asked. "I need some guidance."

"Of course, but I'm afraid I don't have Vincent's panache. I can't promise to punctuate my comments with a meatball." We laughed, and that made it easier for me to tell her I wasn't prepared for class today. "I've been sick all week," I told her, "and I probably shouldn't use my voice anyway." She shot me a quick look of professional concern. "You didn't strain it, did you? Who's your doctor? Did you check with your throat man?"

Rosie Wilton, I'll love you forever. When I grow up and sing *Bohème* at La Scala, I'll dedicate my opening performance to you. "No," I told her with a deprecating grin. "I went to the same guy who treats Richard's back and does my Pap smears. He told me to take two aspirin and call his answering service in the morning."

She didn't smile. "You don't have a throat man? It isn't wise. Your throat is your living, or will be; you have to take care of it. Ask Vincent—he seems to have confidence in the one he uses."

Eternal fealty, Rosie, to my dying day. *Will be my living.* As sure as that. "That's what I wanted to talk over with you. I'm not at all sure what I should be aiming for."

People were going into the classroom. She followed them with her eyes, checked her watch. "All right," she said, a little absently. "We'll talk at lunch."

But she gave me her total attention at lunch. It made me feel terrific at first, while we were talking in generalities about interrupted careers and I was filling her in on my past history. But as we narrowed in on the present and my immediate future, I got edgy. For one thing, it was a very long time for a conversation to center on me; I kept smiling apologetically and saying things like "Well, I guess everyone has to deal with these conflicts," but she was unswerving. She kept steering right back to dead center.

Finally she put it to me: "Forgetting everything else, would you rather perform or teach? That's what it comes down to. That or administration." I shook my head at that, and she went on. "You could have a very sound career teaching at almost any level, and you could always continue with your choral singing on an amateur basis, if it gives you pleasure. It's a very valid life, and a fulfilling one."

I looked down at the remains of my salad. Unconsciously I'd been running my fingers up and down my water glass, making a track on its sweating, smooth sides. My fingertips were numb. It squeaked in the silence. I stopped and wiped my hand on the napkin. "Or—and only you can decide this—you could go for the singing. Vincent tells me you could have it, if you'd work for it, and he doesn't say that lightly. But performance is an entire life; you have to commit yourself to it. It means lessons and training for as long as you sing, and you really would have to start on it now. Certainly you'd be taking the basic theory classes anyway, and if you wanted to, you could easily turn your training to other uses. But you can't do it the other way; you can't take the academic course and then decide in four years you'd like to sing."

"I have a family," I said. My voice was very tight.

"So does Beverly Sills," she countered. "So do most professionals. It isn't easy, but it can be made to work."

51

I looked up at her and then away. I was suddenly right there on the edge of tears. My throat closed up; I couldn't speak. Beverly Sills. I knew from the easiness of her retort that Rosie Wilton had no kids, and that Beverly Sills's life seemed a normal mother's existence to her. I smiled tightly, from my planet to hers. "Well," I managed. "I guess I have to think it through. Thanks for your time and encouragement." I shifted back in my chair, ready to go. But she wasn't finished with me.

"Let's work it out," she said, "either way. For the first year the courses would be basically the same anyway, and the voice training could be an adjunct."

She flipped briskly through the bulletin, checking off courses and muttering about the virtues of one over another, the availability of the best instructors. I sat in a position of attention, elbow on the table, fingers to my temple, and I fixed a thoughtful look on her and nodded from time to time, but I couldn't listen to the panic and to her both, and the panic was louder. She committed me to ten years' forced labor in Kamchatka. I nodded brightly. She suggested I submit to cancer serum inoculations, see how it worked out. I put an intelligent crease between my eyes and assented. She offered me torture and humiliation at the hands of a band of perverted foreign men. I agreed to the double session. Anything, Rosie, just let me out of here.

When we left the luncheonette I had a year's half-time curriculum in my hand and I hadn't cried, but I was breathing hard around the helium balloon in my chest, to keep it from rising into my throat, and my blouse was plastered to my back and under my skirt four separate lines of sweat were running down the backs of my legs. I hoped it was sweat.

I used the ten minutes before my appointment with Brescia very efficiently. I bolted myself into a stall in the women's room and I cried, silent, pathetic, openmouthed sobs. Mama come and get me, I'm scared. That took about three minutes. I blew my nose, wiped my face, and stripped. Everything but the shoes. I hung it all on the hook and mopped myself off, forehead to calves.

52

It was sweat, nothing worse. Then I put everything back on and emerged cautiously, looking around. No one in there. I washed off the eyeliner from under my eyes and put on fresh makeup. I did what I could with my damp hair. Then I picked up my briefcase and walked out into the hall.

8.

Brescia was coming through the front door with a man I recognized as a faculty member. He stopped to laugh, a melodic tenor arpeggio at full volume. He flung an arm around the man's shoulders and said something in his ear, grinning. Both laughed, Brescia even more loudly than before, and they parted. He was still smiling broadly when he met me at the door to his room.

"Ah, the lady returns," he boomed. "So—you are to seize the bow? *Brava, brava.* We begin *subito,* not to waste another breath."

"I'm not sure," I said in what I intended to be a sprightly voice. "I have some questions to ask you about that. But in any case, I've been sick and I can't sing today." Fast like that, to get it all in.

He tilted his head back and looked at me through narrowed eyes. "Brescia will tell you whether you can sing," he pronounced. "Stand there—" he motioned me to the window. He walked to a door on the other side of the room and pulled it open. It was a cabinet. On the inside of the door was a full-length mirror. Inside the cabinet, at eye level, was a medicine chest whose front was another mirror. Under the chest was a small shelf holding brushes, a spray bottle, a can of hair spray, and a flat liquor bottle —brandy, it looked like. Under that was a little sink. He opened the medicine chest, took some things out, and came toward me with them. They were a small angled mirror on a rod, like a dentist's, and a tiny flashlight. He took my chin in his hand and tilted it back. "Protrude the tongue," he ordered. "Don't breathe, you will cloud the glass." He stuck the mirror into my mouth and shone the flashlight in, squinting. He removed the apparatus. I resumed breathing. "Nothing," he said. "The throat of a newborn. What is this, you cannot sing?" He was rinsing the mirror off at the sink. He patted it dry with a tissue, sprayed it with something, dried it again, put everything away. Before he closed the door of the cabinet he looked sternly into the mirror, lifted his chin to yank at his collar, patted his hair. Then he turned back to me. "Mm?" he demanded.

"I had a viral sore throat all week," I said. "I couldn't speak, let alone sing. I was afraid to strain my voice. So I haven't even looked at the exercises." Listen, I was thinking, I am an adult. I will decide when I can use my voice.

"A moment," he said, putting a hand out like a traffic cop. "You are an adult. You take responsibility for your own development, no?" I nodded. I don't have to, I was thinking. You can't make me. "So if the throat hurts, while you are resting it you work with the music in silence. Half the performance is in the silence anyway, I will teach you that. So you read the music, take it in, play it in your head, find your approach." He was beating time to his imperatives on top of the piano. "All in silence. Even with exercises, you can do this. You mean you never looked at the music?" I shook my head. "There is not so much time for us, that we can throw it away," he said. "Time enough to make a good instrument with work and more work, perhaps—time to be idle, no."

"I've been thinking about that," I put in, "about whether I should go ahead with the voice training. I'm not sure it makes sense for me." I waited, but he said nothing. "I mean, say it really did become . . . a good instrument." I smiled a little at that, but he just stood there looking patiently at me. "Then what?" I

55

pushed on. "I mean, wouldn't I have to travel a lot to get exposure and . . . just to go where the work was? I have children and a husband. I can't just abandon my responsibilities."

He was nodding now. "Responsibilities. What about your responsibility to this voice you have? Always to sing in the amateur chorus, is that responsible? Dear girl, everyone has children. They exist to leave you. Then you are old, and the voice has chipped and cracked and can no longer hold wine. And who is responsible then, that you threw it away? Besides," he said, positioning himself on the piano bench, "let us take our worries in order. Today we worry about making up for the lost week. For the next couple of years we will worry about making the instrument. *Then* we will schedule to worry about your babies and your husband. Meanwhile, let us not look for doors just to close them. Get your music please, we must begin."

I can always take this lesson, I thought, and never come back again. I won't discuss it with *him*, if I decide to stop. Just never come back.

I got the music out of the briefcase and we began.

I was just leaving the room, a long hour later, when he stopped me. "About the chorus," he said. "Lecrief's chorus. It is never bad to sing, and Lecrief is a good man to sing for, but perhaps for you the chorus is too dangerous." I raised my eyebrows in a question. "Yes, exactly. Dangerous. Because you must decide to seize the bow and stay with it. You will say—" he slid into a timid falsetto"—'Well, I can sing in the chorus and take the lessons with Brescia, too, and see which I like better,' and you will be seduced by the safety and the noise of the group, and you will never commit yourself to making music on your own. I think you must leave Lecrief and sing only alone, with me."

"I'll think about that," I promised. "Have a good week," and I escaped, closing the door behind me.

The bus was in the sixties when I remembered the application and the course-choice forms. It was Fifty-seventh Street before I

56

could get out. I walked along Fifty-seventh, trying to decide whether to go back and turn in the application. I didn't really have to commit myself to a professional singing career, Rosie Wilton and Brescia had both said it. For at least a year I could take courses that I could use either way. Anyway, it could never hurt to strengthen my voice, could it? I stood still, thinking, Well, I'll sprint for the uptown bus and I'll give them the application and that'll be that. I'll call the kids and tell them I'll be a little late. I was rummaging through my bag for change for the bus when a kid running down the street knocked into me. I dropped the briefcase and someone stepped on it. I snatched it up and went into a doorway to compose myself. Just take it easy, I told myself, nothing's broken. I wiped the shoeprint off the briefcase and rubbed my hand briskly over the spot to eradicate it. I stood there a minute, holding the briefcase in my arms and saying over and over to myself, It's okay, it's okay. Then I lowered it to marching position and looked into the store window to check myself in the reflection. Let's go, if I'm going, I said to myself, but the colors in the window caught my eye. Pretty floral napkins with scalloped edges, set on a matching bed tray with porcelain tea service. "PORTHAULT," the discreet lettering on the glass informed me. It flashed through my mind that Jackie Onassis or someone ordered all her bed linens from Porthault and I thought of the tattered yellow contour sheets on my bed, and before I thought it through I was inside the store, explaining with fraudulent assurance to the woman who'd opened the door for me that I wanted to look around a bit. "Certainly," she said, and moved away.

How do they know I'm not a Whitney? I thought. I walked over to the display wall. One of the little cocktail napkins, a multicolored floral, had a discreet little square tag that said $8.50. I picked it up. The napkin under it said $8.50, too. *Each?* Jesus. I picked up one from another little pile. $11.50, it said.

I walked around, trying to look mildly interested and comfortable. Eligible. Thick bath towels. Terry robes in patterns to match. Vinyl bed trays to match. Fat little pillows, edged with lace and bearing the embroidered advice, *"Va t'en. Je veux dormir."* The lady was at my elbow. "May I be of service in any way?" she asked. She was wearing a green linen dress, sensible and very well cut. It was completely unwrinkled.

"Yes," I said. "I need some sheets."

"Of course," she said with delicate skepticism. She picked up some keys from a desk. "If you'll come with me."

I followed her through a tiny hall into a tiny elevator, which she opened with the key. It opened out onto another floor. Bed linens. Sample fabrics hung here and there, and there were stacks of patterned sheets on shelves. I walked over and looked at them, not touching. She said nothing. Giving me rope, I thought, and some wellspring of stubbornness began to percolate in my blood. "These are available in other colors?" I asked.

She puckered her brow a little. Maybe I was for real after all? "Well, I think so," she said. "Would you like to see the swatches? If you tell me which pattern you're interested in, I can find out what's available."

She motioned me to a table, seated me in a little upholstered chair, and presented me with a sheaf of fabric swatches. I looked through them in silence. "The room is blue and apricot," I said finally. She arranged a look of polite blankness on her face. Now what? A gaffe? Blue and apricot wasn't up to their standards? Hell with you, lady, I thought. I took the reins again, flipping back to a floral, pink on white. "Do they do this one in apricot?" I asked. "Let me check," she said, and disappeared. I got up and went back to the shelves. All the patterned sheets were in one section. They all had scalloped edges. Over to the right were solid-color sheets. A solitary white one had straight edges and an inset of hemstitch embroidery.

"I'm sorry," she said, materializing noiselessly at my elbow. "They don't do special orders like that anymore. I'm afraid we can only promise to get them in the colors as they're shown." I ran my hand over the top floral sheet. "It seems to me," I said, frowning genteelly, "that the quality of the sheet isn't what it used to be." Take that.

58

She frowned, too, and cocked her head. "The workmanship?" she asked. "Or the fabric?"

"No," I said judiciously, "the workmanship still looks all right. I mean the texture of the fabric. They haven't added synthetics, have they?"

She was obviously relieved. "You're so right," she said. "We can't get the three-hundred-thread count in the florals anymore. But—" she brightened "—I think we can still order the three-hundred count in the solids. It's a very fine cotton still," she added, "and no synthetics, of course."

I ran my hand reflectively over the white sheet. Silken. To lie on this, I thought.

"—quote it both ways," she was saying, "and then we can check with the manager whether you can order the three-hundred-count hemstitch in—" she paused "—apricot."

"Good," I said, sitting down in the little chair again and taking the pen and pad she handed me. "Porthault" was printed on the top of the pad. "The Linen of Queens." Well. Deadpan, I instructed myself, no matter what price she says.

"A king-sized flat sheet," I said.

"In the solid hemstitch," she told me, "one hundred seventy-five dollars, and in the floral, three hundred four dollars."

Three hundred four dollars. Right. Got it. She looked at me inquiringly. And?

"The pair of contour sheets?" I asked.

"Fitted sheets," she said. "In the solid, seventy-nine fifty, and in the floral, one hundred sixty-five dollars."

"Each," I said. I'm a fast learner.

"Each," she assented, waiting.

"And pillowcases?" I asked.

"Seventy-five dollars or ninety-one fifty," she told me. "Each."

I saw it through. We went down in the little elevator, and we checked with the manager. No, the three-hundred-count hemstitched sheets came only in the white. So hard, these days, to arrange special orders. Anyway, delivery time on such an order

59

would be months and months. On the blue floral or the two-hundred-count solids, we could get them in eight weeks. They're all hand finished, you know.

As I was leaving, promising to consider the choices and come back to place an order, a large woman upholstered in a beige silk suit made an entrance. The manager melted from my side and was greeting her in his understated French accent before I realized I'd been abandoned.

"—to see you," he was saying. "—in a long while."

"I know, I *know*," she warbled, "and even now I'm here for just a little nothing. I stopped to pick up a few little napkins and sheets for darling *House & Garden*."

Right, I thought, outside on the sidewalk. No one walks in there and buys two sheets—no one but decorators and imposters. Jackie probably has somebody call and order two dozen sets in her registered patterns. They probably send Queen Elizabeth 200 sets in the white every so often, with her crest. She's right, too, I told myself. The white's the one. I stood there for another minute seeing it: lying on that silken sheet, covered with another, looking down and seeing the regal simplicity of the hand hemstitching. Laying my head on the smoothness. Still, still, in perfect white. Simple white. Childhood white. I folded the little memo sheet and put it carefully in the briefcase. Too late to bring in the application now, I thought. The kids are waiting. Anyway, I ought to discuss it with Richard. I never even asked him about the $50.

I sat on the train, yawning and watching the world pull away backwards, and thinking, just the white. Cover it with the bedspread, too. Not to show them off. Just to have them. Just to lie between them. Mine.

9.

I went upstairs as soon as I got home and stood looking at the bed. Just half an hour, I yearned. I'll tell the kids I'm grabbing a nap and I'll turn off the phone and close the door and just lie down for half an hour. But I went downstairs instead and fixed dinner.

Michael reached over his plate, tipping his chair, to select two long french fries from the serving dish.

"Pig," Randy said. "You still have a whole bunch of french fries on your plate."

"I like the long ones," Michael said. He dunked the end of one of them into his ketchup, then, holding it like a cigar with the red end out, he cleared his throat. "Ahem," he intoned. "Layties and gen-tel-men. Your attention please."

"Don't play with your food," I told him. "Just eat."

"*Michael*, you're dripping ketchup on the table. It's on my part of the table, too. Wipe it up. You're disgusting." Randy put down the french fry she'd been holding and, picking up her fork, favored him with a ladylike look of distaste.

"That's my part."

"Is not, it's mine. You're sitting too close to me, anyway."

"I'll show you." Michael dipped his finger in the ketchup and drew a line from the edge of the table toward the center, next to Randy's plate. "*That*'s your part. So tough."

"Mommy—"

"If you don't both cut it out, you'll leave the table and there'll be no TV for either one of you tonight," I said. "Michael, put that down and use your fork. Randy, sit up. And leave Michael alone."

"Me? All I did was tell him he was dripping. He's a pig."

"I am not. You are. Piggy. Miss Piggy."

"Yeah? Well you know what *you* are."

"One more word—" Richard sounded dangerous "—and you'll both be sorry."

"I'm sorry he was born," Randy said under her breath to no one. Richard turned to her and opened his mouth.

"I went to Mannes today," I said to him. "I have to talk to you. Mrs. Wilton thinks I should be in the diploma program. It would mean a couple of days a week, probably, even just going half time, and tuition, not too much to start out with. And there's a fifty-dollar registration fee."

"Registration for what?"

"For the summer session. To get credit for the courses."

"Whatever you want," he said. "You might as well be doing something. The kids'll be in camp all day. Wish I had the time to take a couple of courses."

"This isn't a couple of courses," I said. "Well, it *is* a couple of courses, because I don't think I'm ready for a full load, but it's really starting on a program. It could take years to get the diploma."

"Diploma?" Now he was paying attention. "What is it, a master's?"

"Sort of. A degree in music."

"What would you do with it?"

"I don't know exactly." There were two string beans lying on top of my untouched slice of London broil. I moved them neatly over to the string bean pile. "Teach, maybe."

62

"Well, why not. You might as well try it, anyway. Will you be able to manage the house and the kids and everything?"

"Sure, I think so. Anyway, I'm not even sure I want to do it. It's a real commitment."

"You can always stop if you don't like it. What's it cost?"

I told him. He raised his eyebrows, but then he smiled indulgently. "What the hell. You're worth it. Isn't she worth it, kids?"

They were quiet, eating peacefully now that they weren't the focus of our attention. "Worth what?" Michael demanded. He hadn't been listening to us. I'd been watching him out of the corner of my eye, lining up his french fries and flying them individually into his mouth, each accompanied by a *sotto voce* "vroom." He was out of french fries now, but the steak and string beans were still on his plate.

"Eat your meat and string beans," I told him. "Want me to cut the steak?"

"Worth *what?*" he demanded again.

"Worth money for tuition," Randy said. She was looking at Richard. "Are you going to be a music teacher?" she asked me, still looking at him.

"I don't know, maybe," I told her. "Anyway, it's a long way off."

"She's going to school *now?*" Michael asked.

"She's not so old," Randy said. "Lots of mothers go to school."

"How old are you?" Michael asked me, wrinkling his forehead quizzically.

"None of your business," Randy said.

"I'll be thirty-three in July," I said. "Hey," I turned to Richard. "I found what you can give me for my birthday." Relieved to change the subject, I gave them all a blow-by-blow account of my hour at Porthault linens. I wound up, dramatically, with the prices of the floral, scalloped sheets.

Richard shook his head in disgust. "A thousand dollars to put some crappy sheets on a bed," he said. "Christ."

"Well, they are beautiful," I said. "All hand finished. And durable. I bet you'd never wear them out."

"Wear them out? Hell, I'd never sleep on them."

"Well, the ones *I* liked were the plain white. They'd never fade. And they're three-hundred-count cotton. They're not so expensive, though they're better cotton than the others, and they have this beautiful hemstitching."

"How much are *they*?" Richard was humoring me. He wanted to hear the punchline.

"The fitted sheets are only seventy-nine fifty," I said. "The big top sheet is one hundred seventy-five dollars. We do need sheets."

"Only five hundred dollars to do the bed," he chuckled. "A bargain. Forget it. Or I'll tell you what," he said, setting up the joke. "You can have the sheets and forget the tuition."

I thought about it. I really did.

10.

I was supposed to go shopping with Caroline Thursday morning for the paper goods for the League luncheon, but I begged off. "I have to see what I can do for Jessie," I told her. "Let me take care of that this morning. I'll meet you after lunch and we'll go to the party shop."

As soon as Michael left for school, I hustled the dishes into the dishwasher, straightened up the downstairs, and went upstairs. I raced through cleaning up Michael's room, closed the door to Randy's, and then made the bed in our room. The contour sheet was wrinkled on my mattress. I got the sewing box and stitched the seam at the corners, crouching on the rug to do it. Then I pulled it taut. It stayed. I put a freshly ironed pillowcase on my pillow and turned down the corner of the quilt. I stood for a minute, reflecting, and then I went down and got the AM/FM radio from the kitchen. I plugged it in behind the bed and set it on the night table. WNCN had the *Appassionata*. Horowitz, I thought, recognizing the phrasing from my own copy of the record. Why is it so much more exciting to hear it on the radio? I thought as I showered. It's like meeting a friend on an unfamiliar street: you didn't expect to see him, so it adds surprise to an old pleasure.

I powdered myself, put on fresh underpants, and slid into bed.

Sheet smooth under me. Taut over me. It was 9:30. I had two and a half hours.

Gideon called before I could dial Jessie's house.

"How was Mannes?" he asked. "Did you apply for next semester?"

"Not yet," I said. "I had to talk with Mrs. Wilton about whether I should go for the singing or just take courses that would prepare me to teach. She worked out a program for me that would cover either choice, but I wanted to think about it before I applied."

"What does Richard say?"

"Well, I didn't mention the singing lessons to him. One thing at a time." Quickly, to change the subject, I told him about Brescia. "Hair spray," I told him, "and brandy, and an antiseptic he spritzed on the mirror. Your complete tenor's dispensary." I hadn't meant to tell him about the part where we discussed my responsibilities, but I did. I told him the whole thing.

"He's right, you know," he said. "You have a responsibility to use your voice. You know it, too. That's why you didn't give them the application. You know you don't belong in the middle of the road. Anyone can teach—you can sing. You have to go for it."

"I can't just go for it. What about the traveling?"

"You might enjoy it."

There was a long, not uncomfortable silence, while several constellations of possible lives went past undiscussed.

"I have two kids," I said to the constellations and to Gideon.

"They'll leave you," he said.

"That's what Brescia said."

"Brescia is right. Men who sing are always right," and he hummed a little passage from the Erb piece. "He says you're okay to sing?" he asked abruptly. "Are you coming tonight?"

"Yes."

"I'll pick you up at seven o'clock. Okay?"

"Fine."

66

I dialed Jessie's number before I had time to think about it. She answered it herself.

"Hi Jessie, it's Beth." Pleasant and slightly upbeat, a note and a half higher than usual. An optimistic key.

"Beth, how are you?" She didn't sound any different.

"I'm all right. How're you doing?"

"Great. I'm just great. Feeling better every day. The only trouble is, as soon as I let them know it they pedal me off and shoot me full of trash, so I'm lying low here, practicing looking peaked. Want to come and spring me? We could head for the bright lights, be a month before they ran us down."

I laughed. "You demon. Why don't you behave and let them take care of you?"

"Horsefeathers. They're taking care of me like the bull takes care of the cow. Only the cow has more fun. Beth, they've got evil potions Fu Manchu never even thought of. But I'll get them. I'm going to come back and haunt them, turn their hypodermics into flying missiles and get 'em all in the keester. Say, how's the luncheon coming? I intend to be up and at 'em, especially at 'em. Hope you've got somebody better than last year's dream merchant."

"No kidding, you think you'll come? We're trying to get Victor Gotbaum."

"Damn right, I'll come. I've got a thing or two to tell *him*. Hey, is there still a ringside seat? I've got a mean right hook, now there's nothing in the way of my swing."

"Jessie, you're impossible. You act civilized or I'll tell Phyllis you asked for your own platter of her pecan surprises."

"You'd do it, too. Okay, I surrender. So what can I do to help? Stuff envelopes? Set tables? Sell memberships? Name it, Cookie."

"I'll let you know. When will I see you?"

"Open house here all hours of the day and night. 'Specially night." There was a haunted overtone to the last two words. I could imagine her nights. "Anyhow, by next week I intend to be up and out. This place is falling apart around me. I've got *things* to do. I've given them just about all the sack time I intend to. Starting next week, they'll have to send a posse after me."

"Well, I'll get over there before you break out. Need anything?"

"A fast man and a slow carriage. How soon can you get 'em here?"

"My luck, I'll find a slow man and a fast carriage. But I'll try. See you soon."

"You'll know me. I'll be the one in the wig."

I sat there with my hand still on the phone. Oh God. Her hair. I looked down at my powdered breasts. Suddenly disgusted with myself, I swung my legs out of bed, pulled up the quilt, threw the pillow into place and went to pull on jeans and a shirt. "Jerk," I said. "Holing up in bed when you're alive and well and can get out and do what you want." Fifteen minutes later I was pulling into Bloomingdale's parking lot.

I found Jessie a pretty blouse, a muted floral chiffon with a high ruffled collar and a lot of gathers from the yoke. I had to take it down to gift-wrapping, in the back of the linen department. Coming back through linens I saw a table spilling over with sheets. "Back to Basics," the sign said. "100% cotton, 200-count thread." I felt the sample. It didn't feel like the ones at Porthault. "Percale," I thought. "The ones my mother got us were percale." I went over to the display area. A bored girl in a trendy Bloomingdale's getup was presiding over the dressed beds and the monogrammed towels. One of the beds was done all in white with openwork lace at the borders. I went over and touched the pillowcase. It felt like canvas. I approached the girl. She was squinting downward at her outstretched fingernails. They were long and curved and squared off. They were blood red. "Which of the sheets are the finest weave?" I asked. "The smoothest?"

"The smoothest?" She considered it, then shrugged. "I really woodint know. You'd have to read the labels." I turned to go. "We have satin," she offered.

So they did. They were hanging in a lurid cascade. I touched

68

them and recoiled. "No," I tried again. "I thought maybe all cotton. Percale."

"We have Supercale." She pointed with one ghoulish finger at the shelves on the wall. Sure enough, Supercale. In the same five pastels they came in when we were married. One hundred percent cotton. All the packages were sealed.

"Can I open one, to feel the fabric?"

"To feel it?" She shrugged. "Go ahead." I slit one as neatly as I could. It wasn't as silky as the Porthault ones, but it wasn't $175 either. The blue was pretty near the blue in our room, but in the end I took a set in white. It came to $60.88.

11.

On the way to St. John's I told Gideon about hearing the Horowitz *Appassionata* on the radio. "There's this funny, nostalgic sound pianos always have on recordings," I said. "Like the performance is coming a long way from the past."

"That's the trouble with recorded performances," he said. "They *are* coming from the past. No risks, no surprises. They're dead."

"That's right! I always think that! I'd rather be at a street performance than hear the Guarneri on a record. There's that feeling, when you're at a live performance, that it's happening on the brink, you know? There's the possibility of mistakes, and the suspense is part of the experience. And there's always the possibility of being there at one of those miraculous moments. You have to be ready because you don't know when it's coming, and you'll never hear it again."

"That's the way it should be between a man and a woman," he said. "Ready for the miracle. But how many marriages do you know like that? Mostly people find a safe technique, tape out the mistakes, and replay the old performance, over and over. No surprises."

Quicksand. I didn't say a word. He touched the back of my neck lightly. "I love to be with you," he said, "because it's always

70

a live performance. Even though you think you're not ready for any miracles—" he ruffled my hair and returned his hand to the wheel "—just the things we talk about together, the fact that I never know what you're going to come out with—that's a miracle. Isn't it?" he demanded. "And don't you tell me things you don't talk to Richard about?"

"We're here," I said, "and we'd better go in. We're just on time."

I worked with total concentration at the rehearsal. I tried to use the things I'd learned with Brescia, but to use them as an instrument in symphony. Not to be a solo voice. It meant holding back, approaching the music with restraint. But it was such a relief to follow Lecrief's baton, to let him make all the choices. Just to follow and—yes—blend in. When it was time for the improvisation, I did a little ten-note exercise from the day before's lesson, and I did let that one rip. A woman from the row in front of me turned around. Gideon caught my eye and winked. I felt my face go hot and I concentrated hard on Lecrief's baton.

I was sweating when we walked out of the chapel. "Wait one minute for me," I told Gideon, and I ducked into the ladies' room. I blotted my face and neck with a tissue and ran a brush through my hair. Automatically, I put on fresh lipstick and then I thought about it and blotted it until the tissue didn't show the imprint. "Next stop, briar patch," I said to myself as I went out to meet Gideon.

"I won't kiss you—" he said as he got into the car.

Serves me right, I thought.

"—unless you say it's all right. I don't want to scare you off. Do I make you nervous?"

"Yes."

"Do you want to be kissed anyway? Once? To be on the brink?"

I shook my head. "Things break when you fall off that brink," I said. "Things that belong to other people."

"I knew that's what you were thinking," he said. "All or nothing. It doesn't have to be like that. We could get to know each

71

other, share something between us, and nothing would have to break. Your life would continue, mine would continue . . . and then there'd be what we had together." He ran a finger lightly along my thigh, took it away. "A live performance."

"That's too complicated for me," I said to my lap. "You'd better take me home."

"I'm not closing any doors," he said. "Think about it. I would love it, Beth, getting to know you."

We talked about other things all the way home. When we got off the highway, he pulled into a side street and, with the engine idling, he leaned over and kissed me, a long, sensual kiss, exploring with his tongue. It shot through my mind that I knew this kiss, then why I knew it. It was the one I'd imagined. The hotel-room kiss. I pulled back, but he put a hand on my neck and finished it. "I wasn't going to do that," he whispered. His breathing was out of sync. "But you'd never have said you wanted it, even if you did. Did you?" I looked away. "Okay. You don't have to say it. I'll take you home."

I lay in bed and played it back, over and over. Every time I did, my body reacted the way it had when he kissed me. Finally I wore myself out and fell asleep.

12.

Jessie looked at the box critically. "Well, I'll take a look, but if you got him at Bloomingdale's he can't be much. And if he's been lying still in this box for any time at all, he's not what I had in mind."

"Are you kidding? You ought to see what's walking around in Bloomingdale's these days."

"And me messing around in Altman's all these years. Damned if I didn't know I was doing something wrong. Twenty-five years of shopping and all I've gotten out of it is linen dish towels and a whole lot of double-knits." She looked at me cagily, the bangs of the brown wig arching stiffly over her tired eyes. "And where's the carriage? You don't expect us to carry on in here, do you? Place looks like a field hospital and smells like a morgue." She waved her good arm vaguely at the dressings, medicines, ice packs, and floral arrangements that seemed to have taken possession of every surface in the room. "If I die quick enough, we can use all these FTD Spring Fling Number Sevens at the funeral. It shouldn't be a total loss." Her eyes broadcast the fear that her voice and her grin denied.

I bounced a smile off her forehead. "Jessie," I said, "you're too mean to die. Besides, if you pop off now, what'll I do with him?" I jerked my chin at the box lying forgotten on her lap.

"You'll think of something," she said. "Well, let's see if he's worth living for."

I helped her with the box and held the blouse up for her to see.

"You know," she said finally, "I haven't gone near my closet since I got home, but it seems like every time I close my eyes, I see every damn blouse and sweater I own. And all those blasted double-knits." Her voice broke but she looked down at the box and fussed with the tissue paper, and when she looked up again she was in control. "And you're the only one who's thought about that, or maybe who's been able to face it. What does a woman wear who's lost half her breastworks?"

"Actually," I said, "I got it for you to wear to the luncheon. I hoped it was ladylike enough so you'd want to live up to it. I don't think our insurance covers unprovoked attacks on the speaker."

She sent me a quick look, almost as though she felt betrayed, but then she hitched up in the bed and grinned at me, her old self again. "You League types," she said. "How'd I ever get mixed up with you, a normal hot-blooded girl like me? You'd do anything, wouldn't you, to maintain order? Well, the hell with that. I'm not promising anything—not for a lousy blouse. Show up with that fella for me and I'll consider it. I can be bought, for the right price."

I made some noises about not wearing her out and coming to see her soon and got up to go. "Don't forget the carriage," she called from the bed as I stood at the door of the room. "And don't spare the horsepower. We'll have to do some traveling. Damned if I'm going to mess around in *your* precinct."

Michael was just coming across the lawn when I pulled into the driveway. I grabbed him and held him, rubbing a flat hand up and down his perfect back. He endured it for a minute, but then he squirmed out of it, shaking himself like a wet puppy. "What's for lunch?" he asked. "I gotta hurry up; Evan's waiting."

While he was eating and chattering to me about the dress rehearsals for his play, I kept seeing Jessie's face—the look on her

74

face when I joked with her about the blouse. When Michael left to pick Evan up, I called Richard.

"Hi there, Mrs. Clahr," Frances said. Frances is Richard's secretary. I send her a gift every Christmas and a gift certificate every once in a while when Richard tells me to, for good behavior. I've never seen her. "What does she look like?" I asked Richard the first time I had to choose a gift for her. He screwed up his face, trying to remember. "Hard to say," he said. "Big. Middle-aged. Not especially good-looking."

"Well, what would she like?" I persisted. "What does she do in her spare time?"

He looked at me as though I'd asked the dimensions of her belly button. "*I* don't know," he said. "How would I know? Just get her something for about twenty-five dollars. Get it somewhere where she can return it." That was a couple of years ago. I knew by now what Frances liked, and where she lived, and all about her nieces and nephews and travel plans. She knew all about my kids, too, because she always asked me how they were and what they were doing. There was always a faint pitying tone in her voice when she talked to me.

"I'm so sorry, dear, but he's all tied up right now. He's asked not to be disturbed."

"Unless he's in at the kill," I told her, "disturb him. Tell him it's me."

There was a little hesitation, then she said softly, "I'll try. Hold on, dear."

"Hi, baby. What's the matter?" Richard's voice was strung tight, but with an overlay of joviality. Must be someone in the office with him.

"I just needed to talk to you." I plunged into a description of my visit with Jessie.

"How much did it cost?" he asked. The joviality had gone. He sounded impatient now.

"What?"

"The blouse."

"Twenty-five dollars."

75

Silence. "Well, it's done, so forget it," he said.

"No—Richard—the thing is I think I understand why she looked so ... let down. She wanted to talk about it, let it out, and I got scared and I turned her off. I was afraid to hear it, I think."

"Listen, I can't talk now. Sal is—I'm in conference with Sal. But you did all you could. Forget it. And don't get dragged into it. You'll wind up with her leaning on you all the way down. That's not your responsibility."

"Yes it is," I said to the empty kitchen. Richard had hung up and I was still leaning against the wall. I was running my fingers through my hair, again and again. "She tried to say it to me. So it is my responsibility." I smoothed the hair repeatedly away from my eyes, trying to decide whether to get into bed or call her first, from here.

Summer. Backyard smells of grass and sweetness. The hammock swung easy, back and forth like waves. Stretched out flat in it, I couldn't reach one end with my toes, the other with my fingers. I couldn't make it go or stop it. It swung and took me with it. I didn't want it to stop. The drowsy fear that it might stop, that she might get tired and stop, made every motion seem like a present. I fluttered my eyes so she wouldn't think I was sleeping and go away.

"You sleeping, Bethie?"

"Sing."

It bumped once, stopped. The stillness was like hunger.

"Sing?"

"Sing."

She put a hand on my hair. Gentle. Smoothed it away from my face, smoothed it, smoothed it, sang the song. Toora Loora. And I swung and she smoothed it away, all of it away.

Not from my bed, I thought. Not that call. I'll do it now, get it over with, then I can be in bed.

"You wanted to talk about it and I didn't give you a chance," I said to her. "I realized it when I got home. I'm sorry, Jessie. It must be scary as hell."

"The worst part is that everyone's scared I'll act scared," she said. "So they come all over cheerful when I try to talk about it. 'Cancer,' I say, and they say, 'Hey, did you hear the one about the surgeon and nurse?' 'Malignant,' I say, and everyone starts in about the weather. All at once. 'Lost a breast,' I say, and people leave in droves. Empties the house every time. No one looks at me either. It's a whole epidemic of chuckles and sliding eyeballs. Don't feel bad; you're in good company. I never got so many laughs in my life, and I'm hardly even trying."

"I got you the blouse," I said slowly, "because you've lost a breast and it'll be a while before you can have a prosthesis made, or whatever, and because I wanted you to have something pretty to wear in the meantime that would camouflage the situation. I thought about it very clearly, but when you started talking about it, I panicked and changed the subject. I don't know why it was scarier when you said it than when I thought about it."

"Only little kids don't look away when someone's crying or showing fear or doing something else embarrassing. Like dying. Maybe it's a thing we all have about privacy. Or maybe we think pain is catching. I don't know. All I know is I'm suddenly responsible for keeping 'em rolling in the aisles and it's wearing as hell."

"You don't have to keep me rolling."

"You skinny types don't roll anyhow."

"I mean I'll listen."

"Thanks. You'll be sorry you said that."

I was sorry, as soon as I hung up the phone. More than sorry—terrified. Now I'd have to hear it all. And I didn't want to hear any of it. Images strafed my mind, of operating tables, knives, spinal needles, nausea and dizziness, huge X-ray machines, pain, fear, hospitals, nameless treatments, terror, terror, terror. I squeezed my eyes closed and willed it all away. I'm okay, I thought. The children are okay. Everyone is safe. Then, to my

77

horror, I found myself slipping into my Wednesday-morning check-list. I was saying it over like a prayer. So I started to sing. I sang the Cherubini, all through my shower and while I was putting on fresh underpants and powdering myself. When I finished it, I would count three beats and start it over. I sang it until I set the alarm and slipped between the sheets, and then it was time to be quiet. I reached over and switched the phone to "off." I lay down flat on my stomach. Smooth under me. I pulled the sheet high up away from my body and let it settle gently down. I didn't touch it at all after that. Didn't move, didn't stir. Lay quiet, quiet and safe.

Richard was standing in the kitchen, waiting for the kids to sit down for dinner that night. "Where'd you go this afternoon?" he asked.

"Me? Nowhere. Stayed right here."

"I tried you at two o'clock."

"You did?"

"I wanted you to get something out of the bank vault before it closed."

"Oh." 2:00. The phone was off. I was in bed. "I ran out to the market. Needed onions. You must have just missed me."

After dinner I ran upstairs and turned the phone back to "on." When you turn off the alarm from now on, turn on the phone, I told myself. Don't forget. Alarm off, phone *on*.

13.

Because by now I was admitting to myself that I wasn't just taking a little nap when I was tired in the afternoons. It wasn't a nap at all. It was something else, and whatever it was, it was worth protecting in ways I wouldn't have thought of a few weeks before. I thought of it then as an indulgence. I smiled to myself a little when I thought about it. A funny kind of clandestine oasis in my day.

But without really noticing it, I'd come to consider the bed as my place, and Richard began to seem a kind of intruder. I had the bed pretty much the way I wanted it, now. I'd taken the new sheets and put them through the washer and drier over and over the day I got them. Then I'd ironed them and put them on the bed, making it a kind of ritual of tender precision. It was nearly perfect. The sheets were white and crisp and smooth and fresh smelling. I'd gradually brought things upstairs: the good radio was on my night table permanently now; I'd bought a little transistor for the kitchen that stayed tuned to Richard's news station. Mine was exactly positioned for the clearest reception of WNCN. I'd made room on the night table for a stack of music books and a pencil holder, and for my League files. I'd had to move a bunch of photographs of the kids over to Richard's night table to make room for them. I was thinking then of the bed as a place where

I could work in peace, and I wanted everything where I could reach it, but actually I hadn't done any League work or homework from the bed yet; when I settled in for that hour of—whatever it was—I turned off the radio and just lay there, still in the silence.

When Richard got into bed at night, he sat up and watched the news on television, usually, and ate an apple or an orange. He'd be wearing his shirt, most nights, so he brought street smells and food smells and crunching and canned laughter and professional voices into the bed. He usually had the paper, too, and he got newsprint on the sheets. And even when he turned off the TV and the light and went to sleep, he fidgeted and thumped and yanked at the top sheet. But all that was over on his side. I moved over as far as I could onto my side, glad of the twin mattresses, and blocked out what I could. But there were the nights he moved over to my side, and it felt, suddenly, like an invasion.

Take the night after Michael's dress rehearsal: Monday. We were in bed and I was telling Richard about the scene Michael had made that morning when I was helping him into his fox costume. He was standing in the corridor outside his classroom, in Randy's brown tights and brown Danskin shirt, fidgeting while I adjusted the safety pins that held the tail on. He'd made a production of getting the tights on so they didn't wrinkle around his ankles, and he kept yanking at them. "Hurry up," he told me. "I have to go to the makeup mother."

"Well if you'd hold still, I could get this thing on," I said. "Don't move a minute." He let go of the tights and stood stiffly still for a minute, then squirmed abruptly. The pin almost went into his back.

"Michael!"

"I got an itch! Itch it!" he commanded.

"Where?"

"My *back! Itch* it!"

I scratched. "Not there!" He contorted his body around, trying to reach the itch. The tail swept along the floor.

"Michael—hold still! You're messing up the tail!"

80

"Well *itch* it then! You dummy!"

"Where? Here?"

"No! You know where! No! Dummy, dummy! *There.* Over *there.*"

Everyone was watching. I wanted to smack him, but I tried to look serene and loving. I grimaced conspiratorially at the disapproving faces of the makeup mothers, while I scored his back with my nails. Finally I hit the right spot and he subsided. I took him aside and finished pinning on the tail, then I turned him around and smoothed his hair under the fox cap.

"Honey, I didn't know where you itched," I told him. "When you have an itch, no one but you knows where it is." He'd looked disbelieving and a little panicky.

"You know what he said?" I asked Richard. "He said, 'How can you itch if you don't know where it is?' Richard, he broke my heart. He looked so lost, standing there in that dumb fox suit and refusing to believe I didn't feel his itches."

Suddenly Richard started pulling off his shirt and undershirt. "You look very sexy, for the mother of a fox," he said. "Want to scratch my itch? I'll help you find it." For Richard that was an elaborate overture, and there was something urgent in his face that got to me. This was an unscheduled event—no shower, no pajamas, no veiled hints to me to get ready. Just the look, under his smile, that he used to have when he would take my long hair and pull me down onto him. Hunger. Need.

I pulled off my nightgown. He bent over me, nuzzled between my breasts, flicking his mouth from one to the other. He only did that when he was really excited. I touched him. He was very hard. "Wait," I said. "Richard, I'm not ready." He touched me with an exploratory finger. "Oh yes you are," he breathed. He moved the finger, too fast.

"No, I mean I don't have the thing in. Wait."

"You're okay. You're safe. You just finished your period, didn't you? And you are very ready, baby."

I was. But even so, right while he was pumping in me, saying "Oh, my baby, oh my little baby," I thought about the bed. My

81

bed. He was on top of me in my bed, and there was going to be a wet spot on my sheet. I lost my concentration and he made the trip without me. It didn't matter. He didn't know. He never knew. Sometimes I was able to finish before he did, if the concentration was right, but after all these years he never knew the difference. He'd ask, "Good, baby?" as he slid out of me. Usually I lied; sometimes I didn't have to. Anyway, he finished and gave me a little kiss and rolled off. "You are some foxy lady," he said, heading for sleep.

I wiped off the sheet, using Kleenex after Kleenex. Then I spread some fresh Kleenex over the spot. Then I put my nightgown back on and arranged it under me so I couldn't feel the spot. "I'll change the sheet tomorrow," I thought, smelling his smell on the bed and on me and listening to his pre-snore breathing. After a while I fell asleep.

From then on, I changed the linen every time he came over to my side of the bed. But I couldn't shake the feeling that it was an invasion. I tried to maneuver things so that we were on his mattress, but that only worked on Saturday nights when I knew in advance that we'd be making love. He'd shower and put on the pajamas, and I'd wait for him on his side. He thought that was cute. "Afraid I'd forget and go to sleep?" he'd leer. "No way, little girl." But for some reason it wasn't just Saturday nights lately. On any night I might feel him reaching for me. The trouble was that once he started in, he didn't move around much, and if he started by leaning over to kiss me and sliding a hand under my nightgown—and he usually did—he'd be there on my side and fifteen minutes later I'd be lying on a wet spot and planning how to fit a load of laundry into my early-morning schedule.

It was funny about those nights. For the longest time—years, really—he'd been reaching for me in silence, with only a little smile on his face. But lately he'd always have a little line ready that he'd whisper as he ran his hand up my leg. I remember one night it was, "Want to join my club? I'd like to introduce a prominent member." And there was, recently, the urgency in his voice and the look of need on his face.

Strangely, though, instead of making me content those nights left me edgy and unsatisfied. For the first time since the early days of our marriage I went around feeling horny and I spent a lot of time in fantasies. I was putting the diaphragm in every night now, just in case, and when I took it out in the morning, there was always a moment when my hand, almost independent of what I was thinking, found its place and I was tipping over into my most efficient fantasy and, within a minute, coming in spasms sitting on the toilet or even leaning against the wall. Heart pounding, flesh still throbbing, I would finish mopping myself up and go on to the next task—straightening up the bathroom or stripping the bed or getting dressed.

So those parts were getting a lot of traffic, but whether I came at night or—more likely—by myself in the morning, or both, I was hungry for it all the time. But not for Richard; every time he came at me with the whispered gambit and the look, I put myself in his hands and let it go whatever way it was going to go, but if he'd never touched me at all, I wouldn't have missed it, and if he'd made love to me morning and night and twice on Sundays, I'd still have been hungering. Maybe even more so.

I thought about Gideon a lot. About being, just for a little while, out of everyone's reach—on leave, sanctioned, accounted for—and then finding myself thrown together with him in a place where I could arrange safely to yield to him. One climactic time. It wasn't easy to think of a reason for me to be away in a place where he might be, or to figure out how I could be in touch with the kids without being found out, but I worked out a few. I had the hotel-room one. I had one where I went to visit my father and stepmother in Arizona and ran into him at the airport in Chicago when the plane was held overnight because of a snowstorm. And there was one where I set out to hear a series of Bernstein lectures in Boston but ended up instead in a beach house, in his arms. That was my favorite.

We met at the lecture, decided afterward to go for a ride to the beach, walked too close to the surf, got drenched by a wave, and went to his friend's empty house to dry off. I was drying my hair

83

when Gideon came up behind me and took the towel from my hands. He turned me to him and slowly and gently massaged my hair with the towel. Then he dropped the towel and, holding my eyes with his, unbuttoned my wet blouse. There was a big bed in front of the oceanside window, with a soft, warm, clean old quilt on it in blues and pinks, and at first he pulled it around us to warm us, but then he drew it back in a line from my shoulders to my knees. In this one, he was tracing the hollow of my shoulder with the tip of his tongue when I began to go under, and then he came down over me for a kiss, whispering my name.

I pulled those thoughts out at funny times. Driving. Waiting in the car for school to let out. Lying still on the wet spot at night, with my arms around the pillow and my fingers moving in little stroking motions on the pillowcase. One day I was walking from the music store to my car, thinking about the kiss—the real one, last week in the car—and a man walking briskly toward me must have intercepted the heat rays, because he faltered in his step and then turned and caught up with me. I didn't catch on to what was happening until he spoke. "Excuse me," he said, at my elbow, "and I don't believe myself that I'm doing this, but are you busy Friday night?" I must have still been going on the momentum of my thoughts, because I smiled at him like a woman of the world and said, "Yes, I am. With my husband."

"Lucky man," he said gallantly, but he looked confused as he turned away. I quickstepped the rest of the way to the car with my eyes on the sidewalk, thinking, Talk about a bitch in heat, but smiling a little. Bitch.

It was only the end of April, but after that I wore sunglasses whenever I was out.

I was out a lot. We had one unseasonably hot day and the kids tried on all their summer stuff and nothing fit. So they needed clothes, and I had to start thinking about Randy's camp stuff, and the luncheon was coming closer, so there were things to be done for that. Then there was a day when there was just no time for my afternoon retreat, and somehow the next day I chose to look for a pair of sandals instead of taking the time to shower and unmake

84

and remake the bed, and the day after that I didn't even think of it until it was too late to bother. I was a little relieved. It was a silly habit to get into anyway, I thought. But still I kept the radio and my files up there, and changed the linens whenever Richard made love to me. I kept it ready.

14.

Randy came in from school that Tuesday when I was doing an exercise Brescia had given me. It was the first chance I'd had all day to practice. I'd started with what he called the "velvet sigh": I had to start with any high spot my voice could comfortably attain and slide down lightly in a kind of siren sound. It was to develop height in the voice—the falsetto or "high velvet" range.

She burst into the living room, breathing heavily. "What's the matter?"

I stopped. "Nothing," I said. "I'm practicing."

"That's practicing?"

"Yes. Let me finish, honey. Take a snack."

"Okay. Doesn't sound like singing to me. Sounds like you're falling off a cliff."

"It isn't singing. It's vocalizing. Stretching the voice, or giving it depth. Like you limber up to dance, sort of."

"I don't dance."

"I know." I wasn't about to get into that now. "Let me finish, Rand."

"Sure." She turned on her heel and went off toward the kitchen, trying to whistle.

I resumed the exercise, feeling a little silly now, but determined to get the practicing in before Michael got home. The refrigerator door slammed. Randy came in with a glass of milk. "Did you get my jeans shorts?"

I pointed out to the hall, where I'd left the package from Young Corner.

"In the hall?"

I nodded, damned if I was going to interrupt my velvet sighs again. But I was forcing it now, and the velvet sounded like burlap. Randy came back in, holding up a pair of shorts with two fingers of each hand.

"What's *this?*"

I finished my sigh, sighed for real, and said, "Shorts. Randy, please. I'll talk to you in a few minutes."

"Okay, but I'm not wearing these. They're gay."

Beverly Sills, Rosie? Come visit my planet. Bring your space suit. I was about to sound off at Randy when the phone rang and she went running to get it. I heard her giggle and the kitchen door closed.

I stood for a minute with my hands clenched at my sides. Then I unclenched them and interlaced the fingers lightly in front of me, thumbs touching. I took a deep breath, closed my eyes, let the breath out slowly, pushing out the last of it, released the death grip my back teeth had on each other, lowered my shoulders and thought the muscles into relaxation. Then I filled my lungs with air and reached for a note to slide down from. No good. My body was eased, but the vocal cords were thick with tension and the jaw and tongue were tight. So I started all over with the relaxation exercises. I worked my fingers downward over my face, kneading gently over my forehead and eyelids, over the cheek and jawbones, down to the cleft in my throat. I wagged my chin around to get it easy and loose. Then, carefully thinking of nothing, I sang a scale while wiggling my tongue around a fully open mouth. "You cannot do this unless the jaw and tongue are fluid and easy," Brescia had said. "And unless they are fluid and easy, they will hold the note in the mouth. The mouth must be the last place the note passes before you give it to us. It shapes the note, only gently shapes it. So make easy the neck and the jaw and the tongue."

I was on the second scale when I heard a single loud falsetto note of laughter followed by a snicker. I opened my eyes. It was Michael and Evan. Now Michael was guffawing, faking it a little. Evan was looking down, holding his laughter in check, but he glanced sideways at Michael and then he gave in to it again. "What was that?" Michael asked. "The stupid song?" He was still working on the laugh but his eyes were embarrassed and angry. He closed his eyes, held his hands outstretched in a dramatic steeple, and sang a falsetto *vibrato* scale, waving his tongue around wildly. I had looked foolish in front of his friend, and he was leading the attack.

"That will do," I said, in as final and menacing a tone as I could muster. "Evan, go home. Michael, go to your room."

"I can't go home," Evan said, eyes shooting to Michael for corroboration. "My mother isn't there."

"Me and Evan have to rehearse," Michael said. He looked scared. "We gotta do our lines for the play. We *got* to."

The play. Tomorrow was the play. Wednesday, my Mannes day. How could I have forgotten? "All right," I said. "You may rehearse. But I want you to know I'm not happy with you. I don't laugh at you when you practice piano, and I don't expect you to laugh at me when I'm practicing my singing. Ever. Do you understand?"

"Yeah. C'mon, Evan." He turned to go.

"Wait a minute." They stopped.

"What?"

"You owe me something. I'm waiting."

"*What?*"

"An apology." Michael looked at me, stunned. He'd gotten away with much worse. He couldn't figure out this showdown. Neither could I, really. Randy appeared at the doorway.

"What's going on?" she asked. She looked with pleasure at the sight of Michael catching it. "What'd he do?"

"And you," I said. "When you're working, doing your homework, I don't bother you. And you are to respect my practicing in the same way. You can manage to leave me alone for half an hour and not to interrupt me with nonsense. Can't you?"

Astonishment and resentment chased across her face. "Sure," she said. Her voice was brittle. She turned around and ran upstairs. I heard her door slam. I looked at Michael. "Well?"

"Okay," he said.

"And what?" There was a long moment when we stared each other down.

"*Sorr-ee*," he sang. "Let's go, Evan." They burst into giggles on the stairs. I heard the fake-operatic scale again.

"On the other hand, Rosie," I said aloud, "don't come. You wouldn't like it here."

There was no point in trying to finish practicing until I calmed down a little, so I decided to take care of the Wednesday-morning conflict. I dialed Mannes, then stood with my eyes closed, smoothing the hair from my forehead over and over as I waited for someone to answer. "Mannes School," a voice said.

"Mrs. Wilton, please. This is Beth Clahr."

"I'm sorry, Miss Clahr. Mrs. Wilton is with a class now. I can take your number and have her get back to you."

"Would you be sure to do that? It's important that I speak to her today."

"If you'll give me your phone number, please." She was annoyed. I gave her the number and hung up. Then I thought about a place to finish my practicing. I couldn't go back to the living room; it was open to the rest of the house. I needed a room with a door to close. My room. No—Michael's room was across the hall from it and I'd be tense, listening for the giggling and the mocking scales. I went upstairs and knocked on Randy's door.

"Yes?"

"It's me."

She opened the door, walked away from it, and sank back onto the rug. "Yeah?" She wasn't looking at me.

89

"I'm going to be practicing downstairs with the door closed. I want you to get the phone if it rings. If a Mrs. Wilton calls, come and get me. If anyone else calls, take a message and tell them I'll call back."

"Where'll you be?"

"In the downstairs bathroom."

"In the bathroom?" She was looking at me now, a TV-comedy look of disbelief on her face. Archie Bunker listening to Edith.

"In the bathroom. And I don't want to be disturbed for half an hour, unless Mrs. Wilton calls. Got it?"

"Sure. Anything you say." She shrugged for the TV audience and, flopping over into the middle of a spread of papers and books, picked up a pencil.

"Listen, Randy, I want you to understand what happened down there. Look at me. I love you, and I'm happy to do things for you and to answer your questions and be there for you. But today I was practicing, and that's important to me, working on my voice, and you kept interrupting me about those damned shorts when it could have waited. Can't you understand that that made me angry?"

"I guess so. Since when is it so important, about your voice?"

"I'm giving it a try. I'm taking some lessons; I want to find out if I can be any good."

"You're going to be a *singer?*"

"I don't know. All I know right now is that I have a lesson tomorrow and I want to practice for half an hour now."

"Okay. Mom?"

"Mm?"

"Those shorts are the wrong kind. They're too dark and stiff, and they're hemmed across the bottom."

"They're not supposed to be hemmed?"

"No. They're supposed to be . . . you know, just natural."

"Fringed, you mean?"

"Whatever you call it. Like cut."

"All right. So on Thursday or Friday we'll go and get the right kind."

"No, I *need* them for Thursday. That's the first softball practice."

"So wear jeans."

"Nobody wears jeans to practice. Bad enough I can't hit the ball, I don't have to look creepy, too."

Absolute truth. She couldn't afford to look creepy. There were kids who could show up wearing Dr. Dentons and it would be acceptable. But Randy's only hope of surviving those games was to be invisible. Invisible meant the uniform.

I looked at my watch. Almost 4:00. I couldn't go to the village until I heard from Mrs. Wilton, and besides, I couldn't leave Michael and Evan in the house alone. Out of the question to bring them along. "I can't take you today," I said.

"There's tomorrow," Randy offered. "After school. You can pick me up and we'll go. We could get me a skirt, too, if you want."

That was a peace offering. She'd been fighting me bitterly on the question of owning a skirt.

"I can't go tomorrow, honey. It's Wednesday; I have a lesson in the city."

"You're going to Michael's play."

So she'd remembered it was my Mannes day. Checking out how she measured up against Michael in the love playoffs.

"But I can make it in for my lesson after the play. It's a commitment, Randy. I can't just cancel a private lesson."

"It's a private lesson? How much do they cost?"

"I don't question how much your orthodonture or your camp cost—" I broke off. How had I gotten entangled in a defense of my expenditure? More than one bitch in this house, after all. But I had the advantage of more seasons in the field. I pivoted and came at her from another direction.

"What if you went shopping yourself?"

"Me?"

"Sure. You've been asking to do it. You can go to Young Corner or County Men's and Boys' and charge it."

"You said it wasn't safe for me to ride my bike into the village. You said the crazy teenagers were all driving around after school."

A hit. A very palpable hit. "But you're right. I have to start trusting you sometime. If you go with a friend and you're very careful, I guess you can manage it. Or you could even take the bus."

"You said the bus doesn't run often enough and I might not get home until after dark." Found. Another chink. Damn kids have tape recorders in their heads.

"Right. So take your bike. Go with Rebecca. You'll have time to buy the shorts and choose a skirt and have a Coke at the Tin Drum and still get home by four or four-thirty."

Her eyes widened. "The Tin Drum?" That was where the teen-agers hung out. On her last excursion to the village with Rebecca—I'd driven them and picked them up—she'd been forbidden to go in there. I was sure the kids in there were smoking grass.

"Well, if you're old enough to do your own shopping, I guess you're old enough to handle the Tin Drum."

"All *right!* I'll call Rebecca." She scrambled up, stepping on her graph papers and breaking a pencil. "You'll have to give me some money."

"You'll charge the things."

"But for the Tin Drum."

"Nossir. Cokes are on your ticket, not mine."

"Okay." A cedeable negotiating point, but worth a try. She ran out of her room and banged on Michael's door.

"What?"

"Hey Mikey, you'll have to make yourself a date after school tomorrow."

The door opened a crack. His head appeared. "How come?"

"I'm going shopping in the village. I may not be home till late. Mom'll be at her lesson in the city."

"You're going alone?"

"Yup. Well, with Rebecca. It's no fun to go to the Tin Drum alone."

"You are not. The Tin Drum? She's letting you?"

She glowed. "Sure. Why not? Hey, you want anything? I can pick something up for you if you want."

He blinked. "Me? What do you mean?"

"Oh, I dunno. School supplies? Socks? Something from Big Top? As long as I can carry it in my bike basket."

"Yeah. Some baseball cards. But I wanna go and pick them out."

"Sorry." Her voice was ripe with magnanimity. "I can't take you. But you tell me exactly what you want and I'll get it. Well, I gotta go now. Gotta call Rebecca. Have fun playing."

"Yeah." He said it to her back. He was transfixed. "Yeah."

"Nothing beats experience in the field," I said to my image in the bathroom mirror. "Remember that."

15.

Rosie Wilton called when I was finishing up the practicing with scales. I was concentrating on forming vowel sounds without losing the quality of the chest tones when Randy opened the door.

"Mom? Mrs. Wilton's on the phone. *That* sounded like singing," she added as I picked up the phone.

"Your daughter sounds charming," Rosie told me.

"She is," I lied. "Thank you. And thanks for calling back. I wanted to tell you I have a problem for tomorrow. My little boy is going to be in his class play, and to tell you the truth, I just hadn't realized it was on a Wednesday morning. I'll have to miss class. I'm sorry."

"I'll miss you, but of course performers have to support one another. You won't miss your lesson, though?"

"No. I'm going to try to make it."

"Do. You can't let things interfere with your lessons. It's little enough time as it is. Probably you'll have to give them more time next year. By the way, have you applied for the summer program?"

"Not yet."

"That you must do immediately. Speak to Vincent before you do; he may have something to say about the emphasis of your program. Will you let me know?"

"Of course."

I meant to speak to Richard about the singing lessons that evening, but I wasn't about to bring it up while the kids were around, and it took them forever to get to bed. Michael kept getting up and coming down to check on his assemblage of things to take to school for the performance. While he was putting them back into the bag for the tenth time, Marylynn Padou called.

"Beth? Marylynn. Sorry to call at the last minute like this, but I know I can count on you, you're such a trouper."

"What's the problem?"

"No problem, really. But they're having a class party tomorrow and Michael volunteered you to help with the serving. Nothing much to do, really, just pour their little juice and put the cupcakes out on trays. Actually, *yours* you can just bring right on a tray so it'll only be the other batch to arrange, and then to make sure they all get a napkin and—"

"Mine?"

"Pardon?"

"My cupcakes?"

"Yes. I'm saying you can just bring them on a little doily or something, on any old tray and then they'll be r—"

"Back up, Marylynn. What cupcakes? Was I supposed to have made cupcakes?"

"You must have signed up for baking. I have you down right here. 'Cupcakes,' it says. Did you forget?"

"No. And I didn't sign up, either."

"Well, I guess Michael volunteered you. He knows you can always be counted on. Let me tell you, Beth, it's pathetic how few mothers can, anymore. It isn't a problem, is it?"

"Yes. It's a problem. Because this is the first I've heard of it and it's nine o'clock."

"Oh, I *am* sorry. Well, you know you can always just pick some up on your way. These kids don't know homebaked anyway, anymore. And as I said, just set 'em out on a tray, and—"

"I'm sorry, Marylynn, but I can't be at the class party."

"You can't?"

"No. I have to run to the city right after the performance to make a voice lesson. As it is, I'll be missing a class."

"I didn't know you were taking voice lessons. I *am* impressed. All you talented people. And here I sit, with nothing to show for my life but my Theo and my Greg and my Nicky. They do seem to like having me around, though."

One of the three was her husband, and if I remembered right he spent all evening at every PTA social trying to lose her. He always took off his gummed name tag as soon as she put it on him. He liked to introduce himself directly, mostly to the younger mommies.

"I don't know how talented I am, but I do have a lesson and I can't miss it. I'll bring in some cupcakes, though," I added, "—on a tray."

"Y-es. So I guess I'll be serving again. Thought I could share the responsibility this one time, but. . . . Oh well, Nicky will be glad. They do like to have their mommies show an interest, don't they? Silly, I guess. Well, you have a good lesson and be sure and send me a ticket to your debut."

I looked around for Michael, but he'd disappeared. "An instinct for survival," I muttered as I slammed the cupcake tins down on the table and started shoving paper liners into them.

Richard walked in. "What's this?" he asked. "Baking? Now? I thought we'd hit the sack early." He came up behind me and put his hands on my breasts. "I've got something cooking, too."

"Richard, it's only nine o'clock. And I have to make these cupcakes."

"What for?"

I explained what for. "So buy some," he said. He still had his hands on my breasts. He was moving them in circles, and it was hurting. I shrugged away and went to get the measuring cups. "I can't," I said. "I have to make them. It'll take at least two hours, with the icing, and then I'll be tired."

"I'll revive you," he said. It sounded as if he thought he'd be doing me a favor. I didn't answer, just sifted and measured.

96

Randy came into the kitchen. "Michael's playing a record," she said. "Isn't he supposed to be asleep?"

"Tell Michael to turn it off and go to sleep," I said. She turned on a dime and sprinted up the stairs, then thudded down them again almost immediately, yelling, "I'm telling!" Over the noise of the mixer, she told: "Would you like to know what your son said? He told me to f-u-c-k off. Sorry about the word—he said it, not me."

"Tell your brother I will be up to deal with him in a minute. Tell him that record had better be off when I get up there. And if you're finished with your homework, please get to bed."

"I have to wash my hair." She was gone. I poured the batter into the cupcake tins, slammed them into the oven, set the timer, and went grimly up the stairs, leaving Richard behind in the kitchen. Normally he'd have been wading into Michael by now, but he was strangely passive and it was okay, because I had aggressions to spare.

I heard the record as I approached Michael's room and of all things, it was a Sesame Street record. Baby stuff: he hadn't listened to it in two years at least. My voice was deadly against Big Bird's manic cheer: "You were told to turn that off." Silence. Big Bird rattled off the alphabet again. I turned the knob to "off"; the voice moaned to a halt. I looked at Michael's bed, trying to get a fix on him in the dim light from the hall. He wasn't moving. I closed in. "Well?"

"I'm not doing it."

"Doing what?"

"That stupid fox." Panic or tears had pushed his voice up half an octave. I could see him now. He was lying on his bed, the covers up to his chin. Both hands were hidden. I knew where they were. I sat down on the bed, moving him over.

"What are you talking about?"

"The *fox*. I'm not doing it. I'm not gonna be in the play. Just forget it, that's all."

"Who says you're not?"

97

"Me." A hand came up to wipe his nose. I handed him a Kleenex. He swiped impatiently at his face with it, threw it down, and turned on his side, away from me. I put a hand on his shoulder and rolled him back over, not all that gently.

"Michael, what is all this nonsense? Records at ten o'clock, dirty words to your sister? What's with you?"

"I don't know it, that's all, and I'm not doing it."

"You don't know your lines?"

"I got it all wrong in the auditorium today and Mrs. Quintero said if I didn't know it any better than that, they'd have to let Roger do it. He can do it. I'm not even going to school."

"Yes you are. And you do know your lines—I've heard you do them perfectly."

"Yeah? So how come even with Evan I kept forgetting my song about the grapes?"

"Michael, if you were in trouble, why didn't you ask me to help with your lines?"

"You were practicing. Randy said we had to leave you alone."

Look at that. I didn't even have to go out of town to abandon my kids for my career. I touched his hair. It was wet, and I smoothed it back away from his face. "All right." My voice was gentle now. "Let's hear it right now. I bet you know it fine. You come out on stage and you look up at the grapes . . ."

He was midway through his song, morose but letter-perfect, when Richard came in. "What's this, a private concert?" he asked. "Don't you intend to go to sleep at all?"

"Start over, Michael," I said, still smoothing back his hair. "Let Daddy hear it. He won't get to hear you do it tomorrow." Richard never made it to the kids' plays. He was always out in the field or at a meeting. "Oh yes I will," he said. "And I expect a front-row center seat."

"You're coming?" Michael and I both said it.

"Absolutely. How often do I get to see my son in a Greek drama?"

Michael sat up, pulling his hand out of his pajama bottoms and

98

shaking me out of his hair. "Aesop was Greek," he informed me. "Daddy, you're coming?"

"Yes, sir. If you go to sleep now. I'm not coming to watch you napping on the stage."

Michael planted a kiss on Richard's cheek and sank back into bed. "Okay," he said. " 'Night."

Just like that. One word from Richard. "You're comfortable with your lines now, honey? You want me to finish hearing them through?"

"Yeah, I'm comfortable. Anyway, Roger's a poop." I think he was asleep before he finished speaking.

The timer was silent when I got down to the kitchen. It had gone off while I was upstairs. The cupcakes weren't burnt but they were probably dry. Tough. I have an excuse this time, Marylynn. I was doing my job. Mothering. I beat the hell out of the icing.

Richard had followed me downstairs. He stuck a finger into the bowl. "Good," he said. "I always did like sweet things. How about it, sugar?"

"How come you're coming to the play all of a sudden?"

He backed away, looking hurt and—something else—wary. "Can't I come to my son's assembly program? I thought you'd be pleased."

"I am pleased. But don't you have a meeting?"

"No. I don't have a meeting. So is it all right with you if I come?"

"Of course. It would have been all right if you'd come to any of the others before, too—his and Randy's. It would have been very nice." I was spreading icing on the cupcakes and I didn't look at him when I said it. I didn't look up when he left the kitchen. When the cupcakes were all iced, I dug out the tube of yellow lettering icing I used for birthday cakes and made a flower on each one. I arranged them on a doily on my best tray and stuck some yellow straw flowers in the center. I covered the tray carefully

99

with Saran Wrap and left it on the counter. Take that, Marylynn, and stick it in your motherly ear.

When I got upstairs, the light was out and Richard didn't move when I got into bed. I figured he was asleep.

16.

We didn't sit front-row center, of course. We sat way in the back, in the rows reserved for parents, behind all the children. Richard held my seat while I went down to Michael's classroom and gave the tray of cupcakes to Mrs. Quintero.

"Beautiful," she burbled. "You do things so nicely."

"Well," I said, "the kids do like to have their moms show an interest, don't they? I'm awfully sorry to miss the party, but I have an appointment I couldn't—"

"That's just fine," she said absently, checking something off on her list. "Enjoy the show. I know you will, Mrs.—"

"Clahr. Michael's mother."

"Ah, yes. Our fox. He'll be fine, if he thinks a little and speaks slowly."

"He'll be fine," I reported to Richard, "if he thinks a little and speaks slowly. Mrs. Quintero's professional opinion."

"Stupid bitch."

"Shh. I'll go in with you, after the play."

"To the city?"

"It's Wednesday." I waited to see if it connected. It didn't. "My Mannes day."

"Right, right. Hey, great. You can come in with me, see how us poor working folk live."

The houselights went out. For no reason at all, sitting there on the short wooden auditorium seat, I thought of Gideon and the night of the last rehearsal. I heard the catch in his breath when he said, "I wasn't going to do that. But you'd never have said you wanted it, even if you did." I closed my eyes against the wave of pleasure that overtook my body. "No," I whispered to him in the silence behind my eyes. "I can't say it to you." But I touched his hand as I said it, left my fingers on his. "I'll teach you," he said, "to say it."

Richard poked me. "Fox at bat," he whispered. "No runs, no hits, lots of team errors."

He stood stage left, looking up exaggeratedly at the plywood tree and the bunch of grapes that dangled over his head. A skinny fox with a potbelly and a smartly curving tail. I breathed for him. In, out, in . . .

"Oh, how delicious those grapes look," he bellowed. "I will just take some for my lunch." He jumped, reaching for the grapes. The tail stayed on. He put a finger to his temple, thinking. "Hmmm," he said. "Not high enough. I should have had my Wheaties this morning." The adults laughed, drowning out his next line. "I will have to jump higher," I whispered.

He grinned at the audience and did a couple of little practice jumps. "I will have to jump higher," he confided in us. His voice really carried. He wasn't bellowing anymore, either. He had relaxed into it, and he was even hamming it up a little. I sat back in the seat, giving my heart something to pound against.

His efforts having failed, the fox stepped downstage and put his hands angrily on his hips. The piano played two introductory measures. I sat forward again, to help him sing.

"If I can't get them, I don't want them," he sang, tossing his head. His pitch was perfect. Really.

> . . . they were sour anyway.
> Who wants grapes that look so sour?
> I can do better any day.

102

I wasn't even really hungry.
I'm just as full as I can be.
So someone else will have to eat them.
They are much too sour for me.

He waited a second for the applause, then stamped flashily up-stage. A hand held the back curtain open for him. He disappeared into the slit, flicking his tail jauntily as he went.

I caught up with him in the hall, leaving Richard behind as I wove through lines of kids and grandparents with cameras. I grabbed him by his brown shoulders. "You were sensational," I told him. "We heard every word and you sang beautifully. You're a terrific fox, you know that?"

"Yeah," he said. He was looking around the hall. "Where's Daddy?"

"Coming," I said. "Do you want me to undo your costume?"

"No. The costume mothers will. Here he is. Hey Dad, did you like it?"

"Did I like it? Fantastic. You were fantastic. The whole thing was terrific."

"What was best?"

Richard leaned over, whispered in his ear, "You were. But don't tell anyone." Michael beamed.

"I left a tray of cupcakes for your party," I said. "Special ones."

"I know. Well, bye. Thanks for coming."

"Randy will be home to let you in at three," I called to his back. He didn't give any sign he'd heard. I went to follow him, but Richard stopped me. "He'll be fine," he said. "Come on, we'll miss the train."

We bounced along on the 11:06. "You're looking great today," Richard said. "You know you've been looking terrific . . . very sexy, lately. Even with the briefcase, you're sexy."

"Thank you." I sounded prim, even to myself.

He leaned over and whispered, "How about me? Am I still sexy? You still love the old man?"

"Of course," I said. If he'd asked me if his nose was on straight

103

I'd have said "of course" in the same tone. Cold bitch. What was the matter with me? "What's the matter, Richard?" I asked in a warmer voice. "Are you okay?"

"Yeah. I'm fine. Having a hairy couple of weeks out there in the real world, but I've got a handle on it. It'll be fine."

"Trouble at work? What is it?"

"Nothing. Things going a little wrong, going a little too right for other people. It'll swing back, though."

"Going wrong?"

He sat back and crossed his legs and shrugged, smiling. "You know this business. You can go six months without getting a contract. You bid low, someone else bids a little lower, that's all. It happens."

"Six months?"

"Four months, six months. Bids don't go out every week, you know. But don't worry, baby, it'll go my way again. I've got one ready to go out now, and if Russo doesn't screw me, I think I'll get it."

"Why would Russo—"

"He's been giving me the ballbusters to bid lately, and this is a beaut—possibility of water, complications that could eat up the profits—and if he gets nervous enough about losing money on it he could screw around with the PM."

"PM?"

"Profit margin. Listen, you don't have to—"

"Like he did to Grady?"

He winced. I shouldn't have said it. Grady was an older man who'd started out with Russo's father in the business. Richard had told me the story. Grady had underbid a whole string of jobs and they'd had trouble breaking even on the work in some of them. Finally Russo lost confidence in him and started adding a fifteen percent or twenty percent profit margin to his bids instead of the usual ten percent, trying to recoup. "So the guy strikes out, job after job, because he's carrying this extra percentage on his bids," Richard had explained to me. "So on this *last* bid he cuts it to the bone, *under* the bone, and what does Russo do but drop the

PM to seven percent and Grady gets the contract but Russo loses a boodle doing the job." I had met Grady. Russo didn't fire him, but he never estimated jobs anymore. He ran back and forth to the county clerk's offices and kept track of the subcontractors' receipts and permits. He still called Russo "Sal" but he came to work in a sweater and shared a desk with the bookkeeper.

"No, not like Grady. Grady was a turkey Russo inherited from the old man; he was looking to get him out. Me he needs, and he knows it. Anybody can have a dry four months." He recrossed his legs, squeezing them so tightly together that the material in his trousers cut into his legs. I thought of Michael lying in bed with the blanket up to his chin, holding himself under the covers. "Don't you worry, baby, Russo needs me more than I need him. But meanwhile he's making it a little hot for me, that's all. Jerking me around."

"Who's it going so well for?"

"Who's? . . . oh. Walsh. Walsh is having a run. Every job he points his thing at rolls over and opens its legs for him. Russo's gold-plating him these days. But—"

"Richard, are my courses too expensive? I have to write the check for registration, and I was going to ask you about voice lessons. They cost a fortune . . . maybe I should forget it for now."

"You want singing lessons?"

"Well, not if it—"

"When I can't afford to stake you for a couple of lousy lessons—hey listen, we pay for the kids' piano lessons, don't we? You want to sing, baby, you ought to do it. You do enough for us." He put a hand on my thigh. I didn't move away.

"But maybe it's a bad time to have these extra expenses," I said. "Richard, I don't mind stopping. If we can't do it, we can't."

"You want to do it, we can do it. What is it, a couple hundred dollars?"

"It's twenty-five dollars a lesson. If I take two a week, that's fifty dollars a week. I—I've already had two, but one was just . . ."

His eyebrows went up and he straightened, taking his hand off my thigh. He'd left a damp spot on my poplin skirt. Now I moved a little, shifting away in the seat and facing him. "Twenty-five hundred dollars a year," he said. His eyes were open, but he was inside them, thinking. Then he frowned at me. "I thought you said something about teaching," he said. "So what do you need so many singing lessons for?"

"Brescia—that's the voice teacher—says I may be good enough to sing professionally. Well, what he really says is my voice may turn out to be a good instrument. What I do with it then is another thing. But I won't even know whether it's possible unless I give it a good try—enough lessons to see what's there."

"So then what?" He sounded incredulous. "Then you'll be some kind of a singer?"

"Richard, I don't know. I'm just at the beginning. Most likely I'll wind up teaching music, or maybe leading a chorus or something. Anyway, it'd be a couple of years before I'd even know whether the voice was good enough, and longer before I'd be ready to do anything with it. But I'll be taking other courses, too, so I'd be ready to teach or whatever."

"You don't have to, you know. I do pretty well taking care of you."

"Of course you do. But I want to be interesting for you, Rich. You're a dynamic man; I don't want you to wake up and find yourself married to a useless and boring woman who hasn't grown in twenty-five years."

I recognized the melody, but I was shocked to hear myself singing it. I hadn't for a minute thought of the singing or the courses in connection with Richard. He hadn't entered my mind. I waited for him to call me on the lie; it was so blatant, I deserved it. But he relaxed and grinned and said, "Well, at least you don't think you need sables to make you interesting. Maybe twenty-five hundred dollars is cheap at that. If you want to take the lessons, baby, take them. Seems to me once a week ought to do it, though. If you're that good, you don't need so many lessons, right? Anyway, you don't want to push yourself. One of us under the gun is enough."

"But what if I—"

"I said don't worry. You feel like taking singing lessons or dancing lessons, do it, baby. Russo with his PM and Walsh with his gold-plated fucking bids . . . they don't have what I have. They don't have you to come home to." His eyes were red. He cleared his throat and uncrossed his legs. "You just be there at the énd of the day for me and I can handle the rest."

"Grand Central, next station stop, Grand Central. This is our final—"

I put a hand on my briefcase and got ready to stand up. I pitched my voice under the amplified announcement. "Richard, but what if he says doubling the lessons is the best way to go? What should I do?"

"What? Oh, your voice guy you mean." He sniffed and cleared his throat, shifting in his seat and reaching down for his briefcase, but he came up smiling. "We'll manage it if you want it. That's all. Maybe we'll cut out Michael's piano lessons. Kid doesn't practice anyway. He'd probably be glad to get off the hook."

At the corner of Madison, where I stopped for the uptown bus, I reached up to kiss his cheek, but he pulled me in and kissed me on the mouth. "My girl," he said. His breath was sour. "See you tonight."

On the bus I thought about Michael's piano lessons. It was true about the practicing, but I couldn't let him stop. He couldn't grow up with no music in his life like Richard, and I wasn't going to take the lessons at his expense. There was the money my mother had left me. Not much, but enough for a few years of lessons. I'd always figured on using it to send the kids to Europe when they were in college, but maybe by then we'd be able to afford to do it without that money. I liked it, anyway, the idea of paying for my lessons myself. I liked it very much, now that I thought of it.

17.

"Open, open," Brescia commanded. "Keep the cords open. You have to let the air through, to get the velvet. Easy, airy, light. Let it float down on the air. When you push it out like that, you strangle it." He put a hand to his throat and, popping his eyes as though he were strangling, emitted a falsetto squeal. I smiled sheepishly and tried again. It wasn't even as good as yesterday in the bathroom. "I did it better practicing," I told him.

"Of course, because you were alone; Brescia was not there with his whip. We are all magnificent, alone. But what, you will sing in a closet? The voice is for *me* and for others—strangers, critics, the ones who listen. You know what it is, singing? It's an encounter with a lover: if the electricity between you and the lover doesn't make you struggle beyond yourself, why trouble to see him? It's easier to stay alone, no? And safer. If you are not desperate to sing and be heard, *cara*, if you do not ride that tension between yourself and those who listen, you are not a singer but a lady who hums in a closet. So think about Brescia listening, fear me, and then open the cords and sing for me, and the singing will be better than your virginal concert in the closet."

At the end of the hour, he said, "You see? Already it is working. You are using me, and there is a quality to the voice that

was not there before. Sing, sing all the time. Whatever you are doing, sing. But when you sing for me, you will go a little beyond.
That's what it is."

"I can't sing all the time. I can hardly find time to practice. I
have to steal it, almost."

"Steal it." His voice was flat. "Steal it back from whatever you
have given it to. One has got to be ruthless to sing. And we
shall need more time. Rosie tells me you have not yet enrolled.
That's good. It's easier for me to rewrite your program before the
machines get it than after. Have you got it?" I handed it over.
"What is this?" He took the pencil he'd been marking my music
with and impatiently crossed something out, then something else.
"Courses for librarians," he said. "Forget them. You will have
two hours with me instead. This one you can keep. It may be of
some use to us. The rest of the time you will use for singing."

"I had those courses in there because Mrs. Wilton said they'd
prepare me for teaching or another career if the singing didn't
work out," I told him.

"Ah, wait," he said, looking up with an expression of innocent surprise and holding up his hand like a traffic cop. "There is
something here you have not told me. You are immortal? You are
planning to live forever? Then definitely, you have time to take
this course and that one—any you like. And whenever you like,
you can develop the voice. Take your time. When Brescia dies,
there will be other teachers. Prepare yourself by all means to be a
musical archivist and the teacher of kindergarten bands. Safety
first, no? Then, with all that time before you, *then* perhaps you
will sing."

We stared at each other for a minute. You will die first, you
paunchy blusterer, I thought. But I had folded my arms across
my chest while he was speaking, and my breasts were tender
where I pressed into them, and Jessie flashed into my mind. And
Mama. I closed my eyes against the thought of Mama. And for
some reason I thought of Richard with his sour breath calling
me baby and telling me I didn't have to be under the gun. "All
right," I said. My face automatically offered up a smile, but I

cut it off and met his look soberly. "I'll do it that way. I'll emphasize the singing for this year. But you'll have to tell me as soon as you know whether it makes sense for me to keep at it."

"No," he said. "You will have to tell me. Meanwhile, we shall work. It is the only way I know to make a voice. Ah, here is another victim for Brescia's whip. Come in, come in."

A young girl came in, maybe twenty. She had some battered-looking music in her hand, and she moved impatiently into the room and put it on top of the piano. She tossed her hair back and looked at Brescia, then politely at me. I held out my hand to him for my program, and now I did smile at him. "Thanks for being tough," I said. "I will steal the time back." But he only nodded absently. His mind was already on her. Too late now for my smile. I left.

18.

I entered the tuition deposit in the checkbook, steadying it on the briefcase as the train lurched out of Grand Central. Twenty years old, hasn't cut her hair yet, I thought. Still uses it as a lure. Got that intense look grafted on her face, but she uses it all. And doesn't he just respond on cue. Then I smiled. Hey, jealous? She's paying for his time and she's entitled to an hour of his attention, just like anyone else. Just like me. But she's only twenty, I thought. No kids, no ties, and all the time in the world. I let him buffalo me into a singing program, but even if the voice is there, how many of *her* will there be, just as good or better? And she can go anywhere in the world to sing. No kids, no guilt.

Kids. Oh Christ, I never gave them a thought. Walked away from Michael this morning and forgot either one of them existed. In a panic I ran through it. Michael. Lunch. Oh Jesus, I never packed him a lunch. So busy with those damned cupcakes, I completely forgot it. I closed my eyes, seeing him coming home at lunchtime, ringing the bell, waiting, ringing again, realizing in terror that no one was there. Fighting tears, whimpering, holding his crotch—then what? Would he go to Evan's? What if Evan wasn't home? Maybe he'd have remembered I was going to the

111

city. I looked at my watch. 3:30. Randy would be home by now. No point worrying about lunch—it was over. But I kept going back, trying to rewrite it, make it come out differently. No, stop it. Whatever happened happened three hours ago. Go on, Randy had lunch. Sandwich in the bag, bag in the knapsack. Key in the hiding place. Burners. . . .

No. Randy was not home. She went to the village with Rebecca. Right now Michael was coming home and no one was there for him. I looked wildly out the window. Where were we? Somewhere between 125th Street and Fordham. Twenty minutes till I got off the train, ten more minutes home. I could get off at Fordham and call Laura, tell her to look out for him. I grabbed my briefcase and looked around for the conductor. Not in this car. I ran to the end of the car, tried to open the door to go through, but the cars were crashing together and sliding away at an angle and I couldn't do it. A man who was sitting near the door got up. "Can I help?" he asked. He was wearing jeans and a work shirt. There was a camera around his neck. The case said NIKON. He had wire-rimmed glasses on. "Have you seen the conductor?" I asked him. "Do you know which end of the train he'd be in?"

"In the back, probably—the other end. He usually works through. He'll be back."

"Yes, but I need to ask him, before Fordham—"

"What?"

"When the next train stops there. I may have to get out to make a phone call."

"Well, how about the schedule? Here, I'll look it up."

Of course. I had a schedule, too, but I wasn't about to say so after all that. I stood there and let him pull the schedule out of his wallet and run a finger down until he found it. "Aha. Three-thirty . . . that's this one; it does stop at Fordham. Three-forty-eight . . . no, they don't stop at Fordham again until . . . the four-thirty-two stops there at four-fifty-two." He looked up. "You're not ill, are you? Or in trouble? Maybe I can—"

"No, I'm fine. Thank you. I've done something dumb, that's all, and I'm trying to think how to . . . well, thanks for being so helpful." He was still standing up, leaning against the seat and maneuvering his wallet back into his pocket. And looking at me. He was checking me out. He was a little heavy for his jeans, but he held his body easily, shifting against the motion of the train. His look was open and calm.

"How dumb?"

"Pardon?"

"How dumb is the thing you've done? Does it involve your life—or your job? You seem panicked."

"It's my . . ." It's my little boy, I was about to say. I've forgotten to make arrangements for him and he's only seven and . . . but somehow I couldn't admit my neglect, even to this stranger. Anyway, I thought I might cry, so I just shook my head and tightened my face against the tears.

"I think I understand. Stay there, all right? Just stay there. Here, sit in my seat." He was off, dancing against the lurching of the train to the rear door, shouldering it open, and disappearing into the clash and squeal beyond it.

Okay. Fordham, I thought. I'll call Laura, tell her to look out for him. Or Evan's mother. Both. What'll I tell them? Not that I forgot. Stuck in midtown traffic, that'll do. Please give this boy a home. Okay, okay. Don't overdo this. He's not sick or dying. But scared, he's scared and it's my fault. 3:37. He's home by now. I told him Randy would be there. House is empty, no car in the driveway. Mommy. Where are you when you're suddenly not there? Where am I, then? Mama, my God, Mama come for me.

Toora loora loora, toora l—

Stop. He's okay. It isn't even raining. We'll be at Fordham in a few minutes. It'll only be for—what?—fifteen minutes that he's *scared. It isn't funny, Mama. Please—*

"Okay. They'll hold it for you at Fordham. You'll make your call—"

"What?"

"The train. They'll hold it a minute at Fordham and you'll make your call, and then you'll be home by—where do you live?"

I told him.

"You'll be home by . . . four-oh-eight, add a couple minutes for the delay . . . by four-twelve, say. Relax. Got a dime?"

"What do you mean? They'll hold the whole train for my phone call?"

"I know this conductor. He's a very nice guy. I told him it was a medical emergency. Here—here's some change for the phone."

"But then the whole run will be off schedule. I can't—"

"Are you kidding? The Penn Central? Who would notice? Relax, okay? You'll be at the phone in four minutes. What could you possibly have done that you can't at least neutralize with a quick phone call? If he won't give you till four-fifteen, when you can straighten it out, he isn't worth—"

"I don't even know if I can get to him with a phone call now, and by four-fifteen he'll be desperate."

"I imagine so." He smiled. "Here, take the change." I received a handful of coins. They were warm.

"No . . . I have change. You've done enough, anyway. Look, please sit here." I stopped, hearing what he'd said. "You don't think—you think it's my—a man?"

"No? Okay. But it *was* a fairly logical assumption. I mean, you seem *very*—"

"Fordham, this stop. This station stop is—"

I stood, looked at the door, back at him. "Should I really?"

"Of course. Quick, now. Don't worry. The train will be here when your three minutes are up."

I called Laura first. No, she hadn't seen him at lunchtime. "But I wasn't looking for him, either. Want me to look out and see if he's there?"

"Could you? I'm in a pay phone and they're—I'm in a pay phone."

She came back after an endless static interval to report that Michael wasn't at the house. But she promised to watch for him. "I can give him dinner if you'd like."

"Dinner! No! I'll be there by four-thirty. Just give him a home base for a few minutes, would you?"

114

"Well, I mean if you'd like to stay out a while longer—"

"Laura, I'm on my way *home*. I got stuck, that's all."

"Happens to us all." It never happened to her. She was always there, taking in the strays and keeping score. I paid off the first installment of gratitude and hung up.

No one answered at Evan's house.

When I got back into the train, the end seat where my Galahad had been sitting had a stranger in it. I looked around. He was in a seat in the middle of the car, half standing up and waving. I went over. There was a seat next to him.

"Sit down. Everything all right?"

Now was the time for me to explain that it was my child, nothing more exotic than that. But some perverse impulse kept me from doing it. He thought it was a love entanglement, saw me as a woman who might have a lover, a career, God knows what. With images of Michael sending shooting stars through my bloodstream, with stray worries about Randy flickering in the background, I fanned that little flame. I smiled, a demure and sadly secret smile. "Everything's on hold, anyway. Thank you."

He pursued it, of course. Problems at work? He glanced at the briefcase. What did I do? Studying voice, I said. His eyes widened a little and he nodded, impressed. "That's got to be expensive, though. How do you manage to keep eating?"

My husband feeds me, I could have said. But I smiled, a strong, womanly smile, holding the residual secret sadness in the eyes. "All kinds of stuff. I manage." Oh Beth. Oh Beth. "What do you do?" I figured him for a writer or teacher.

"OB, GYN." He saw me looking at the jeans and work shirt. He touched the camera. "Wednesday. Doctor's day off."

"So you told the conductor it was a medical emergency—"

"Right. And he stopped the train. It *was* a medical emergency. You were about to hyperventilate. But I suppose you live on the thin edge all the time, in your kind of life."

Thin edge. Doctor, I am a charter inhabitant of the broad and

115

even way. "I guess maybe I do. I never think of it that way." Another poignant smile.

I kept it up all the way to Bronxville, where he got out. It required constant alertness not to allude to Richard or the kids or the house, just to sustain by omission the illusion that I was a free soul who sang and somehow kept herself going. But it helped use up the adrenaline and keep the panic at bay. At the Fleetwood stop, he asked my name. I hesitated. "Perhaps we could get together," he said, rather timidly.

"I'd like it," I said. "You've been unbelievable. But . . . my life is pretty complicated right now." Strike me dead. Lying bitch.

"So I see. Well . . . so long. Hope it works out." He stood up, walked a couple of feet toward the door, then came back, pulling a little white card out of his wallet. "I—maybe you'd—if things straighten out—maybe you'd want to have dinner one night. Can I give you this?"

"Daniel Block, M.D." it said. I took it. "Maybe," I said, with a last shadowed smile. "Anyway, you're a very kind man. Thank you." The train threw him forward, yanked him back as it stopped. He nodded brusquely and left.

As soon as he left, it closed in. I shut my eyes and took them in order. Michael. No lunch. Don't think about lunch. Had his sweatshirt, didn't he? Warm out anyway. Home at 3:30. No. Don't think. Laura will get him. Randy. Randy. Sandwich in the bag, bag in the knapsack. Right? Didn't I? Yes, turkey and lettuce. In town now, with Rebecca. I never asked if she had money. Didn't even tell her what time to be home. Big Top is across the railroad bridge. Did she ride her bike there? Teenage drivers. Don't think. Big Top. Baseball cards. Michael. Maybe he's in the backyard where Laura won't see him. On the jungle gym. Falling. . . . Stop. Laura will *get* him. It's Randy's turn. Randy. Tin Drum. Can't worry about that. Riding home from the village. Brakes okay on the bike? Coming down Sycamore, losing control, flying—neck snapped, back. . . . Stop. She rides it every day. Bike is fine. Randy is fine. House. Burners off? . . .

116

Laura was sitting on her front step. I swung out of the car, ran up to her. "Is he here?"

"Hiya. Nope. Haven't seen him at all. And I've been sitting right here since you called. Did you have a good day?"

"I had a lesson. It was okay. Did you check the backyard?" I'd already half turned to go.

"Of course I did. Don't worry. Kids have a way of taking care of themselves when they have to."

I ran, scattering thanks behind me as I went. The house was empty and quiet. I looked all over for signs that he'd been home, even walking uselessly around in the yard, looking for sneaker patterns in the mud under the swings. No, think. He's got to be somewhere. 4:20. Still no answer at Evan's. I tried one or two other kids, explaining briefly to the mothers and dealing as quickly as I could with the disapproving sympathy and the offers of help. The third kid I called—Robby—answered the phone himself. "Yeah," he said, "I think he went home with Nicky."

"Nicky Padou?" Jesus, no.

"Yeah. Him and his mother."

"Robby, was Michael upset?"

"Huh?"

"Did he—was he—never mind. Thank you, honey."

"Sure."

The phone rang five times before she picked it up.

"Hello." She sounded cheerful and breathless.

"Hi, Marylynn. It's Beth Clahr. Where'd I pull you from?"

"Oh, I was just out in the yard pitching to the boys. None of us is exactly star material. Speaking of stars, Michael was just adorable this morning. And he enjoyed the class party so much."

"Marylynn, is Michael with you?"

"Yes, and he's a delight to have. We ought to get them together more often."

"You're an angel to have taken him. How—I mean, did he—"

"He just came right up to me at the party and said, 'I have to

117

have a play date after school because no one is home: Can I come home with Nicky?' And of course I said that was fine, whatever little appointments I had I could postpone. But wasn't that cute, to be so independent and arrange his own afternoon?"

I closed my eyes. Hit me again, I'm still moving. "I hope you didn't cancel anything important."

"No, just the optometrist. But I'd have dragged poor Nicky along and he'd much rather be playing with Michael, so it's fine."

"Well, let me take Nicky whenever you've rescheduled your appointment. It's the least I can do."

"Don't be silly. And your son is a pleasure to feed."

"Feed?"

"Lunch. He ate a whole bowl of macaroni and cheese, even after the party."

"You gave him lunch, too. I don't know how to thank you. I don't know where my head was. I'm usually—"

"You had your singing to think about. It was fine, no problem at all. When he asked about playing at three, I said, 'What are you doing about lunch?' and Beth, he was so cute. 'Oops,' he said, 'I guess my mom forgot about lunch. I hate to eat in school anyway.' Wasn't that cute? 'Oops, I guess she forgot,' with that wonderful grin of his. Nicky was delighted to have him. And how was your lesson?"

I couldn't even remember having the lesson. "Fine," I said. Then I launched into a long explanation of how I'd forgotten and where Randy was, and how terrible I felt. When I'd groveled long enough and she'd absolved me in the name of responsible motherhood, I offered to come and get Michael.

"Oh no, let me drop him off. I promised to take them for ice cream. We were just waiting to hear from you, so you wouldn't worry. I'll drop him off in an hour or so, okay?"

Help me, doctor, I think I've been patted to death. It's all internal bleeding.

I walked across the street to tell Laura that Michael was okay. Randy was just turning the corner on her bike as I came back across.

118

"Hi, Mom."

All in one piece. No visible signs of debauchery. Bag from Young Corner flopping from the handlebars. "I got the shorts and a skirt and some rainbow suspenders. And baseball cards for Michael and the new *TV Guide*. You owe me two dollars and twenty-nine cents."

"You had enough money?"

"I took my own. And I'm home by four-forty-five, and I didn't get killed. See?" She was flushed and exuberant. "I didn't even smoke any pot."

"Very funny." I moved in, to touch her, then stopped with my hand out. Sweat. A meaty, heavy smell of sweat. I remembered it . . . Jackie Tanedo in the sixth grade. She was bigger than the rest of us, and she had breasts. She smelled like that when the rest of us smelled of Juicy Fruit and nothing else. I sat next to her and caught that pungent, mellow smell whenever she lifted her arm, showing tufts of black hair where I had puckery skin. I kind of liked it. It was solid and comforting, like stew cooking. Randy smelled like Jackie Tanedo.

"What's the matter?"

"Nothing. Hi, world traveler." I kissed her. Her breath was invasive, too. Cheesy. I put a hand on her forehead. Cool. It wasn't the intense breath of fever, anyway. Mouthwash, I thought, and deodorant. She's cooking and the juices are running.

Funny. I'd been braced in pregnancy for the smells—diapers, vomit, what my friends in the development called "cheesing." I'd worried about it, how to take the smells without being disgusted by the baby. But although I'd tell her, "Phew. You stink, little stinker," holding her heels up with one hand and swabbing off shit with the other, she never did stink, not even when she was eighteen months old and walking around with a ripening load in her ruffled pants. An identifiable smell, but not repugnant to me. So I was shocked, changing a friend's baby, to find myself gagging, violently repelled by the stench. Randy's smells, Michael's smells, were part of a set of signals I was keyed to—the message they triggered in me was "Self. Okay."

119

Now they'd changed the signals on me. Odors from Randy, traveling the subterranean passage between us, were bringing the message: not self, other. Ah, love, good-bye.

"Did you brush your teeth this morning?" That isn't it. Gone, she's gone.

"Of course. Why, do I smell bad?"

"Well, you're growing up. You may want to start using a mouthwash."

She pulled her face away from mine. "What's growing up got to do with it? You think growing up is some kind of sickness that makes people smell?" Red-faced, she poked furiously around in the Young Corner bag until she found the baseball cards and the *TV Guide*. "Here. This stuff is yours. Two twenty-nine you owe me. Want to open the garage, please?"

The door lifted, she coasted in on the bike and lowered it between us.

19.

"I'm a heavy loser in the potlatch exchange," I told Richard at dinner.

"Potlatch? What's that?" Michael asked Randy.

"How should I know? Ask her."

Richard turned on Randy. "Who's 'her'? Are you referring to your mother?"

"Yes."

"Then say so. Don't say 'her' as if she weren't here."

Randy pushed back her chair. "I'm going upstairs," she said, voice tight. "I have a headache." She pushed past my chair and ran out of the kitchen. Richard threw his napkin on the table, scraped back in his chair.

"Don't," I said. "Let her go."

"What's a potlatch?" Michael demanded again. "What did you lose?"

"There's a tribe of people in Africa or somewhere—"

"American Indians," Richard said. "Vancouver." He was still looking at the doorway where Randy had fled. Now he returned his attention to his salad, letting out an audible, exasperated sigh.

"Okay, Indians. They have this system. I give you a gift. Maybe a chicken. But it's not like a birthday present or something where you say 'thank you very much' and that's that. Because now you

121

owe *me* a gift, and it had better be at least a chicken. If you can give me two chickens, now you're one chicken up on me. See? If you give me a chicken and I give you back a cow, look out. You have to go hungry, trade away things you need, maybe, to give me back a cow's worth of presents. If I really want to get you, I give you such a big gift that it knocks you out of the game altogether."

Michael was fascinated. "So then what?"

"That's what I want to know," I said to Richard. "I've had fourteen chickens and a stud bull dumped on me today. Now what? Do they drum me out of the tribe?"

"Who dumped what on you?"

I told him about Laura sitting watch for Michael, and about Marylynn. "First I couldn't do the class party, so she did it, and then she takes him for lunch *and* after school. And misses an optometrist appointment. She'll probably drive into a truck because her glasses are wrong, and I'll have her widower and orphans on my chest for the rest of my life."

"That randy little peapicker gets near your chest, I'll put him out of the running. Make the neighborhood safe for the girls."

"I lose extra points because I didn't even ask if she'd take Michael," I said. "Out of the goodness of her heart, Marylynn took my poor abandoned child. And I already owe Laura, too, for the casserole. I can't hope to beat her anyway—she's the champion. Do you know she brought dinner to John Handler after Jessie's operation and he doesn't even know her?"

"Mother? Would you come up here?"

"I'll go," Richard said. "*Her* crap you don't have to put up with."

"Mother?"

"Coming. Richard, you tell Michael about the potlatch losers. I've forgotten how it ends, and I don't think I want to know."

She was in the bathroom, sitting on the toilet and staring disconsolately down at her underpants, stained brown and red. "Look."

"Do you know what it is?" I asked gingerly.

"Of course I know. What do I do about this mess?"

"I'll show you." I pulled the hair away from her face, kissed her. "That's why you had a headache, probably, and why your breath was funny. Be glad, honey—you're a woman."

She blushed and grinned a little, but fought the grin down and said crankily, "Whoopee. Now I get to have this disgusting mess every month. Why do women always have to be the ones? You know what they were talking about at the Tin Drum?"

"Who?"

"Stephie Vail and some other kids. We sat with them." Stephie baby-sat for us. The kids liked her so much, I was a little suspicious. "They said, this girl? She got in trouble and had to get an abortion. *She* has to have the needles and stuff, *she* has to have this thing done, and *she* gets to be the murderer. Sixteen years old and already she's a killer."

"You think she's a murderer?"

"Sure. Hey, a baby's a person. Even a whatchamacallit, a—"

"Fetus."

"Yeah."

"So what should she have done?"

"Had the kid. Then someone would adopt it and it would get to have a life. Or she could keep it."

"What about her life?"

"Yeah, see? Great, being a woman. Either you're a murderer or your life is ruined. And every month, you're gross."

I opened my mouth, closed it again, and went to get the starter kit I'd stashed on my closet shelf. After she was cleaned up and sitting on her bed, awkwardly astride the Kotex, I sat down next to her and said, "You're not gross. It isn't gross. It's natural. It's easy to keep it from showing or being a nuisance. And it's lovely being a woman. You get to have the babies and to nurse them—both wonderful things to experience. Hey, look, I've never had an abortion and my life isn't ruined. That girl was very unlucky, and pretty stupid."

123

"Well I'd never get an abortion, I'll tell you that—" She broke off, hearing Richard on the stairs. "Don't tell him," she whispered wildly. "Swear you won't tell."

"I won't."

"Your daughter is a woman," I said to him during a commercial break in the 11:00 news.

He looked at me blankly for a moment, mind still on the sports section of the paper. Then he understood. "The headache," he said.

"Right."

"Holy shit, I'm outnumbered. I'll be floating in bloody little packages."

I turned over, pushed my pillow between our heads, and lay flat on the edge of my bed. Later, when he turned off the light and put a hand on my leg, I pretended I was asleep.

The waves are breaking against the rocks, somewhere under the window. He holds me, wrapped in the quilt. Soft cotton against my back and his hands, moving over it, chafing me slowly against the cold. Then he folds it back, down to my knees, looks at me. I don't move. He is over me, mouth against the hollow of my shoulder. More. Beth, he says. I open my eyes, hold them open for him. Let him in. Lift to him, the *andante*. I am coming, I turn my head away, bury my face against his arm. "Where are you?" he whispers. I turn my face to look at him. It's all there, he sees it. "Yes," he says. "Come. Now, with me." Ah, my God. Now.

20.

I sent Randy off to school with four Kotex in the bottom of her bookbag, each camouflaged in tinfoil, and two Midols in a little plastic bag. She was wearing her baggiest overalls, and she tied a sweatshirt around her waist so it dangled down over her bottom.

"You'll think the whole world knows," I told her, "but no one will. Absolutely no one. Just take it easy. If you're uncomfortable, take the Midol."

"I don't take drugs."

"Randy, Midol isn't a big-time drug. It's like aspirin, for cramps. If you need it, take it."

"Can I have a gym excuse?"

Got me. But I came back with the party line: "Really, exercise is the best thing—keeps the blood zipping around in your veins." But she was exuding misery and I relented. "I'll write it and you decide whether to use it. See how you feel."

Dear Mrs. Reynolds. Please don't hurt her. She's only a little girl, and she's bleeding as it is.

She took the note, stuck it in a pocket, walked out tentatively, on sea legs. Swim, Randy. Swim, dammit.

Michael left, too, and the house was quiet. I wanted it that way—no music until I did the seven stations of the cross.

125

First leg, Marylynn. I called and begged to take Nicky so she could go to the optometrist. "Go out for lunch; make a day of it," I wheedled.

"Well, maybe I really will. Maybe I'll meet Theo for lunch. He gets a little jealous, I sometimes think, because I put so much of myself into the boys. Can't forget to save a little for Daddy, can we?"

"Never forget that," I said numbly. A picture flashed through my mind—a diagram of Marylynn, segmented by dotted lines like the side of beef in the cooking charts. Instead of "loin" and "chuck," the areas were labeled with names. The head and arms and legs and the motherly bosom said "GREG" and "NICKY," in absolutely even apportionment. The hands and feet said "COMMUNITY." Then there was a dotted circle that said "THEO." I superimposed it over the belly and crotch. Lucky Theo, I thought. "Well, you have a lovely long day with Theo," I said. "I can give Nicky dinner, too, if you'd like." Look out, Marylynn, here come three chickens and a goat. But she was too smart for me.

"Oh, no, I'll be missing the boys by four-thirty."

We called it a draw at lunch and a play date after school on Friday.

Second station: I called Laura and asked if I could take her to lunch next week. "That'd be gorgeous," she said. "I really never see you these days. Lutèce at noon?"

"I was going to suggest the diner at one," I said, "but seeing that you fed my family in our hour of need and looked out for my abandoned boy, I'll compromise. Le Bistro at twelve-thirty next Monday?"

"Done. You settled too quick; you could have talked me down to House of Tokyo at one-fifteen."

"The very thought of raw anything on a plate makes me ill," I said, and actually I felt myself getting queasy. I swallowed hard and ended the conversation. All this penance, I thought, I'm getting light-headed.

126

So I called the florist next. That was an easy one. I had him make up a bouquet of deep pink roses and daisies and baby's breath to be delivered to Randy after school. I had him write on the card, "You're getting there! Welcome—it's a nice place to be, and it's lovely to have you here. Love, Mom."

Now what? You know what, I told myself. Jessie. But first I pulled on jeans and a sweatshirt and ran to the toy store. I got Michael a Star Wars calendar with stickers to paste on important days. I had them gift wrap it and I put a little card on it that said, "For my big boy, who is a great fox and a real star, and who makes his own appointments when Mommy forgets."

Four down. Jessie is five. And Richard, Richard is six. Must it be seven? Well, anyway, Jessie counts for two.

I called Richard first. Frances sounded harried and depressed already, and it was only 10:00. "I'll have to put you on hold, dear," she said, "and hope he picks it up." He did, after a couple of minutes of Muzak.

"I hate that damned canned music," I said. "Why do they do that?"

"What music? Listen, babe, I'm up to here this morning. What's up?"

"I wanted to tell you," I said, "that I'm going to pay for the singing lessons myself, with the legacy from my mother."

He'll say, "Forget it; I can take care of my girl," I thought. Then I'll say, "But I want to help . . ."

"Great," he said. "That's a fantastic idea. I was thinking of using some of that money for the bills, but this is just as good. You'll take a lesson a week, and it should cover for a year or two. By then, who knows what you'll be into?"

My money? The *bills?* Mama's legacy to me? You wooden son of a bitch, I thought. I was stunned to hear the words in my head. The shock and the anger and the rising nausea left me graceless.

"Two lessons a week," I said tightly.

"What?"

127

"I'll be taking two lessons a week, but it won't cost you. Mama will treat me to them for a few years and maybe by then I can pay for them myself."

"We'll talk about it tonight," he said. "On those new sheets of yours. Maybe you'll convince me to go for the two lessons."

I got to the bathroom before I vomited. I wiped my face and sat down on the edge of the tub, rocking a little. My hands were very cold, but I kept running one through my hair over and over, smoothing it back. When I heard myself humming "Toora Loora" I stood up and squared off. "You really are nuts," I told myself.

Just Jessie now. And it wasn't so bad. "Hey there," she said. "Thought you fell off the edge of the world. I was going to call you. . . . Want to go on a mission of mercy?"

No. "Where are we going?"

"We are going to take me to the body shop. I need to get my bump replaced."

"Prosthesis? Sure, I'll go with you. Are you healed enough? When do you want to do it?"

"I can go in another week. Say next Thursday; that'll be after the luncheon. And I'll be ready. Will I ever. . . . Well, gotta go now, Cookie. I'm on my way to the chemical factory for my weekly juicing. I can hardly wait—got it all worked out who I'm going to throw up on."

"Want company? Shall I come with you?" No. Please, no.

"No, Toots. You are a love, though, to offer. John never has. That's what we're paying the White Tornado for. That and so she can tell me how fine I am. In fact," she said thoughtfully, "maybe I'll save it this time and throw up on her. It's my only weapon, but it's a beaut."

"All I know is, I'm going to stay on your good side."

"That's the left one, and you're on it. Bye."

So it was Richard who counted for two stations, I thought, not Jessie. I wrote it all down on the calendar: lunch with Laura, Nicky here for the day, Jessie on the twenty-first.

21.

It was 10:45. I stripped down and got into the shower. Because I'm grubby, I thought—not to go to bed. I ran the water very hot and used a lot of soap. I was thinking I'd get busy on the table arrangements for the luncheon and was planning them in my head when it happened. I was soaping my breasts and they were so tender, I jerked my hand away. Then, cautiously, I touched one again. Checking. A little tender, no lump. The other. More tender . . . and there was something. A mass, or a lump. I felt for it over and over, until I couldn't be sure what I was feeling.

I thought about absolutely nothing as the water ran over me, washing off the soap, as I stood wrapped in a towel, waiting to be warm, as I surrendered the towel, patted on the powder, got into bed still not warm. The sheet was flat under me, taut over me, but I was shivering so that I pulled sheet and quilt around me and huddled encased in them, rocking a little against the cold. Anyway, it's not working, I thought. It doesn't make me safe. Mama.

Inside my wrapping, I put a hand up to touch the breast. My hand was dead cold, but I probed gently and as steadily as I could. It was still there, a mass on the outer side of the left breast. Michael is seven, I thought, Randy is twelve. Maybe I can hold on for three or four years, till they're—no, that's not long enough. Not long enough to pilot her through until she finds someone to—is it catching? Jessie—oh damn you, Jessie, why didn't you die alone? Needles, piercing the soft flesh like deadly straws, sucking out cells. I cradled it tenderly in the dead-cold hand, cooling the breast, warming the fingers. Chemicals, nausea, impotent terror. Not me. Not to me.

I turned over, pulling the phone off the night table and onto the bed and, still shivering in my wrappings, dialed Monroe's number.

Valerie, his nurse, answered. "I'm sorry, Mrs. Clahr, Dr. Lippzer is away," she said.

"When will he be back?"

"Not until Monday. Is it urgent? Dr. Sloan is covering."

"Here's the problem," I said. "I was examining myself and I seem to have a little mass in the left breast—thought I'd better have it checked."

"Definitely. Well, you *could* wait till Monday—"

"Not and keep breathing, I couldn't."

"I understand. Well, Dr. Sloan is—"

"I don't know him."

"How about your gynecologist?"

"I don't have one. Dr. Lippzer does all that." How could you forget, Valerie? You're the production assistant.

In the end, she gave me the names of three gynecologists, which I scribbled down on the back of an old photo I pulled out of the night table drawer. I looked at them: Montgomery, Zaret, and Hoffman. Montgomery sounded shallow to me, and cold. Zaret sounded old. I couldn't decide about Hoffman. I turned the picture over: me, at the beach, with Michael. No inspiration there. Just pick one, I told myself, and call him. Then I remembered Daniel Block. I dialed information. "Dr. Daniel Block, B-l-o-c-k," I said. "In Bronxville."

"I wonder if I could speak to the doctor," I entreated the voice that answered.

"Doctor is in surgery," she crooned. "What is your problem? Maybe I can—"

"When is he due in?"

"By eleven o'clock, but he—"

"Could he see me then? It's urgent."

"What is the nature of your—"

"A lump in the breast that must be seen immediately. My doctor sent me to him."

"I see, and who is your doctor?"

We fenced for a while, and finally she said I could come in at 1:00 and he'd try to fit me in.

There were two very young women in the office, one hugely pregnant and dealing unsuccessfully with a whiny two-year-old. The girls chatted cheerfully about baby nurses and play groups. An elderly woman sat straight up in a soft chair in the corner of the waiting room, turning the pages of a magazine.

At 1:20 he walked into the waiting room. He was wearing a suit. He nodded pleasantly at the young mothers, then stopped as he saw me. "Hello!" he said. "How are you?"

"Scared to death," I said. He looked at me for a second, then quickly around at the other three women in the room. "Just half a second," he said. He went through the door to the offices and bent over to say something to the receptionist. Behind the glass, she frowned and jerked her chin toward the very pregnant woman, clearly pointing out that she should be attended to first. He said something back and disappeared.

She opened the door. "Mrs. Clahr," she said grimly.

I followed her through the door, clutching the magazine I'd been holding. She took it from me. "In there first," she said. "Urine specimen, please. Then the yellow room. Disrobe entirely and put on the white gown, opening in the front please."

"But he won't need a urine—"

"That's our procedure, Mrs. Clahr. Doctor will see you in the yellow room."

131

It was very warm in the yellow room. There was a chart of fetal development on the wall. A trim little nurse with shiny black hair came in. She took some vital information and weighed me. "Date of your last period?" she asked.

"Two . . . no, almost three weeks ago."

"Good. Doctor will be right in." She was gone.

He came in looking down at my chart. Then he looked up and smiled professionally. I pulled the gown more tightly around myself.

"The AMA will ride me out of town on a rail," he said. "Soliciting patients in a public vehicle."

"I'll never tell," I said. "And I was very glad to have your name. My G.P. is away and I have no regular gynecologist . . . and I figured if you could stop a train, you could move mountains. Or masses, as the case may be. Is." I tapered off.

He nodded, four beats to the bar. "You've had a bad week—" he looked at the chart again "—Beth. Is it . . . *Mrs.* Clahr?"

"Beth. Yes, Mrs." I didn't explain; he didn't pursue it.

"So what's the trouble? What's scaring you?"

I told him. Then I looked intently at the ceiling, pushing air in and out of my lungs, which had forgotten how to operate independently, as he probed with light, dancing fingers. You could do that in Carnegie Hall, I thought, if we could only work out the acoustics.

"That's fibrous tissue," he said finally. "Not a malignancy, or even the threat of one. Why it should be inflamed just now— you say the breasts are tender? Are you premenstrual?"

"Not yet."

"Let's do a pelvic, see what's going on. The nurse will get you ready." He left, then opened the door again. "Unless you'd rather . . . my partner could—"

"No, please," I said, "you do it."

He shrugged, looking uncomfortable, and then nodded and was gone again.

So much for mystery, I thought minutes later, as he grabbed

my womb from inside and pressed from outside. Talk about being unveiled. Talk about your speedy retribution.

"It's too early to tell for sure this way," he said when the excavation equipment had been removed and I was sitting up, dripping K-Y jelly on the paper table-liner. "I'd like you to bring in a urine specimen."

"I just . . . left one."

"No. A clean one. No food or liquids after six P.M., collect a specimen first thing in the morning, before breakfast. Janet will give you a specimen flask." He looked down at the chart. "Will this be a complication for you? In your . . . home situation?"

"Why? Am I contaminated?"

"Of course not. But . . . a pregnancy—"

"A what? *Me?*"

"Well, yes, that's what I'm saying it looks like. Early to tell without the urine test, of course—it could be some other hormonal disturbance. . . ."

I looked at him in horror.

"Listen," he said, "at least it isn't breast cancer. Right?"

"Right. Pregnancy was my second least-favored choice, though. If I'd thought of it, which I hadn't."

"A much lesser evil." He smiled.

"Not terminal, but a life sentence," I said. "For me, at this time."

"Let's not get excited until we know," he said. "Bring in the specimen tomorrow morning."

"Then when will I know?"

"Right away."

Not wooden enough, Richard, you son of a bitch, I thought as I drove home. Oh you're fine, baby, you're safe. I thought vicious thoughts all the way home, even saying some of it aloud. It didn't help.

I crept out of bed in the morning before Richard was even up, got the flask from the laundry hamper where I'd secreted it in a plastic bag, and filled it, listening nervously for Richard. I put the plastic cap on it, put it back in the plastic bag, and stashed it carefully, upright, in the hamper again. I covered it with clothes and left it. Then I eased back into bed and lay there listening to my heart pound and trying to remember what people said abortions cost. Before you buy me singing lessons, Mama, I thought, you may have to bail me out of this.

22.

Daniel Block's office was homey, if not beautiful. There were openweave curtains at the windows and a red Oriental rug on the floor. No photos of wife and kids. A rock collection on two shelves, flanked by medical books. He came in and closed the door carefully behind him. He was wearing a gray suit.

"The test says you're pregnant," he said from behind his desk. "When it's positive it's trustworthy, even this early. It's when it's negative that we question it."

There were two goldfish in a bowl on the windowsill. I watched them moving in the sunlight, gliding, then flicking, then gliding again. One of them was always distorted by the angle of the glass. I watched, waiting to see them both centered at once.

"—want this?"

The object he was holding out to me came clear, because he held it very still. It was a Kleenex.

"I'm not going to cry," I said.

"It's all right if you do."

"Hmm?" They were crossing paths, coming and going. I tried to will them to be still, even for a moment, to see them both undistorted at once.

"It's all right if you cry. Or curse, kick and scream."

"I did that—yesterday. It didn't help. Does it hurt?"

135

"What?"

"Having an abortion."

"Yes. I see. No, I'm told it isn't painful. There's some discomfort afterward. . . ." He was turning the Kleenex over and over on the desk, making tiny folds and smoothing them over with a fingernail. It looked like a fan.

"I used to do that. If you put a bobby pin in the middle now, and separated the layers, you'd have a flower. Listen, it's not so bad. What if you were telling me I had terminal whatever?" Why am I comforting him?

"I'm supposed to be saying that to you."

"You did. You said it yesterday. It's about the best that can be said, actually, for this mess."

"Listen, don't jump to abortion so fast. Wouldn't you like to have a child?"

"I have two." He flinched. I said, more gently, "It's out of the question for me to have this one."

"I see. They're how old? Oh, I see." He found it on my record. "Normal births? Good. No, it's not painful, particularly not if it's done this early." He was still looking down at the folder. "There are various methods, of course, some less pleasant than others. I'll send you to a clinic where you'll be comfortable, and the atmosphere is . . . not too oppressive. You'll be—"

"Couldn't you do it?"

"Yes, but I'd rather you went to this place. They're set up for it."

There was silence, then we both started talking at once.

"How soon could I—"

"The procedure there is—"

He stopped and waited. I went first. "I was asking how soon I could . . . go ahead with it."

"The sooner the better. Perhaps you want to choose a day when your husband can—"

"Richard? Does he have to—"

"No. Take it easy. He doesn't have to—anything. You don't need his consent, and if you paid in cash, he wouldn't even be billed. But someone should—you shouldn't be alone." He looked at me straight. "They won't know or care who's with you. They won't ask any questions. But if for no other reason than to drive you home. . . ."

His phone rang. He picked it up, punched a button, and said, "I told you to hold the calls. . . . All right, I'll take it. But hold the rest, will you please? Ten minutes more." He punched another button, said, "Hiya, Nat. What's up?" and launched into a conversation about medications and procedures that I didn't want to hear. The fish had slowed down and were moving lazily around the bowl. For a moment they were both suspended in the center of it, but one was in front of the other, so I could still only see one. The other one looked like a bright shadow.

"—was going to tell you about the procedure there, so you'd know what to expect," he was saying. He was talking to me again.

He told me all about it, more than I wanted to know. I made notes: "Corner of Maple and Fulton, two-story brick bldg. Be there by 8:30 A.M. No breakfast. Know date of last period. Home by 4:00, 4:30. *Don't drive.* $250. Get box of super Kotex for after."

"They use a short-duration anaesthetic," he said.

"Isn't there a risk?"

"There's a miniscule risk with any anaesthesia, but the other way you can hear what's going on, and you do feel it. It's better to be out." He called the place himself, made the appointment for me for the following Friday. He gave them my name as Beth Clahr, no Miss or Mrs. "It's completely confidential," he said. "Your name will never leave that office."

I stood up to go. "Thanks," I said. "That's twice in a week you've bailed me out. You really are unbelievably—"

"There'll be someone to drive you home?" He was standing too, looking sternly at me. His face was red. "I don't want to tell you about your rights, but surely—"

"Thanks," I said, softly again, as though he were the pregnant woman. "I'll be taken care of."

137

Driving home, I went over the list in my head. Richard. Laura. Jessie. Richard's sister, Dot. I wasn't about to tell any of them, that was for sure. Finally I decided to have the clinic call me a cab. Two hundred fifty dollars for the abortion, another $10 for cabs. I hadn't had any breakfast and I was starved, but I stopped at the bank and withdrew $275 from my savings account. That's eleven lessons, Mama, I thought, driving home. That's okay. This is a lesson, too, isn't it?

23.

I put the money in my lingerie drawer, folded inside a slip. Then I went down and fixed myself some breakfast. The phone rang before I could take a bite.

"Are you ready?"

"Gideon?"

"I'll assume that question was rhetorical. Are you ready?"

"Ready?" I'll never be ready again. For any of it, not even you.

"This is Gideon. You are Beth. You sing soprano, coloratura when the stars are right. I asked you whether you were ready for the concert tonight. Now *you* say—"

"Tonight. Oh, God."

"You forgot? Beth, are you okay?"

Would you like the long answer or a lie? I chose for him. "I'm fine," I lied. "It's been . . . a crazy week. I did forget it was tonight. Good thing you called."

"That's the first kind thing you've said. Let's start over. How are you? I've missed you. I'm looking forward to tonight, even if it slipped your mind. Shall I pick you up?"

"I—my family was planning to come. They wanted to hear me sing." Why did I say that? They had only the vaguest idea that there *was* a concert. None of them had ever said anything about hearing me sing.

"Oh. Of course. Well, in that case, break a leg. I'll be listening for you during the improvisation; give 'em hell." He was gone.

Really gone, I figured, dejectedly sitting down at the table. The raisin bran was soggy. I picked out a few raisins, then pushed the bowl away. I played it back, hearing the chill come into his voice. Gone. I clinked the spoon around in the mug. The coffee was cold; the cream lay on top in a greasy film. Fighting nausea, I threw it all out and made some tea and toast. The tea was scalding, but I drank it. Too bad for you, Goldilocks, I thought. Too cold, too hot—and just when you're thinking of trying a different bed, you slam the door in your own face. You ought to have had enough of beds to hold you for a while anyhow, I told myself, resolutely swallowing toast.

The toast, or the ghost of it, was still sticking in my throat when I called Richard. He answered the phone himself.

"Where's Frances?" I asked.

"She's—I'm sharing her with Walsh for a couple of weeks. They're a little shorthanded. What's up?" He sounded brusque. Probably angry about last night, I thought. He'd turned the TV off early and started pushing my nightgown up, murmuring, "What's the deal about the lessons? You're not going to knock yourself out, are you? Take it easy, babe; save a little for me." A picture of me, carved up like Marylynn in sections, had flashed into my mind. But there was a fetus in the womb, where Theo's section of Marylynn had been. There's nothing left for you, I thought poisonously. And get *off* me. But what I said, moving away from his hand, was, "If I have a life, Richard, it doesn't take anything away from you. So please don't tell me what to do with my time and my money." I pulled the nightgown back down over my legs, pretending I didn't see his stricken look. "You don't worry about my wearing myself out doing housework or taking care of the kids. So why the sudden concern for my energy level?" It worked; he moved away, saying only, "Good night, Beth." "Good night, Richard," I said. "Sleep well."

140

"I'm calling to remind you about the concert," I said now. I made my voice warm and soft.

"What concert?"

"The chorus is singing at St. John's tonight, remember? I'd really like you and the kids to be there. Be my audience."

Two and a half beats. "You didn't want any part of me last night."

"I had a horrible day yesterday, Rich, and I wasn't feeling very well. You wouldn't want me to fake it, would you?" How would he know? "I'm sorry."

"Okay. You're entitled to an off day. But you said some lousy things. Did you mean it, about my denying you your own time?"

"No, of course not." The lying was getting easy. "I was just feeling bitchy. Will you come home early for dinner? The concert's at eight."

"How long will it take?"

"I don't know. Two hours, maybe. Why?"

"It's pretty late for the kids, then."

"It's Friday. They can sleep late. I'd think you'd want to—" A phone rang and suddenly I was hearing the Mantovani strings. Then he was back.

"Right," he said. "That'll be fine."

"Me?"

"What?"

"You saying that to me? What'll be fine?"

"Your concert. Pick me up at six-fifteen, okay? Gotta go, babe." I was left with a handful of silence.

Nicky Padou was wearing brown corduroy pants and a brown plaid Levi shirt with mother-of-pearl buttons, tucked in and belted. His hair was shiny clean. "Oh, good," he said, "macaroni and cheese. We never get to have the kind out of the box."

"It was good at your house," Michael said. "Better than this."

"Some things I like when my mom makes them," Nicky said. "Like pizza. She puts anchovies on, and extra cheese."

"Your mother *makes* pizza?" Michael, who had been threading orange elbow macaronis onto the tines of his fork, froze in awe. "Herself?"

"Yeah. She lets me put on the anchovies. Last time I got to mush the tomato stuff around on top of the crust."

"I'm singing in a concert tonight," I said to Michael. "And you and Daddy and Randy are coming to hear it. You'll be staying up pretty late."

"I don't wanna," Michael said, sucking one piece of macaroni off his fork. "The Hulk is on tonight. Get me a baby-sitter. Get Steve."

"Not tonight, honey. This is special; you'll be in a pretty church at night, in the city, watching Mommy sing. It's a very grown-up thing."

He swung around in his chair. "You mean I *hafta* go? I'll hate it. I'll be bored stiff. I won't go. Get me Steve and that's that." He swung back around and stuck the fork into his mouth, watching Nicky from the corner of his eye.

"We'll talk about it later," I said. "Eat your lunch. Nicky, does your mommy have any hobbies? Does she sew or play tennis or anything?"

"I don't know. Yeah, she sews. And she teaches something at the church. Greek, I think."

"Greek cooking?"

"No, *Greek*. Talking Greek. Something like that."

"Greek! Aesop was Greek!" Michael said.

"I know. She read me some of it. It sounded—" he rattled off a string of nonsense syllables. Michael snorted, then barked a laugh, shooting half-chewed macaroni across the table.

"Clean it up," I said, "and apologize to your friend for your manners."

"La la la," he sang, as he swiped at the table with his napkin. "Loo-o-o-o la la la." He was waving his tongue around and crossing his eyes. Nicky laughed politely.

"Sit down and finish your lunch," I said, one word to a measure. He ate, grinning at Nicky. Then he got up and grabbed two

142

Ring Dings from the cupboard and gave one to Nicky. "Let's go," he said. They ran out, slamming the screen door. "And I'm not going," he shouted back to me.

"Ring Dings!" I heard Nicky say as they turned their bikes around in the driveway. "We *never* get Ring Dings!"

24.

Randy came in when I was greasing the brownie pan. "You're wrong," she announced, dumping her bookbag with a thud. "It's gross. It's disgusting. I had to change—you know—the thing, today and I had to go to the girls' room three times before I could be alone in there."

"Why did you have to be alone?"

"So I could use the *machine*."

"You had to buy one? How come?"

"I forgot to bring them. They're so *big*, and the boys take people's bags and go through them, and what if they found them?"

"How about tampons?"

"Whats?"

"Tampax? They're little—"

"Oh, *gross*. Sticking something in*side*?"

"—Yeah. Well, you really don't feel it. They don't show at all, and you can carry them in your overalls pocket, even. They're much less trouble, really. Listen, I'm not going to tell you what to do. If you want to try them, I'll buy you a box of Juniors."

"Well it's finished now anyhow, thank God. You can buy them if you want to, but don't tell me it isn't disgusting." She put the milk on the table and got a box of Mallomars from the cupboard. Delicately she began peeling the chocolate off the top of one.

"I'm singing in a concert tonight," I said. "I thought you and Daddy and Michael might come to hear it."

"I really don't—"

"I mentioned it to Michael and he made a big fuss—said he'd rather watch the Hulk."

Behind her eyes, as she nibbled the cookie part off the marshmallow, she did an about-face. "He would," she said. "Do you have a solo?" Friend to friend, regret for the Hulk hovering in a quirk of her chocolaty mouth.

"No. We have three professionals coming in to do the solos."

"You're a professional."

"No, I'm not. I'm a long way off from it. But it's exciting to be singing *with* the pros, and for an audience. Anyway, it's at St. John's in the city and it doesn't even begin until eight o'clock, so you'd be up kind of late. Think you'd want to come?"

"Of course. Does Michael have to come?"

"Yes, I want him to."

"Why don't you get a sitter? It'll be too late for him anyhow."

"He'll manage. I don't expect him to appreciate it the way you can, of course, but even if he's a little cranky, I think he should see what I do, don't you?"

"He won't pay attention. He'll just spoil it for all of us. What are you doing? Are we having company?"

I was stirring melted butter and chocolate with one hand and groping in the drawer for the beaters with the other. "No company. Just making some brownies. The boys'll be home in half an hour."

"You're making brownies for *Michael?* Just for a snack?"

"For you, too."

"How come?"

"Just felt like it. With nuts or without?"

"With, I guess. Aren't you supposed to be resting and drinking honey or something? For your voice?"

145

Not with Nicky Padou coming over. I'm still behind on the chickens and goats—damn kid's not going to report home that all he had was macaroni and cheese out of a box and Ring Dings. "Nah," I said, "only stars do that. Hand me the sifter."

The brownies were cooling in the pan when the boys came home. "What do I smell?" Michael yelled through the screen door. "Ma?"

"Brownies," I said, taking Nicky's baseball jacket and books. "Want some?"

"Now?"

"Aren't you hungry? They're just out of the oven."

"But we nev—"

"Nicky? Want a brownie?" I propelled him toward the kitchen. He stopped at the door to look around for Michael and caught sight of the Mallomars on the table.

"Mallomars," he breathed. "Can I have one of those?"

While the boys tore into the box of Mallomars, I grimly scrubbed burnt chocolate off the stove and swept up spilled sugar.

"You eat the top first?" Michael was saying. "I eat all around the sides, then the chocolate off the top, then the bottom, *then* the top." He demonstrated, licking chocolate off his fingers, then wiping them on his shirt.

Randy came in. "*Michael*," she said in exaggerated repulsion, "you are dis*gust*ing. Use a napkin." She pried the first brownie out of the pan, crunched through the pile of crumbs the broom had collected, and sat down at the table. "And you better not act up at the concert tonight," she told him. "I'm not sitting with you if you do."

"Not going," Michael said cheerfully around a mouthful of Mallomar.

The phone rang. It was Marylynn. "Am I pulling you from your work?" she asked. "Just wondered how the little fellows were."

"They're great," I said, walking into the den and closing the door on the phone cord so she couldn't hear Michael and Randy

146

screaming at each other. "I'm just giving them their snack. I baked some brownies, but they—"

"Grand. I just wanted to ask you—we were thinking of taking the boys bowling after supper. It's not a school night and I thought maybe Michael—"

We're full up with goats, Marylynn: forget it. "How nice of you," I cooed. "But I'm singing tonight and Michael really wants to come and hear it."

"How wonderful! Where?"

"At St. John's in the city. It's just a choral concert; I sing with the Philharmonia Chorale. But the kids are all excited. They think it's big-time stuff." I felt my nose. It wasn't growing.

The kids were still screaming when I went in to hang the phone up. "And that's final," Michael was shouting. "You fartie." Nicky was peacefully eating the bottom off another Mallomar. I went upstairs to wash my hair.

25.

Richard was still lecturing Michael when we got out of the car at St. John's. "You will sit there like a human being and listen," he said. "You hear me? And there will not be a sound from you. Your mother does plenty for you, and she wants you to hear this thing, you're going to hear it. Is that—"

"—clear?" I heard in my head, running to the stage entrance. "Do you understand me, young man? Because if you don't—" *because if you don't, young lady, I know a way to make you understand. Daddy, don't. I didn't, I won't, I'm sor—*

"Why?"

Gideon, with both hands on my shoulders. I must have been saying it aloud.

"Why sorry? Beth, you look—what is it?"

"Nothing. I'm sorry. . . . I was awful on the phone yesterday. It's been—"

"Hey, everybody's got a family. Don't look like that. I don't scare off so easy. Will you be home on Monday? I'll—"

"—rybody, please." It was Lecrief, in a tux, standing on a chair in the corridor, steadying himself against the wall with the fingertips of one hand. "Two things. One, this is our final meeting of the season. I say it every year, but it's even truer this year: we've never sounded better. I'm proud of you, before you even

148

begin to sing, and I'm already looking forward to the fall. Our pieces for next year will be even more complex than the Erb—" cheerful groans from the chorus members, who were crowded into the corridor "—but we're ready for them. The nature of the works demands that we modify our usual setup of choral unity with professionals for the solo parts. We'll still use professionals, but because of the intricacy of the choral score, I'm naming a lead soprano, Beth Clahr, and a lead baritone, Sam Solender." People craned around to smile at me. I felt my face go hot.

"Two: remember, I want each section to sound like a single instrument. One—"

"ONE VOICE!" Everyone shouted his pet phrase back at him, through grins.

"Okay, I guess you have it. Break a leg." Hands steadied him as he got down off the chair. He headed down the corridor toward the stage. The space was filled with bodies; I couldn't get through to him.

"Lead soprano!" I looked helplessly at Gideon. "I was going to tell him tonight that I won't be singing with the chorus next year."

"Maybe this will make it worth your while to stay. I hope so." He put a casual hand on my waist, propelled me forward with the crowd. There was no time for us to say anything else.

The professionals stood downstage left. From the riser I stood on, I could see them clearly in profile. One baritone, one tenor, one soprano. The tenor was very young, but the baritone was paunchy and gray, and the soprano, although her hair fell youthfully down her back, was haggard in the stage lights. She had on too much makeup, and it only exaggerated the lines in her face and neck.

Our backups, a cellist and a pianist, took their places. The cello tuned a bit. The houselights dimmed and Lecrief walked out. There was that long moment of rustling in the underbrush—nylon shifting against silk, murmuring, coughs—and the little hush. For me, I thought. They're mine. To love me. I raised my head and

149

looked commandingly out at them. Ready. A glance at Lecrief. Ready.

But Lecrief was looking at the altos, giving them the count, ticking them in. They began. I lowered my eyes to watch Lecrief's hands and listened for our measure. We came in on the millisecond, one voice. When McCormack, who was always weak in the high ranges, wavered on a high D-flat, we anticipated it and swelled in concert to cover her. She cracked and dropped out for a measure or two, and we held the volume until she picked up again. It was the first movement, which is tight and crisp, and we were fine. A single, sustained voice with a cutting edge. But the second movement, a pastoral passage with allusions to hymns and Appalachian songs, started mellow with the baritones and basses and "requires of the sopranos," as Lecrief kept saying, "roundness and sweetness." I knew, or I was beginning to know, how to get that sound, but the others thought all it meant was putting a smile in their voices. "Okay," I telegraphed to the back of Lecrief's head, "catch this."

The baritones and basses gave us two measures and we came in. I started low and silky, opened up so gradually that at first no one noticed. Lecrief did, two bars in, because I was really doing it. It was sweet and round and pervasive, and the rest of them were ordinary voices with smiles in them. Lecrief nodded to me, with a little smile, and I felt them shifting a little on the risers around me, but I kept opening it up. Now I raised my head again, to them out there. To gather them in. They were moving around a little, too, some of them; I could hear them. They were looking for me, for the voice. I tossed my head on the crescendo, just a little. No hair flew behind me, but it was the same. Snare them all. Catch it, boys, it's for you, if you listen. To me. I glanced back to Lecrief. He was looking at me. He smiled a little, but he patted the air with his right hand, pat, pat, pat. Hold it down, Beth. They were shifting around me, indignation coming through the smiles in their voices. I missed a measure, came in then like the rest of them. They settled down, and we finished the movement, one smiling voice.

150

The improvisation came and went without me. I opened my mouth, but mouthed silence. Sulking, Bethie? They went their separate ways around me, wondered at my silence, the hell with them.

I maneuvered through the corridor, head down. "Hey." Gideon's voice from behind me. I edged between two men and kept going. He put a heavy hand on my shoulder, stopped me. "*Hey*," he said. "You were really going there, then you shut off all of a sudden. I didn't hear you at all in the improv. Where were you?"

"I was told to keep quiet," I said, "so I kept quiet. I'm quitting, Gideon. Brescia's right; you can't take the bow and pull in the galley, both."

"What? Who told you to keep quiet?"

"Lecrief. He gave me the sign. And he's right. Soloists are soloists, and the chorus is—a chorus. I have to quit."

"Listen." His voice was pitched low and he held me still with a steady look. They were pushing past us, calling to their families, who were coming in the other way. "Listen to me. You're good, and getting better all the time. If you have to quit, okay, you have to. But don't do it tonight. You're furious, and Lecrief will know it in a minute, and he'll figure you're leaving in a temperamental fit. You may need him someday, Beth."

"Ma-a-a!" I whipped my head around. It was Michael, tunneling through the crowd, calling steadily as he came toward us.

"I'll call you Monday," Gideon said. "*Don't quit tonight.* Promise?"

"All right," I smiled. "Thanks."

"Monday." He said it like a loveword, then turned away just as Michael made it through.

"I was *calling* you," he said.

"I know, honey. Let's find Daddy and Randy." I picked him up and used him as a flying wedge to get out of the corridor.

26.

"Well?" Richard's voice was jovial against the unnatural silence. The kids had shuffled to the car without a word and sat so quietly in the back that I looked around to see if they were awake. I felt a twinge in my back. "Michael's too heavy for me to carry around anymore," I said to Richard. "I think I dislocated my back."

"What were you carrying him for? He's a big kid, aren't you, Mikey? Hey, kids, how *was* it?"

"You were there." Michael's voice was sullen.

"It was okay," Randy said. "I mean, you were fine, Mom, but the music was a little weird. How come you don't sing something good?"

"Well, if they sang something ordinary, no one would know how clever the conductor was," Richard said. "You couldn't accuse him of picking this thing for the way it sounds: it's a showcase for his Delicate Mee-usical Sensibilities, right?" He hung a limp wrist in the air, then put his hand on my thigh.

"To people who know music," I said, "this piece is difficult but important—and even beautiful, in its own way." I looked out the window, to close the subject, and thought with surprise that it was true. I found the piece beautiful. It's like writing a paper

152

on the sonnets of Keats or something, I thought. You take them apart, find a way to understand them, say what you know, then you own them. They're yours, so you love them. Like the kids. I looked out at the river going by under us. I might never have chosen these two, I thought, but I've been working on them for twelve years, so they're mine, so I love them. I put a hand on my belly. What about that one? Cut it out, I thought, then grinned sourly to myself. Just what I figured on doing, Mr. Bones, I thought—cutting it out.

Not just my back but my whole body was aching when I crawled into bed. I was so tired, suddenly, that even the muscles in my face were drawing. My eyes closed and I felt the slow spiraling. Like the anaesthetic will be, I thought, and I saw Daniel Block in his white coat. He came toward me, holding something in his hand. "Wait," I told him, "I'm not ready."

"—ready? Beth? You going to sleep already?" It was Richard. His face was enormous. I closed my eyes again and turned over, but he pursued me. He was over me, pulling.

"What? Richard, *what?*"

"Boy, it really takes it out of you, doesn't it? You going to be this zonked every time you sing?"

I was awake now. "No. But it was a very long day."

"Mine, too. I had an estimate to get out—an important one —and Frances was tied up with Walsh, and I really had to break my tail to get out on time tonight. But I got there for you, didn't I?"

Tell the man thank you. "Yes, you did. Thank you."

He snaked a hand into my nightgown, closed on a breast. "I wouldn't sit through that stuff for just anyone, you know."

I thought for a minute, then I wriggled out of my nightgown and lay back, waiting.

"Not all that tired, huh, baby? You okay? Got your thing in?" He was pulling off his underpants. It was erect and quivering. It brushed against my leg as he swung over me. It was hard and warm, but I felt it like a dead thing. "I'm safe," I said, and I closed my eyes. He pushed it into me and I squeezed my eyes tighter shut, against a panic that came up through my throat. The patterns moved behind my eyelids. I'll never be safe again, I thought.

27.

I spent all day Saturday and most of Sunday with Caroline Cook and Leone Taub, making centerpieces and doing the seating chart and placecards for the luncheon. A lot of people who never came to meetings were coming to hear Gotbaum, and we tried to seat them with active members. "Break up the cabal and do a little recruiting," Leone said.

"The ones with young kids won't need much recruiting," I said. "They're ripe—it's the loneliest time in their lives, and they're starved for companionship and desperate with boredom. They'll do anything to have an adult to talk to." Caroline and Leone looked at me.

"I don't think that's very—"

"That's certainly not why I—"

"Come on," I said. "You think all those mothers of three-year-olds who become active do it because they're fascinated with sewage disposal and one hundred percent assessment? They're not old enough for PTA and they need a fix too badly to wait."

"Well, if that's all they wanted they could go bowling," Caroline said.

"Not in this community. League *is* bowling in this town." Four beats of silence. "How about Jackie Kerwin at table six?" I asked. "She's dynamite." I glanced up in time to catch them looking at each other.

"Super," they said. One voice.

I was practicing five-note jumps when the phone rang, Monday morning. It was Gideon.

"You still have the music in your voice," he said. "You're high and sweet this morning."

"I was practicing intervals," I told him. "It's murder, hitting precise pitch and keeping the muscles relaxed enough not to choke the tone."

"You were doing it Friday night. You sounded better than the *grande dame* we paid. She was pushing so hard I thought she'd hemorrhage."

"She had a very rich lower range," I said, "but she did strain on the high notes. No volume. I kept thinking—that'll be me in ten or fifteen years, an aging, semidecent singer hacking with local choruses and losing range every year."

"Scared this morning? What happened? You were blazing Friday night: seize the bow, no more choruses. You were right, too; I thought about it. I seem to spend a lot of time thinking about you." He jumped to it without warning, his voice suddenly intimate. I said nothing. "Here's what I think," he said, business again. "You're right. Brescia's right. If you're going to psych yourself to sing solo, you can't keep sabotaging it by trying to fit back into a chorus, even as lead soprano. I fought the idea there for a little while, because half the reason—more than half the reason —I sing in that chorus is so I can see you. But there are other ways we can see each other, and other places. . . . Beth? You still there?"

*A motel somewhere, I thought. A quickie, off the road. Who does he think I am? "Gideon, I have two children," I began. I was forming the next sentences carefully in my mind: and I don't just . . . see . . . people. You're very attractive, but my life. . . .

"I saw them," he said, before I could get it out, "as you went out. The girl—"

"—Randy."

"—Randy—is going to be like you. Willowy and sexy. She's sexy already."

Randy? Willowy? *Sexy?* I smiled, seeing her clumping up the stairs, tripping over herself. Then I had a sudden picture in my mind of her in shorts and a T-shirt, with those long, young legs, and the high budding mounds, tossing her hair. I pulled in my stomach, breathed a little velvet into my voice. Just a little.

"Sexy's in the eye of the beholder," I said.

"I know. Would you like to know how I see you? I know you have two kids, you keep telling me. But I see you making a way for yourself alone—surrounded but alone—pretty, sexy and ripening so fast, in so many ways, you don't know how to handle it. Like Randy, only you're a woman, not a little girl, and the allure —for me—is tremendous. Tremendous. I know you don't think of yourself as alone, and I know you're not out looking for anyone. But there's something about you that calls to me. Does that scare you? Offend you?"

"Offend me, no. Scare me, yes." Randy faded back to clumpy twelve, faded out altogether. I saw the bed by the oceanside window, felt his hands. *Tell him to go away. Beth?*

"I told you, I won't push you into anything. But I remember a moment when it was pretty clear there was something between us. Do you remember? Beth?"

"Yes." More. Tell me more.

"So do I. Vividly. Beth, should we meet?"

Tell him no. "Not . . . right now."

"All right. Not now. But you don't want me to stop calling? You'll be talking to Lecrief—when?"

"I don't know. Today or tomorrow."

"I'll call later in the week, see how it went. Listen, what are you going to tell him?"

"Just what Brescia said, I thought. They know each other; he'll respect Brescia's position."

157

"Okay. Later, then. And Beth?"

"Yes?"

"Think about it."

The intervals were easy when I went back to practicing. Even the high ones.

I wore a new silk shirt and a straight skirt and spiky sandals to lunch with Laura. As we walked along the sidewalk to the restaurant, with one part of my mind I checked to see whether the men we passed were looking at me, and with the other I ordered myself again not to tell Laura about the abortion, or even allude to a problem. She'll ferret it out and then she'll feed on it forever, I told myself. Chauffeuring, broth, little meals for the family, phone checks—and underneath it, contempt. She'd never do it. Abortion. Murder.

We sat at a table in the corner. "No kidding, let's go dutch," she said. "It's nice to see you and to be out to lunch; you don't have to pay for my meal."

"I absolutely am and that's that," I said. "And no little salad. I may be too cheap to go for Lutèce, but at Le Bistro the sky's the limit." I set an example by ordering wine for both of us, and consommé and a veal dish. It sounded like a meal I could get down. She ordered snails ("They should know I've been around") and choucroute.

The snails came while I was telling her about Marylynn Padou.

"—and then after I baked the damn things, the kid went for the Mallomars. I bet he never even told her I made them. So now she thinks—" I stopped because she had speared a snail in its shell and was holding it suspended, listening to me. It was gray and glistening, like mucus. I looked past her, toward the bar, and swallowed hard. My glance landed on a man at the bar and he looked back. I slid my eyes away, back to Laura. She was pushing the snail around in the sauce.

"What's the matter?" she asked. "You okay?"

158

"Fine," I said. "Tell me about your pottery. How's it going?"

She worked away at the snails while she told me about glazing and firing. She must have seen me staring at the snail on her fork, because she held it out to me. "Want one? They're terrific."

I shook my head.

"Come on, one little one won't kill you. How much garlic butter—hey, are you sick? Beth? Wait, I'll come with you."

I motioned her to stay and made blindly for the ladies' room. On the way back, as I passed the bar, the man I'd seen before smiled at me. I gave him one murderous look and stalked to the table. Smile, now.

"Honey? You okay? Should we go home?"

"No, I'm fine. Sorry about that. But really, I'm fine now."

"But if it's a stomach thing—"

"It isn't, believe me. I'm fine. Hungry, even." I took a piece of bread and nibbled on it to prove the point.

"It isn't a stomach thing and now you're hungry? You do this every day at lunch or what?"

"No, just lucky today. Forget it. Let's eat."

The waiter picked up her plate, looked questioningly at my untouched consommé and at me. I nodded for him to take it. He came back with our main course, hers steaming piles of sausage and sauerkraut, mine medallions of veal in a light sauce. I really was hungry, and I started in on it. She sat back and watched me. Suddenly she leaned forward. "Oh my God, I know," she gasped. "You're pregnant, aren't you?"

Tell a lie, your mother dies. "Give the lady a cigar," I said. Oh, Beth.

"Don't hand out cigars so fast. What are you going to do about it?"

"Do?"

"Beth, listen to me. Do you really need this now? Diapers, playgrounds, play groups, car pools—you'll be a grandmother, practically, before you get loose again. How'd you get in this mess?"

"Caught unarmed."

"Well, Jesus Christ. I mean, passion is great, but you two are old enough to—well what does Richard say about it? He's crowing, I suppose."

"He doesn't know."

She pulled her chin in and looked at me with unblinking eyes. Steam from the sauerkraut made a ribbon around her nose and forehead. Then her eyes narrowed a little and she moved her head to get me from another angle. "It isn't his," she said finally. "Oh Jesus, Beth."

"Of course it's his. My God, Laura."

"Then how come—"

"I just found out. It's only a couple of weeks along, and I haven't—I don't know—"

"You poor kid."

"You just had me a grandmother."

"Later. Right now you're a poor kid. When are you going to tell him? Will he want it?"

"I don't know." Richard? It was a new idea. What did his wanting it have to do with my abortion?

"Don't tell him."

"Don't tell him?"

"No. Look, Beth, I know you think that's a horrible thing to suggest—you two are so close and all that. No, listen, I see it. The way he looks at you—you know he's always saying to people, 'How's my girl look? Not bad, eh?' Obviously he adores you and I understand you'd want to tell him everything, but don't do it. Don't tell him, this one time. Just go and have it done, and that's all. I told Len and I've been sorry ever since."

"About—you had an abortion?"

"Sure did. Two years ago. The worst possible way, and—well, I made two mistakes. One, how it was done, and two, I told Len. I couldn't see myself going through it alone, you know? And it was late in our lives already. I mean, that's why I didn't even figure it out until I was eight weeks along—figured it was, you know, irregular, onset of menopause. So I said, 'Look, honey, I seem to be pregnant, we'll have to arrange for an abortion,' and

160

he said, 'Abortion? *Why?*' " She sat upright, mimicking Len, a combination of pomposity and preening. It was a bitterly funny characterization. I smiled.

"Yeah, laugh," she said. "I told him *why*, in words of one syllable, and you know what he said? 'It'll be a joy in our old age.' He actually said it! 'It'll be living proof my cock still works,' that's what he meant. Can't you see me trotting along on kindergarten class trips at fifty? Not me, kid."

Laura? "So what did you do?"

"Well, you know, I kind of purred around and played with his hair and said how now we were free to be *alone* together and all that, wouldn't a little kid kind of get in the way—you know, kind of prop up the old cock from another angle. He fell over like a tenpin—cleared his throat and said how if it was best for me, and my health, and so on. . . . So *then* we didn't know where to go. It was before it was all organized, you know? Legal, but still kind of hole-and-corner. My doctor didn't even want to recommend anyone. So I heard about this place. Listen, when I die, I'm going to skip hell and move right over on to purgatory, 'cause kiddo, I've *been* there. It was this *house*; I mean someone's *home*. A little ranch with linoleum floors and the office is in the rumpus room? You went in the back entrance, down some stairs, and there was this big, dark waiting room, paneled—the rec room, right?—and sitting around on threadbare couches are about six other women, all black, in pairs, and Len and me. Those other dames were smart; they left the men out of it and brought a *friend*. There's one other white lady—the nurse. I go over to her and she sits me down and pulls out a long white form. 'Name?' she says. Well, I don't want to shout out my name, obviously, so I say, 'I'll fill it in.' She looks at me—you know how they do—and says, 'Name, please?' like that. So I tell her and she spells it out, slowly, at a million decibels. 'Address?' she says, and so on, all the details. *Then* she gives me this thing to sign. It's a waiver, you know? And in enormous letters on line two it says ABORTION. You know—before you murder this infant, do you know what you're doing? Len had to sign, too. They really rub your face

161

in it. But we sign and I pay her the blood money—yeah, up front —and I figure that's the worst; it's over now. While all of this is going on, two of the other women have been called in. We wait forever and then they call this other woman and me. Eat, it's getting cold."

She'd been working steadily at the choucroute as she talked, but I'd forgotten about my veal. I started on it. She watched me for a minute, then nodded and went on.

"So next was the enema."

"Enema."

"Yeah, what do you think? And prepping, the whole thing. There was another nurse who did that. She was a little nicer. Black. Been through it herself, I suppose. So then she hitches you up, legs in the stirrups, and in comes—"

"On a table? Like for a Pap smear? You're awake?"

"Oh, yes ma'am. Wide open, wide awake. And in he comes. He's about twenty, face hasn't cleared up yet, thin as a rail, and while he hooks you up to the machine, he's cracking jokes."

"What machine?" My hands were cold and sweaty. I wiped them surreptitiously on the tablecloth and exchanged the day-old oxygen in my throat for another batch.

"It's this dinky box—he tells me he pilfered it from the army and I believe him—and it has a hose on it, a small black hose. They use water and they suction you out. I'll spare you the details; you look half dead. Believe me, I wouldn't be telling you all this if I didn't know yours will be different. Yeah, and I'm wide awake and I *hear* it all, clackety-clack, swurgle glush. Never mind what it feels like. Then all of a sudden it's over and you're lying in a room, wrapped up like a goddamned mummy—that's good, mummy—and you're alone. Back to square one and feeling like if that blankety-blank who got you into this ever so much as looks at you again, you'll kill him." She broke off, made herself busy with the last of the meat and a piece of bread, then looked up, hard lines around her grin.

"Funny thing is, it was such a long time before he even *tried* to touch me that I was chewing on the walls. You're depressed

162

afterward, you know, like it was a childbirth—as far as your body's concerned, it is—and you're in no shape to pay *him* any attention. Then one day you look at him and he's shell-shocked, like. They can't take it like we can, you know—pain, guilt, that stuff. Took me months to bring him around and even now to get him going I have to—are you eating or not? Don't dream you'll do me out of dessert on grounds of time. *Eat.* Okay. Well, anyway, yours'll be a cinch. They have it down to a fine art now. Bunnies on the wall, Muzak, the works. And you're so early on, it'll be like nothing. Only tell me you'll profit from my tale of woe and leave Richard out of it. I'll go with you; he'll never have to know. Yes, I'll have . . . um, how's the mousse? Okay, I'll have the mousse. Beth?"

"Just tea, please."

"She'll have the cheesecake, and tea. Coffee for me. No cream. Got any Sweet'n Low? Good. No cream and two Sweet'n Lows, please. You're not thinking seriously of having it, are you? No kidding."

"No. I figure you'll eat them both."

"The *baby*, dummy. You don't really want it?"

"No, I guess you're right. I hadn't—"

"Believe me, I'm right. So make an appointment—I know someone I can call, she knows a great place—and tell me when, and we'll go. That's all. I'll call her when I get home. This is *good*; try it."

"Laura, I—my doctor said he knew a good clinic, if I—I think if I do it, I'll let him—"

"Great. Just tell me where and when."

"You're an angel, I don't know how to thank you . . . but I think I'm better off alone. I'm much braver that way. If I need you to drive me home, can I call?"

We argued it back and forth while she finished the desserts, and by the time we pulled into my driveway it was settled: I'd go alone, but swore to call her the minute I wanted her. She'd be ready at a moment's notice, and she was definitely coming to bring me home, I should call her and tell her when. Okay, I wouldn't tell Richard, if she really thought it was best. I could tell him later it was an emergency D&C ("It *is*," she said). She would provide dinner. Goats and chickens everywhere I looked, and after I'd sworn myself to silence, but still I figured I hadn't done badly on this one: she thought she'd convinced me to do the deed. Oh, Beth, what a clever bitch you are.

28.

The silk shirt had wide sweat stains under the arms and streaks of sweat on the back, so I couldn't wear it to the luncheon on Tuesday. I wanted to be demure, anyway, so I put on my shapeless khaki poplin skirt and jacket, with a green T-shirt. Then I remembered about Jessie and buttoned the jacket over the T-shirt.

She came in early, while I was running around with the placecards and conferring with Caroline about the salad dressing. I didn't know she was there until I heard the businesslike staccato in the room change to a chorus of stroking melodies near the doorway.

"—good to *see* you—"

"—look fabulous!"

"—you were coming—"

She was standing in the archway, flushed and smiling shyly, oddly passive for Jessie. The sunlight from the wall of windows in the lobby made a bright line all down her left side and shone brassily off the brown wig. Just then everyone stopped talking at once and the clatter of dishes from the kitchen suddenly seemed unbearably loud. I ran over.

"Check this woman for sidearms," I said. "She's a known perpetrator." They looked at me in relief. The uncertainty in Jessie's eyes changed to wicked glee.

"Who knows what evil lurks in the hearts of persons?" she

cackled. "You can surround me, Cranston, but you'll never thwart my plan."

"What's she up to now?" Only a beat and a half. Not bad, Leone. "Undermining the nonpartisan school-board elections again? Seat her near the kitchen."

"Worse than that," I said. "She has designs on Gotbaum's person."

"I don't blame her a bit," put in Caroline, still holding the olive oil and mustard. "He doesn't have a half-bad person. Jessie, can I help? But listen, don't you think firearms is a bit . . . pushy? We could probably do better with a little—" she finished the sentence with her ample hips.

"You go right on talking dirty," I said, taking the oil and mustard out of Caroline's hands, "and *I* will make the dressing."

"Calm yourself, woman," Jessie was saying to Caroline as I walked back across the room. "It's mayhem I had in mind, not lust. Although come to think of it, if he took the two of us on, it would probably—"

Leone followed me into the kitchen, waited until the door swung closed before she spoke. "What a shock," she said. "She looks awful. Awful." She shuddered and hugged herself.

"She does? I picked the blouse myself. I think it kind of—"

"You know what I mean. She's lost weight and her *color*, and that wig. I don't know. . . . I hope she's going to—" she shook her head grimly, hunching her shoulders and holding herself tighter. "Well." She looked around the kitchen. "How's it coming? The dressing?"

Jessie insisted on helping with the cleanup after the luncheon. I passed her carrying a stack of dishes on her left side. "Don't mess up the blouse," I said. "It looks sensational. Go do something clean. Help with the money or something."

"Who told you money is clean? Anyhow, they know better than to let me near the profits."

I took the dishes from her. "You behaved very well, actually," I told her.

166

"Yeah, well I decided Caroline had a point. Be more fun to kill him with kindness. Besides, I figured if I popped him one you might get miffed and break our date Thursday." It was her usual bantering tone, but the look she shot me was almost pleading. Leone was right. Her color was bad.

"Shall we do it right?" I asked. "Have lunch? What the hell, after Phyllis's pecan surprises. . . ."

"Best idea I've heard all day, not that the competition was much. You're on. I'll go count money; if enough of it sticks to my fingers, lunch'll be on me."

Leone was in the kitchen, counting pitchers. "—Louise had two, that's twelve. Right. She hardly ate a thing, did you notice?"

"Jessie?"

"Mm. I can't tell you how it upsets me to see that. When Jerry's sister was—"

"How was the take?"

"The what? Oh, we're all paid up but two. Membership's up, they don't have a final count yet, and we have all the voters' service booths manned. It's a bad sign, that's all I'm saying. Jerry's sister was like that, and then it was only—"

"Leone, I want to tell you while you can still—you asked me to sit on the board, and I want you to know what an honor—" I stumbled through that part for a while. "—anything to help, you know that, but between the kids and school, and I'm spending a lot of time studying voice and practicing. . . . I just don't think I have the time to do it justice. I'm sorry, I—"

She was unperturbed. "We thought you might say that, after your remarks the other day. Well, League's not for everyone. We wish you all kinds of success with your career. And thanks for your help, Beth. The luncheon was smashing. Really super." I was dismissed.

I drove home near tears, feeling irrationally that it was I who had been shut out of the game.

167

29.

When the train stopped in Bronxville, I was just finishing my checklist, second time through. . . . weather's great, he'll walk home. Randy will be there to let him in. The stew is ready . . . and that's *that*, I told myself. Stop it. Looking up casually, I scanned the crowd on the platform and checked the people getting on, but I didn't see Daniel Block. Just as well, I thought; you sure don't have any games left to play with him. To shut out the picture of myself in the receiving position and Daniel Block gripping my womb with that look of impersonal concentration, I pulled the music for Rosie's class out of my briefcase and began to work on sight transposition. The train bucked out of the station, then settled into its rhythm for the long pull into the city. I closed my eyes for a minute to hear the music in the new key.

A small darkened room. I am alone, wrapped in a white sheet, white blanket, hair tousled on the pillow. Quite still. No, sleeping. Fingertips smoothing hair from my forehead wake me. I open my eyes, look up. Daniel Block, in his white coat, standing over me in the dim light. Was it his touch? He sits down next to my bed. "How are you?" he asks softly. "Is it over?" I ask him. "Why are you here?" "It's over, and everything is fine," he tells me.

168

"You sleep sweetly," he adds, "like a child." I feel myself flushing. I nuzzle my cheek into the pillow to hide it. "I've been here most of the morning," he says to the sheet. "I couldn't let you be alone." "I'm not alone," I say bravely. "There are people—" "You are alone on this one," he says quietly. "Aren't you?" I nod. "Okay. For whatever reason, whoever is . . . in your life . . . isn't here now. Maybe you want it that way." I look away from him. "But I couldn't let you wake up alone, travel home alone."

"But your office," I say. "Your patients—" I wince.

"Does it hurt?"

I nod.

"Okay. Shh, okay," although I'm saying nothing at all. "Here. Take this." He puts an arm under me, raises me a little to take the pill, lowers me back gently. My hospital gown has fallen open. He pulls it gently closed, lets his fingers linger for a second on the swell of a breast, draws the white covers up over me. "Well," I smile, "no mysteries there." "That's wrong," he says. "You can't know how wrong." The pill is getting to me. I turn my cheek to the pillow again, very near his shoulder. My eyes close and open again slowly. "Sleep," he says. "I'm here. I'll be here when you wake up." I fall asleep feeling his fingers in my hair.

I sat for a moment after the train pulled into the station, not wanting to move. When I did get up and move out of the car, my breasts felt so full against my T-shirt and there was such a feeling of readiness all over my body that I put my sunglasses on, even in the darkness.

All the way to Mannes I tried to work it out, how I could keep Laura from coming to pick me up and interfering with our time alone together in the darkening afternoon. Stage-managing your daydreams, I said to myself. You're crazy, lady. But by the time I sat down in Rosie's class, I had it worked out. Laura would call the clinic and he would answer and tell her that he was my doctor, and that he would take care of it. He would take care of everything.

169

I called Lecrief from the pay phone, after Rosie's class. I figured it was a safe time to call, but I was wrong. He was home.

"It's Beth Clahr," I said. "I wanted to tell you—"

"You were in marvelous voice Friday, weren't you? Quite a sound you gave us. I've always believed there is a connection between one's state of mind and the quality of the voice, but that was really graphic proof. At seven-fifty you're named lead soprano, and at eight-fifteen you're singing like an angel. Don't worry, you know, that you got a little carried away. It's understandable and next year, I hope, there'll be a place for—"

"I wanted to tell you," I said, "that I'm going to have to quit the chorus." I forged on before he could say anything. "I've been studying voice these past few months with Vincent Brescia—"

"Good man, Brescia. I knew him when he had hopes of making the Met."

"He said you were a good musician, too, and that if I were going to sing in any chorus, yours was a great one, but if I'm going —he says if I'm going to develop as a singer, it's not a good idea to try to sing in a chorus. Just now."

"Brescia told you that? Curious. He himself—"

"He's my teacher. I really have to follow his advice if I'm going to—"

"Absolutely, absolutely. Well, I admire your courage. It's no easy thing, cracking the music world, even if one started out young. But all good luck to you, and my best to Vincent."

"I'll tell him. And thank you. I've learned a lot singing with you. I'll come to all your concerts next season." Gracious Beth.

"We'll look for you. And any time—well, perhaps you'll be back with us one day. As soloist, of course."

Never, you bitch, I thought, walking down the hall to Brescia's room. I'll take a vow of silence first.

Brescia was surprised by my intensity that lesson. "Eh," he laughed, "now it's you who drive me! Gently, gently; we cannot

170

make the voice in a day. And anyway, to do battle with the instrument is not the way. Seduce it, prepare the way for it, and it will open in time. That much time we have."

I rehearsed it in the train, how I would tell Gideon, when he called, about Lecrief and about the lesson with Brescia.

"He made me sit on the rug, right then, in the middle of the lesson, with my legs crossed and my eyes closed and my wrists on my knees, palm up, and breathe," I would say. "So while I was sitting there I told him I'd quit chorus. You know what he said?"

"What?" A loving smile in his voice. He's seeing me, the mock lotus.

"He said, 'Quiet, please. Only breathe. It's good you quit, but why so late? No wonder you are on fire today. Now you will be ready to sing. *Breathe.*' He wasn't even surprised that I quit. He expected it."

"Because he sees what you don't see," he would say, "that you're something special. He's going to expect a lot from you. Be ready for that. So do I," he would say, with the lover's hum in his voice. "I know there are things in you you've never thought of, or never dared. I want to be there when you dare them. Right there."

When the train stopped, I went to put on my sunglasses and found they were already on. Just as well.

171

30.

I was supposed to pick Jessie up at 10:00. I got going early, dressing carefully in pants and a billowy shirt. You couldn't even tell I had two breasts in that shirt, and I buttoned it all the way up. I was ready by 8:45 so that when Gideon called I could talk without worrying about the time. I tackled Randy's room while I waited, not running the vacuum or even playing the radio, so I'd hear the phone.

It rang at 9:05. "Hello?" I said. Sweet, a little throaty. Warm.

"Hiya, Toots. All set?" It was Jessie.

"Yup, I'll beep for you at ten."

"Yeah—hey listen, that's why I called. Think you could come in for a minute before we go? Something I want you to see. Actually, I should tell you—"

"Absolutely." I cut her off. "I'll ring your bell at ten. Okay?"

"Sure—"

"Great. See you then."

"—Yeah. Okay."

It was 9:08. It seemed silly to start again in Randy's room; I'd no sooner dig in, probably, than he'd call. But I was restless, just waiting, so I went back in there anyway. I looked around helplessly. A pile of clean laundry lay on the floor, scattered out and

172

laced with books, papers, shoes, and parts of a Scrabble set. Dirty underwear and twisted sweaters were everywhere. I started with those, pushed them into her already full hamper. Then I tackled the clean stuff. I was starting to put underwear away in the top drawer of her dresser when I saw something in the corner of the drawer. An envelope. I picked it up. It wasn't sealed. In it was a sheet of paper, folded up small. It was divided into two columns. The first line, in her round, even printing, said:

Drive 16
Smoke cigarettes . . . . Never

I looked down the rest of the sheet, smoothing it flat.

Smoke pot . . . . 16 or 17
Drugs (Heroin, coke, etc.) . . . . Never
Drink . . . . ? 18? Practice first
Make out
    Kissing . . . . Any time
    French kissing 15
    Touching—on top 17
               on bottom . . . . 17 or 18
    BJ [*BJ? BJ? Blow job. My God.*] . . . Never! ! !
    All the way . . . . College probably
Married . . . . After college
Kids, etc. . . . . NEVER.

Under all that she had drawn a double line. Then she had written:

   THINGS TO DO NOW
    1) Stop biting nails.
    2) Stop picking at zits, wash face 2ᵗ a day.
    3) Exercise *every day*.
    4) Stop doing It.

The phone rang. Still holding the paper, I ran to get it. Easy, now. Casual, throaty. "Hello?"

"Hi, baby. How are you?"

"Richard? What's the matter?" I looked at the clock. 9:36.

"Nothing's the matter. Can't I call and say hello?"

"Of course."

"What are you doing?"

"Cleaning up Randy's room a little."

"Randy is thirteen, she can—"

"Twelve."

"Okay, twelve. She can clean up her own room. You should make her do it."

We went back and forth on that for a while. Then there was a pause. I looked at the clock: 9:40. "Listen," I said, "I have to pick Jessie up now. I'd better get going."

"You going out?" He sounded edgy.

"Yes, I told you. Why?"

"Nothing. I figured I'd maybe come home early, after they open the bids."

"That's what you're doing? Waiting to hear about the bid?"

"Right."

"What do you usually do when they're opening them?" 9:42.

"Work on another, but Russo—it's a little quiet right now, and I need secretarial help, anyhow, for the desk work."

"Where's Frances?"

"With Walsh."

"Still? How come?"

"Walsh is busy." He meant it to sound breezy, but it came out tight.

"Well, I think you ought to enjoy the lull. Take a walk, go shopping. I've got to go, okay?"

"Sure. Listen—"

"Yes?"

"—I'll call you if I can get home early."

"Okay. Bye." 9:45. Damn. I ran into Randy's room with the sheet of paper. Writing on the other side caught my eye as I was folding it up. I opened it again. Another list, headed:

SNOBS   WIMPS   OKAY

There was a list of names under each heading. SNOBS was the longest list. A couple of names had been moved from one category to another: Mindy from SNOBS to OKAY, Robin from WIMPS to SNOBS, Alyssa and Sharon from OKAY to SNOBS. I put the paper back in the envelope, left the envelope where I'd found it,

174

put her clean underwear back in the pile on the floor, and closed the drawer. Randy. Keeping score for a game she couldn't control, writing herself rules for whenever they let her in it. I left the room the way it was.

At 9:52 I picked up the phone for a second to make sure there was a dial tone. There was. When I finally left the house at 10:05, he still hadn't called. I waited outside the front door for a second, listening, then got into the car and screeched out of the driveway. The hell with him.

Jessie opened the door as soon as I rang the bell. She was wearing a skirt and sandals and the blouse I'd given her, and her makeup was on, but she hadn't finished dressing. The blouse hung out over the skirt.

"Aren't you elegant," she said. "Come on in. Want a cup of coffee? Piece of coffeecake?" Chipper and polite. She put a hand on my arm to bring me inside. Her hand was icy.

"Not a thing," I said. "I'm saving up for lunch. Where are we going? White Plains?"

"Yes. The New You, the place is called. Well. What did you think of the luncheon yesterday?"

"It's over; that's the best part. And I'm excused from further duty. I'll tell you about it at lunch. But we'd better get going. You wanted to show me something?"

"Mm. Well, no, it's okay. You really don't have to—"

"Jessie, what is it? Come on."

She looked wretchedly at me for a moment, then down at her feet. She pulled in a long breath, let it out raggedly. "It's a hell of a thing to—why should I burden—"

Leone is right, I thought, terror coming up into my throat from between my ribs. Jessie is dying. Wants me to go with her to the border. Oh Christ, get me out of here. "Hey," I said, touching her arm. "It's me, remember? What is it, Jess?" Don't tell me, don't—

"I was going to ask you if you would—it's silly, but I have to know if I'm re—" tears now, sliding out of the corners of her eyes and down along her struggling mouth "—pulsive."

175

I put my arms around her, careful of the breast, careful of the wig. She was rigid. "You want to show me how it looks?"

She nodded, the wig bouncing against my cheek. I pulled back a little. "What a relief. I thought it was a new style, the blouse out over the skirt like that, and I was missing it. What's the big deal? Show me."

I followed her up the stairs to her bedroom. I felt my breasts move with every step, felt lesions open in them, craters, worms boring through, deadly mushrooms growing under the nipples. Don't make me look. Please.

Sunlight was spilling into the room. It was company-clean, bedspread precisely drawn, rug freshly vacuumed, closet doors closed, magazines in drill order on the night table. I sat down on the little armchair. She turned away from me, unbuttoning the blouse, shrugging out of it, fumbling with the bra. "Ready?" she asked. "It isn't pretty."

"I'm ready. Let's have it." Pictures in my mind of an empty bag of skin, the flesh scooped out of it like melon balls, and a dangling, empty nipple. I looked. It was just a scar, a carefully welted crescent of red on taut, white skin. "It's not bad," I said in real relief. "It just looks . . . neat, and kind of blank. I'm surprised, Jess. I thought it would be . . . hard to look at."

She searched my face. "Really?"

"Really. Something's missing, of course, but it's not like something ugly is in its place."

"You wouldn't believe how much time I spend looking at it. In the morning—before I get dressed?—I sneak looks at it if I pass a mirror: I have to know if it's horrible when you see it unexpectedly. It isn't?"

"No, it really isn't. And anyhow, these people see mastectomies all day. It's their business."

"What people? Oh, The New You, you mean. I'm not worried about *them*."

"Then?—"

She pushed her mouth into a tight smile, eyes brightening, shrugged and shook her head. She turned away and put on the bra again, and the blouse. "Did you ever live with someone who couldn't look at you?" Her voice was thin and tight, like the smile.

"John?"

She nodded, jabbing the blouse into the waistband of the skirt. "Instant invisibility. If I could bottle it, I'd be richer than God." Her mouth pulled out of her control, a dowsing rod to the tears spilling down past it. "I make him sick. Just the idea makes him sick. Won't look, won't touch. He won't even come into the room if he thinks I'm undressed. He calls from the hall—'Jessie? What are you doing?' If I say I'm getting dressed, he's gone. You know what he says all the time?"

I shook my head.

" 'How are you feeling?' Every fifteen minutes. 'Scared to death,' I want to tell him; 'Hold me.' But I'm afraid if he thought he was actually going to have to *touch* it, he'd go up in smoke. Or leave for real. So I say, 'Great. I feel fabulous,' and I dress in the bathroom and put on my makeup and perfume—the works. Then he looks past me and says, 'How are you feeling?' "

She walked into the bathroom. I heard her blowing her nose, then the clicks of metal and glass on tile. I followed her. She was methodically repairing her makeup. "I mean, look, we've been married forever—twenty-eight years—and it's not like we're the last of the red-hot lovers or anything, but it was *nice*. He thought I was hot stuff, too; he was always grabbing a feel, even if he was just passing through the kitchen. But since I'm home from the hospital, the only part of me he touches is my elbow. The left one. Not my most erogenous zone—although, I'll tell you, I'm working on it." She grinned weakly at me in the mirror. I grinned back, avoiding my reflection. She turned around to me. "I even told him once that my doctor said it was okay for us to . . . have relations. He said, 'Well, when you're a little stronger.' "

"Maybe he's afraid he'll hurt you."

"He is hurting me, damn it. He's killing me."

She motioned me out of the bathroom and we went downstairs. She stopped at the hall mirror, checked her lipstick. "*Any-*

177

way, Toots, here's what I figure. They have nightgowns, you know, with the form built in, nipple and everything. I don't know how they work it so you don't wake up with a boob sticking out of your shoulder, but they tell me it stays put. So I'll get one of those, and I'll wear it to bed and when he's asleep, I'll—well, I'll work it out so he wakes up interested—and maybe he'll complete the pass before he remembers. I'll leave the nightgown on, see, so it'll feel like I'm . . . all there. Then maybe if he gets through it once . . ." she rummaged through her canvas handbag, found the house keys, nodded to me to go outside. "I may have to make love wearing a rubber boob all the rest of my days, but it's got to be better than being an untouchable. Let's go, Cookie, and don't spare the horses."

31.

The shop was upstairs. It was pretty, all green and white, with wicker chairs and a glass coffee table covered with *Vogues* and *Glamours*. A blond, athletic-looking woman came into the room from a curtained area in the back. "I'm Mrs. Handler," Jessie began.

"Yes. Jessie, right? Hi, Jessie. I'm Alix. How are you doing?"

"I have my ups and my downs. The ups I can handle. I brought the major down to you." She waved a hand past her flat right side.

"Great. We'll fix you up so no one'll know the ups from the downs. Your surgery was six weeks ago?"

"Right."

"Good. So you came right in. You'd be surprised how many people wait for months, or a year, even. I shouldn't talk. I hid in my house for a whole summer."

"You have—you had a mastectomy?"

"Eight years ago."

"You don't look like you were old enough to *have* breasts eight years ago."

She laughed. "I did. A matched pair, and I'd had 'em for years. Jan, my partner, had the surgery, too. That's why we opened the shop; we were desperate for the right things to wear. You know

179

how hard it was, eight years ago, to find a bathing suit? Let alone the forms. And in the suburbs, forget it." She pointed to racks of clothing in a mirrored alcove. "But we really have everything now. I'll show you. Want to come in with me and we'll start with the forms?"

Jessie started toward the curtained area, then turned and signaled to me with her eyebrows: come with me. I followed them through the curtains. Alix, chattering to Jessie, turned and saw me. She smiled. "The space is a little limited back here. Why don't you have a seat out there and we'll come and model for you. Okay, Jessie?" She shepherded Jessie toward a dressing room, then escorted me back out through the curtains, waiting to make sure I was going to stay put. "She may think she wants you in there," she said to me in a low voice, "but really, she's better off going through this with a stranger. You're her daughter?"

I was perversely glad to be able to correct her. "Her friend."

"Oh. I thought—well, even more reason to let her have her privacy. Make yourself comfortable; we'll be out in a few minutes."

When they emerged, I had leafed through two magazines and read the ads and releases scattered around the room, and was going through the clothing on the rack.

"They have great things," I said to Jessie, who was wearing a bathing suit and looking uncomfortable. "I found a shirt to go with my white jeans."

Alix directed a chilly smile at me. "I'm afraid we can't sell it to you. Store policy. It's a struggle finding attractive things for our customers, especially summer things, and if we sell to the . . . other people who come in, we'll have nothing left. What do you think of Jessie in this suit? Isn't it smashing?"

The suit was royal blue. It fit closely around her bust and was wrapped at the hip. Outside its Spandex tautness, Jessie's arms and legs looked white and doughy. Her three reflections turned and posed, turned again. She jiggled experimentally. Both breasts bounced.

180

"Raise your arms," I told her. She did. Both breasts rose; nothing showed at the side. "Incredible," I said. "You'd never know."

She looked doubtful. "It comes up so high. I hate to give up my cleavage—it was my best feature. But it looks okay?"

"Dynamite," I said. "Really." She brightened and followed Alix happily into the back, coming out at intervals to show me two nightgowns, a sundress, a jersey dress, and a couple of summer blouses. By the time she got to the dresses, they were laughing and murmuring appraisals to each other, a club of two. I stood by while Jessie wrote a check and accepted the two glossy green and white shopping bags. "This was a real binge," she said to Alix. "I hope this stuff looks sensational, because when John sees the checkbook he'll probably throw me out and I'll have to take up hooking. Of course," she added, "if I fall right, I'll bounce."

Alix put a hand on her shoulder. "He won't throw you out," she said. "Remember what I told you; we all go through it. Just have a little patience. He'll come around."

"You told her?" I asked, when we were stowing the bags in the trunk of the car.

"It sort of came up in the conversation. Seems it's not all that unusual." She didn't say any more about it, and she didn't mention Alix again, except once when we were waiting for our omelets at Sassafras. "Eight years," she said suddenly. "She really has it beat." That was all.

"The saleswoman thought Jessie was my mother," I told Richard that evening. "Can you imagine?"

"Well, she is older to begin with, and with the surgery and everything, she probably looked old enough to be your mother."

"But my mother—well, of course this woman couldn't know, but she was so elegant and so beautiful."

He looked at me oddly. "Yes," he said carefully, "she was a nice-looking woman."

He had come in early, interrupting Randy's outburst. It had started quietly. She was already home when I walked in, standing

181

by the open cupboard eating handfuls of potato chips out of the bag. I poured myself a glass of iced tea and sat down heavily at the table.

"Come sit down," I said. "And eat those things one at a time. Tastes just as good and you eat less."

She sat, shaking a pile of potato chips out on the table and picking through it for the big ones. "What's the matter?" she asked. "You look mad."

"I'm not mad, I'm upset," I told her. "Nothing to do with you. I spent the day with Mrs. Handler—you know her—and, well, you know, she's been sick—"

"Cancer," she said knowingly. "She had a breast removed, right?"

"How did you know?"

"I heard you talking to someone on the phone. Is she going to die? Does she have kids?"

"Two sons, both grown up. I don't know if she's going to die. She seems okay right now."

"So why are you upset?"

"I don't know. It was a hard kind of day." Without meaning to, I began to tell her about it. "She's my friend and I want to help her, but it's scary. When you're with someone who's very sick and frightened, you feel vulnerable yourself. I guess nurses and doctors get used to it, but it's tough. For me, anyway."

Suddenly she got up and came at me. She put her arms around me, pressed my head to her breast, patting my hair. "Don't worry," she said. "It'll be okay." Her small breasts rose and fell against my cheek, and smells of potato chips and sweat surrounded me. "It's okay," she said. "Really." She patted my hair lightly and I sat quietly for a moment, but it wasn't anything like my mother's touch. I pulled away gently, running a hand back over my hair to wipe off the potato chip crumbs. "Anyway," she said, reaching for the milk, "her kids are grown up, right?"

"So she might as well lie down and die?"

"No, but it's not like—I mean, if a real young person dies, or someone with young kids, it's, like, a tragedy. But someone who's in their fifties . . ." She shrugged. "The worst is when a little kid dies," she finished.

"What's the turning point? When can kids do without their mother, for example?" I could die tomorrow, I thought, under the anaesthetic. Michael is seven, Randy is twelve.

"Well . . . I mean, it's not that you don't always love your mother, but once you're in college . . ." She blushed. "*I* don't know," she said desperately. "There's a difference between *loving* somebody and *needing* them. You know?"

I let her off the hook. "Of course. And Jessie—Mrs. Handler—doesn't have young children who need her, that's true. But there are people who love her and who would miss her terribly if she—if they had to do without her."

"I decided I'm never going to have kids."

"You have?"

"Yes. Look, if you don't have kids—if you don't waste all those years feeding them and running around after them and that stuff, then you can get somewhere yourself. So when you die, *everyone* cares. Like Thurman Munson."

"He was a man."

"Yeah, see?"

I could see it, on her schedule: "Kids, etc. . . . NEVER." Then I thought of the list on the other side of the sheet.

"Rand?"

"Hm?"

"Are you happy in school? I mean, with the kids?"

"What do you mean?"

"Well, I mean . . . besides Rebecca, who are your friends? Do you still see Sharon and Alyssa?"

She looked at me suspiciously. "Why?"

"Just wondered."

"I see them."

"Well, who're your special friends now? Are you still close to Jody Emerson and Robin?"

She turned on me, flushing bright red, eyes narrowed. "Did you sneak in my drawer?"

183

"Of course not. Sneak what?"

"You did!" She was screaming. "I'll never ever trust you again. There's nothing safe in this house—"

That was when Richard walked in. Randy ran out of the kitchen, thundered up the stairs and slammed her door. Michael appeared, breathless, behind Richard.

"What'd she do? Why's Daddy home? Is she getting punished?"

"No. She's angry with me, that's all."

Richard picked Michael up, stepping back under his weight. "Whaddaya say?" he asked him. "How was school? How about we go out and hit a few?" Michael grinned widely, kissed him on the side of his neck and slid down. He ran to the hall closet, came back with his ball, bat and glove. "C'mon!" he yelled.

"Wait a second, champ. Gotta have a word with your sister first." He went upstairs, peeling off his jacket and tie. I heard him knock on her door.

"Randy? What was all that?"

"Ask her."

"Your mother?" Silence. "I asked you something: are you talking about your mother?" He must have pushed the door open; her voice was suddenly louder.

"Ask *your wife* if a person can have any privacy in this house when people go snooping around where they *have no right*. Ask her what a person has to do to have a life of their own." The door closed; I heard her sobbing, Richard talking. I went down to the basement to fold laundry. When I came up, Richard and Michael had gone out and the house was quiet.

I went upstairs and began, stealthily, to get ready. I rummaged around until I found my best underpants and bra and a pair of stockings with no runs. I put them in my scarf drawer, the money under them. I chose a denim skirt and a T-shirt, laid them out over the chair. I checked out the window: Richard and Michael were running bases on the lawn. I closed the bedroom door, locked myself into the bathroom and shaved my legs and underarms and clipped my toenails. Okay, doctor, I pass inspection.

Nurse, is her underwear clean? Yes, doctor, spotless. Cash on the button? Yes, doctor, in large bills. Blood type acceptable?

Blood type. I stopped with my jeans halfway on, busyness turning to fear. Needles, of course, for the blood test, and what did he say about the anaesthetic? A shot? Intravenous? I squeezed my eyes shut against the picture of the needle nosing around in the bulging vein, instruments scoring secret flesh, a bodiless hand with a threaded needle, sewing—Jesus—sewing it closed. No, that's an episiotomy, that was childbirth. No, Beth, shh, it's okay, you won't feel it, they won't do it. Shh.

I was making a sound behind my teeth, rocking against the towel hanging in the corner, jeans around my ankles. Stop. People have them every day. This time tomorrow, it'll be all over.

For the ten thousandth time, I prodded with a finger, looked at it hopefully. No blood. Let go, damn you, float out. I pictured it, tenacious fetus, clinging to its honeycomb wall. We're bringing in the big guns, kid, come out with your . . .

Does it have hands? Don't be silly, two weeks old. Three. Just a glob of cells. Sorry, kid, it's you or me, and I—

I saw it beached, torn from its hold, drowning in the air. Stop it, Beth. If you could push a button, you'd do it this second. It's only because it will hurt . . .

It will, that's all. Just stop.

I pulled on my jeans, washed my face, put back the razor and nail clippers and rinsed out the sink. No traces. Then I went out to call Evan's mother and make a lunch date for Michael.

"I may not be here when you get home from school," I said. Randy sat sullenly, pushing a piece of chicken around with her knife.

"Where'll you be? It isn't Wednesday." Michael's hair was plastered to his head with sweat, his face and his hands—to the wrist—scrubbed clean.

"I have a checkup. I'll be home as soon as I can."

"Seeing Monroe?" Richard asked.

"Mm."

"How come?"

"Just a checkup."

Richard leaned over to me that night in bed during a commercial. Touch me, you prick, and I'll bite your Adam's apple out. "You know, babe, you're getting too involved with the Handler dame. I told you, she'll wind up dragging you with her to the grave."

"She's not going to the grave. She's fine. And that's what it means, being a friend. Being there, even if it's unpleasant."

"Trouble is, you don't have friends your age. Who do you have? Jessie? Laura? They're both old enough to be your mother, you said it yourself. They begin to fall apart, you going to nurse them all?"

"How come you had no work to do this afternoon?"

"What? Oh, I told you, I was waiting for the bid."

"Did you get it?"

"What? Yeah. Half of it."

"Half?"

"Well, it was in two parts. We got one." He sighed. "It's tight out there now. The governor cracked down on the cities, the feds shut off appropriations; no one's building. Somehow, though, the last few weeks, everything Walsh touches is golden, and I—well, today was a turnaround, maybe. I have a meeting tomorrow with some people from New Jersey. . . . I think I can get a handle on that market." He swallowed. "You're my rock. You know that?" He reached for me.

I lay still. Sperm in the passage, I thought. They'll go in there to do an abortion and what do they find but fresh sperm? I pushed him away, not roughly. "My back," I said.

"Your back? You mean it still hurts?"

"Not as much, but I think I'd better just go to sleep. Okay?"

"We could work it so your back wouldn't be—"

"It hurts no matter what position I'm in. Night, hon." I gave him a kiss, avoiding meeting his eyes, and rolled over to my side of the bed, groaning quietly for the effect. Lying flat. Safe.

186

32.

I had the taxi let me off half a block from the clinic and waited until it pulled away before I made my move, quickstep, head down, to the brick building. Inside, I ran a quick check: no one I knew. The place was clean-looking and cheerful—yellow walls, tweedy couches, nondescript watercolors. The receptionist sat behind a glass enclosure. I walked over and waited humbly until she slid open the little glass partition. I wondered, briefly, whether it was bulletproof like the ones in city cabs. She looked up and smiled. "Beth Clahr," I said, *sotto voce*.

"Will you come around here, please? The door on your left."

I went in and she turned and motioned me to a desk where a young black woman sat. "Sit down," she smiled, taking a form from a pile on her desk. "This is just a brief interview, no hard questions."

We got through name and address, statistics, form of payment. "Check, Medicaid, American Express, MasterCharge?" she asked, but she didn't flinch when I handed her the wad of bills, just counted it, nodded, checked off a box on the form, and laid the pile of money on her desk. "Now," she said, "what was the date of onset of your last period?"

I told her. "Good," she said. "You're in plenty of time. Why do you think you're pregnant?" I explained, and she wrote Dr.

Block's name and address on the form. "Do you know what will happen in this procedure, Beth?"

"I think so."

"Let's be sure. This is termination of pregnancy, accomplished by use of saline solution. What it means is you'll be put to sleep and, in effect, a miscarriage will be induced. When you wake up, you'll no longer be pregnant. Do you understand?"

"You mean you get people in here who think they're going to have a tooth filled?"

She didn't smile. "We have to go through this; it's state law. Do you understand?"

"Yes."

"Will you sign here, please?"

Here it comes, I thought, taking the paper and scanning it for the accusing word. But all there was, was a statement, in italic type, of what she had just explained. I signed. Then there was a release. I signed that, too.

"All right, Beth, if you'll have a seat in the waiting room, it won't be too long."

"Will they—do they have to call my name?"

"No, if you'd prefer, I can send the nurse in to get you. No problem."

Lifting my eyes furtively from the magazine in my lap, I looked around. Laura was right; they were all women. One pair of girls in their twenties, in tight jeans and high-heeled sandals; two very young girls, each obviously with her mother. One mother and daughter sat stolidly looking at the floor. The other girl had her head on her mother's shoulder. The mother was absently stroking her hair. *Mama.* She looked over, feeling my eyes on her, and stared me down. I retreated to the magazine.

About twenty minutes later, after one of the girls in jeans had strolled in alone and each of the mother-daughter pairs had been called in, a nurse came in to get me. By now there were other people in the waiting room. I walked in briskly.

188

It was just an examining room. I sat on the table, dangling bare legs, while the nurse took blood and checked my blood pressure and pulse. She weighed me. "The doctor will be in, in a minute," she said.

"What's his name?"

She looked startled, answered defensively. "I'm not sure which one. Dr. Karlow, I think. Feet in the stirrups, move your body down, please."

He was balding and aquiline, but suntanned, athletic-looking. I waited two beats, three, but he said nothing, busying himself with a tray of instruments. "Good morning," I said finally, when he approached me.

"Good morning." He looked at his clipboard. "Beth Clahr?"

"Yes."

"You know this procedure is to terminate a pregnancy?"

I knew better than to try the quip again, but I allowed myself a rueful glance at my sheeted, upraised knees. "Yes. Is the—"

"You know, if the pregnancy is more than thirteen weeks advanced, we can do nothing?"

"Yes, but it's only three—"

"We'll see. You had a question?" The cold steel spoons opened me up, clicked into position. I tried to see what he was reaching for. "Is the anaesthetic local or—"

"We use an intravenous. You won't feel anything. Relax, please. You're tightening up."

"The intravenous is in—?"

"The arm." He sounded bored and annoyed. Drop dead, I thought. I'm not the one who murders hundreds of babies a week. But I tried once more to make him see me, catching his eyes as I sat up again, feet gracefully tucked to the side, hospital gown innocently held by a flat hand. "What's the recovery period? I have—"

"You'll be here three to five hours after the procedure."

"No, I mean afterward. I'm a singer and I have voice lessons—"

"You'll be up and around tomorrow. No effect on the voice. Prep her, please, Arlene."

189

When he left, I looked at the nurse. "Is he always this cuddly?"

She smiled. "He's nice, really. Will you lie down, please? I have to prepare the area."

When she finished, I lay waiting on the table, covered with a clean sheet and surrounded now with lights. I tried not to look at the tray of instruments.

"Just relax now," she said, touching my arm. "It'll be over before you know it."

I didn't look at him when he came in, kept my face cool even when he swabbed my arm and found the vein. Let him come to me, I thought, falling in circles. Tumble to me—

Randy was missing. Not in her room, not in the kitchen. Potato chips fallen on the table, on the floor, but no Randy. I walked around the swing set, looking—even, cleverly, checked under the slide. No. Ask Laura. But now I couldn't leave the house, couldn't get out, couldn't get to Laura. The intravenous cord wouldn't reach. I made it to the window, screamed for Laura. No answer. Right. Laura is so old, too old to—

the phone. Call Richard. Answer it, Richard, oh God, let him

Richard, listen to me. Please . . . I'm not, I'm not raising my voice. Please, you have to listen—Randy is gone, you have to—

No—sobbing to Frances—get him out of his meeting—Richard, please, I'll do it every night only listen

Richard, *Randy. Is. Gone.* I think she's in the Tin Drum. They're drugging her, you know what it means, breasts now and they'll

Randy, Richard. The Tin Drum. Get her. Please, I have to see her before I

dying, Randy, and I can't tell you. I won't be there when you— the key is in the hiding place, burners are off

Randy, baby in her crib, screaming, with breasts, and I'll never, it won't reach—

190

"—now? Beth? Want to move to a more comfortable room now? Know where you are?"

I nodded.

"Okay. Lean on me, we'll just take a . . . ride . . . easy . . . here we are. Want to climb into bed? How's the pad, okay? Wait, I'll change it. . . . *There* you are. Cold? Here's another blanket. Better? Good. Just rest." Hand on my wrist, listening, write it on the chart, she's gone.

A ward. Bright, sunny. Other bodies in the beds. Jesus, what a dream. It was a dream? Wait. Stop. Randy.

I pushed back to the morning. She was wearing shorts and a red T-shirt, packing her knapsack, still sullen. "Randy?"

"What."

"Remember, I won't be home at three. You come right home so you can let Michael in. Okay?"

"Sure."

Can't let her go like that. Not today. I touched her arm, held tighter when she twisted away. "Listen, honey, I'm not sure why you're so angry. I didn't—snoop—in your room. You know I wouldn't do that. I don't even know what I'm supposed to have seen." Nothing more sincere than a mother's lies.

"So how'd you know those names?"

"Your friends? Those kids have been your friends for years. Whose names would I say?"

She looked down, flushing. "Okay. I'm sorry I yelled."

"It's okay. I love you, Rand. Friends?"

"Yeah." Tears caught in her throat. A hug.

So it was only a dream. Randy gone, me dying.

Like Mama. Like I was gone when Mama died.

"Mouth dry? Want some tea and cookies?" It was a grinning dark-haired girl, wheeling a tray. I sat up and took the mug.

"How are the little girls? They get through it okay?"

191

"Oh, sure. You mean the two teenagers? They do better than anyone."

"You mean you get a lot of them that young?"

"All the time. How's about you? Any cramps?"

"Not yet. I've been too busy thinking to notice."

"No point thinking too hard. Cheer up. Enjoy your tea."

Dr. Sattenburg had said that. "No point torturing yourself thinking about it, Beth. Your mother never knew what happened. Wouldn't have made a bit of difference if you'd been here."

He said it with a heavy arm on my shoulder, holding out the prescription to me. Serenity in pills. You let her die, I thought, sick at his touch, but I smiled and said thank you and left holding the prescription.

They called at dusk, the phone startling us both as we lay naked on the bed. I had my hand on him, touching the smoothness of it.

"Who knows us in Bermuda?"

"Answer it. Maybe we're the honeymoon couple of the year."

So I rolled a little, picked it up, laughing. "Overseas operator," a voice said. "Mrs. Beth Clahr?"

"I sure am. Uh, speaking. Hello?"

"Beth?"

"Dad, hi!" I snatched my hand away from Richard.

"Listen, Beth, I—your mother—"

Noises. Dead. Mama.

"—embolism. So sudden, you know—"

No. No she isn't. Can't be, Mama—

"—yesterday. We didn't want to interrupt your honeymoon, you kids—"

"What? Dad? What did you do yesterday?"

"The funeral, honey. It's all ov—" another voice on the phone. "Hi, Beth? It's Uncle Jack. Your dad's here with us. He's okay, only it gets him sometimes, you know? He wanted to wait till you got home to tell you, but we thought you'd—"

"Uncle Jack? She's—they had the funeral? Is that what he said?"

"Yes, honey. Yesterday, it was. Should have·seen how many

192

people came out. Bob and Sheila Tanner, remember them, from Chicago? They—"

I gave the phone to Richard, walked naked to the window, trying to make a sound come through the heavings. "—yes, sir, I'm awfully sorry. Anything we can—? No, I guess you're right. No point, now. We'll be back Monday. Yes, see you then. We will, thank you. Beth? Honey?"

When I came out of the bathroom, I started folding things up—my things—and putting them into one of the suitcases. Lady's 26-inch pullman.

"What are you doing?"

"Packing. I have to go home. Will you call the airport?"

"Honey, we don't have to go. It's over. There's nothing we can—"

"You don't have to go."

"Why would I stay here alone? Beth, listen, it's irrational. She's dead, honey, and the funeral is over. They purposely called now because they didn't want us to—Beth? What can you do there?"

I went to Uncle Jack and Aunt Ruth, not to my father. I was still wearing honeymoon clothes. Aunt Ruth put a sweater over my shoulders.

"What is she wearing, Uncle Jack?"

"Your mother? She had on . . . I don't know, she was shopping, I think, when it—"

"Now. In her—where she is. What is she wearing?"

He looked helplessly at Aunt Ruth. "What difference does it—"

"Her navy, honey, the one with the ruching at the sleeves. She looked—"

"It's satin?"

"What, her dress? No, peau de soie, I think."

"What she's lying on. It's satin? White?"

"Now let me . . . yes, of course it was satin. Gray, I think."

"Is there a pillow?"

"I don't know if I noticed, honey. . . ."

"Show me, how is she lying? Please, Aunt Ruth."

"Now Beth, I really don't—you ought to be—"

In the end, she told me. She was lying on her back, head straight, hands folded on her rib cage. The man at the mortuary, when I called him, told me about the pillow. Pearl gray satin, filled with batting.

In bed that night, my old bed in my mother's house, Richard, who had been tight-lipped ever since our quarrel in the room in Bermuda, reached for me. I pulled away, but when I closed my eyes I saw her, closed in the box, blackness, no air, things moving, trapped, defiled, face etched and mouth filled with—

I reached for him and made love, sobbing, but it didn't help. I could still see it.

Some time in the night I phoned Aunt Ruth.

"Aunt Ruth? You know the shee—the satin . . . thing . . . under my mother?"

"Beth? Honey? What is it?"

"Just tell me, please Aunt Ruth. The satin thing my mother is lying on—is it smooth?"

"Smooth? It's satin, Beth, I told you."

"I mean is it—did they straighten it out? Is it smooth under her?"

"My God, Beth, I don't know. What does it—I think it was, you know, kind of tufted. I really didn't look."

I would have looked. If I'd been there, I'd have made sure. Mama.

The next morning my father, groping in the refrigerator for the juice, said that he'd made an appointment for me to see Dr. Sattenburg. "Aunt Ruth called me this morning. Says you're . . . upset."

"How am I supposed to be?"

"Don't get fresh with me, young lady. Just don't—upset is one thing. Creating scenes, calling people at three in the morning, that's something else. Ten o'clock you'll see him. You be on time, don't keep him waiting. And don't try any of your lip on him. He doesn't expect that from us."

I left Dr. Sattenburg's office with the prescription in my hand. When I walked into the beauty parlor and the girl at the white and gold table looked up, I handed it to her. She looked it over, laughed uneasily. "We don't fill these, honey. We just do hair."

I snatched it back. "Of course. Sorry, I wasn't—I'm Cynthia Wheelock's daughter. Can I get a haircut?"

They hadn't heard she was dead. "Sure. Lemme see who's free."

They washed it and put a cream rinse on it and combed it out carefully, gentling out the knots. It was heavy, lying wet down my back.

"You want to cut it? Beautiful hair. You sure?"

"Please cut it."

"How do you want it cut? Got a style in mind? You could look in the books; take your time."

"You decide."

It took him a long time to cut it. I watched for a while, then I closed my eyes. That was a mistake. He snipped a little, lifted the hair, let it fall, lifted it again. Ran two hands gently through the hair at the temples. Like hers. Like her hands. I heard her singing, Toora loora. Sleeping, Bethie? As it left his fingers, the tears ran rebelliously down my face. They wouldn't stop.

"Ah. See, you shouldn't have done it. You didn't really want it cut. I knew it. Every time—"

"No. It's okay. I really do want it cut. It looks fine. Are you done?"

When he let me go, I went back to father and Richard. Nobody's girl now.

"Try to wake up. Beth? Come on, you didn't have your tea. Try to wake up now. How's your pad? Good. How's about sitting up now? I'll get you some hot—"

———

195

Kneeling on the floor, head in her lap. Much too big for that . . . floor so hard, knees keening pain, but her hands in my hair, smoothing it. Quiet, both of us. Just quiet.

"—get you in the chair, here. Here's your hot tea; you can chat with the other girls. People, this is Beth. Beth, that's Sharleen, and Tracy, and that's—"

In the mornings, then, there was the panic. I would lie quite still when Richard got up and went into the bathroom: let it not come today, but it would rise up, crowding my lungs, closing my throat. So I began to make the lists. Things to do, it was then. Tick them off, step from one to the next, no cracks. I got them all done, made more to do, pulled hand over frozen hand through the days. Mama lay violated on gray tufts and I smoothed them out, smoothed them, they wouldn't stay so I had to smooth them again, but it was never done, she screamed to me and I couldn't make the words come out.

So I had Randy and then it was—

"Boy, you're a tough case, aren't you? Sleeping sitting up? Come on. I'm going to stand right here while you drink that tea. That's the girl. Hey, you hungry? It's lunchtime. How about it? Soup? Girls, you keep her up. I'll see about—"

—so I had Randy and then it was easier. Only when I left her in her crib there were the other lists, litanies they became, of horrors held off another time: pins are closed, I checked, clicked the pink top down, did it again to be sure, both sides. Nightgown is smooth under her. Taut flannel sheet, I checked the elastic, can't come up and smother her. Bars are narrow, she can't get her head wedged through. Blanket is away—isn't it?—yes, folded back, away from her face. She can breathe. Sleep, Randy. Breathe.

After lunch, and after they checked our pulses and blood pressures and temperatures and rates of flow a last time, they told us

196

to get dressed. In a slow line we followed the nurse. She took us to another yellow room, sat us around a conference table. We smiled shyly at each other. The teenagers sat together, snorting laughter behind secret hands. When the doctor began to talk about contraceptives, they seemed not to be listening, but he started with condoms and one of them, looking up with swift scorn, said, "Yeah, shit. That how come I'm here." He didn't laugh with the rest of us. Karlow.

When he finished about contraceptives, he talked briefly about sterilization, looking at me. I smiled mysteriously and sadly at the table, but he went on to discuss postabortion and didn't look at me again.

"—expect the bleeding to continue for about a week. But no intercourse, please, for six full weeks. . . ."

Okay. Six easy weeks. Wait. What about Richard? Then he'll have to know. No. When the lesson was over and the group was breaking up, I headed for the doorway to cut off Dr. Karlow before he could escape, but one of the mothers came in and got to him first. I waited, pretending not to hear their conversation as she tried to wheedle a once-a-month contraceptive out of him for her daughter.

"—can't nobody get that child to do *nothin'* every day regular, except if it's—"

When she left and he strode after her, I politely blocked the door. "Dr. Karlow?"

He waited.

"You said—did you say there should be a six-week period of abstinence?"

"Yes."

"Should be or had to be?"

He looked at me with distaste. Of all these persons, you, madam, are the one so consumed with lust that—nurse, did you say her underwear was clean?

Yes, doctor, clean and nice. No rips, no safety pins even.

You just can't tell these days. Sluts.

197

"—your own decision, of course, but six weeks is the time it takes the tissues to heal, and that is the period I would strongly advise. If you can manage it."

Yes, I can manage it, you sanctimonious prick. I could manage for much longer.

Still, I stopped behind the door to the waiting room, relaxed my face, letting the anger slide off it. Looking soft and sad and a little weakened, I walked out into the waiting room. But Daniel Block was not there, and there were no messages. So I called Laura. When she came, I didn't say a word. Just leaned on her arm and let her take me home.

"Richard?"

"Why are you in your robe? What'd Monroe—"

"I didn't go to Monroe. I—we lost a baby today, Rich. I had a miscarriage."

"But where—"

"I went to Laura's gynecologist, a Dr. Block. It happened right in his office. Remember my back was hurting?"

"Sure. But I didn't even—just like that? Ah, babe. . . ." A hand out to touch my belly. I moved away before it touched.

"That was it."

"But are you—"

"I'm okay. It was a mess, Rich. But Laura was very kind and brought me home. Look, she even fixed us dinner."

Later, I told him about the six weeks. He just swallowed hard again and told me not to worry about anything.

33.

When I woke up the next morning, Randy was standing over me.

"Bye, Mom."

"Rand? What time is it?"

"Almost ten. I'm—"

"You're late!" I sat up. "What's the—"

"It's Saturday." I lay back down. She peered at me from a height. "You okay?"

"I'm okay. Just dopey. Where's—"

"Dad went to the office for a couple of hours. I'm going to Michael's softball game. Feel better." The stripes in her T-shirt curved under her breasts. She swung her hair away from her face.

"Michael?"

"He's dressed. I gave him breakfast. Just relax—"

"You gave him breakfast? What did he have?"

"Cheerios and a banana and milk. I wouldn't let him have a doughnut. Okay?"

"Wow. Sure. Send him up, honey. Rand? What about lunch?"

"I'll take him to the deli. Dad gave me money. See you later. MICHAEL. MOM WANTS YOU."

He bounced into the room. He was wearing his Disneyworld shirt. It was too small.

199

"Daddy said to pick my own clothes. Randy makes lousy cereal. She put too much milk in it and it got all mushy-mooshy. You getting up?"

I did, but not until after they left. Lying tangled in the quilt, I became aware of the stickiness between my legs and the unfamiliar, medicinal smells. I rolled cautiously out of bed, but it was too late; there was a wet, red patch on the sheet that had imprinted itself on my leg. I was moving slowly, logily, but before I got into the shower I stripped the bed and started the washer. It took the cold water from my shower in random raids, but I stood under the beating water anyway for a long time, washing myself over and over again like a demented cat.

When I got out, straddling a fresh Kotex and wrapped in a towel, I pulled the sheets out of the washer and looked anxiously for the stain. I'd gotten it in time. Just to be sure, I scrubbed the spot where I thought it had been and rinsed it before dumping the sheets into the drier. I was shaky when I got back into the bathroom, but I methodically dried my hair and cleaned my ears. Then I scrubbed my face and brushed my teeth and clipped my fingernails straight across. I got out a white cotton nightgown.

The sheets were still warm when I made the bed. I thought I could see the faintest yellow stain on one of the mattress covers and one of the bottom sheets. I put those on Richard's bed.

I brought a bowl of cereal and a banana and some juice up from the kitchen. Then I powdered myself all over and put on a fresh Kotex and the nightgown. Clean girl. I got into bed carefully, not to jar the Kotex out of place. No leaks: seal is secure. Sheet smooth under me, warm and clean. No wrinkles. I pulled the quilt up, let it ease down onto my tingling legs. I ate the cereal slowly but steadily, timing it so that I didn't rush and spill any but the last bites weren't soggy. I didn't think I'd still be hungry but I was. I ate the banana, too.

When Richard came home from the city in the afternoon, he came up to see me. He sat on the edge of the bed, pulling ridges into the sheet and quilt and unbalancing me. I moved a little, away from the downward pull. He smelled of the city. It's not fair, I thought. I have time out. You're not supposed to be on my bed for six weeks. But he was telling me the hopeful news about New Jersey highway reconstruction, and I made a listening face.

—guy in Trenton, knew him from the Schenectady deal, contract for ten million bucks' worth of—pretty sure thing—Russo will pee in his pants—Walsh in his place—Frances back full time . . .

Frances. The spoils of war. The maiden prize. So we're .winning again. Whose side is up?

He drifted away finally, and when he came back up, bringing in smells of hot dogs and coffee, I pretended to be asleep.

I would have stayed in bed Sunday, too, but they were coming into the room in shifts, bouncing on my bed and touching the sheet with sticky fingers, so I went downstairs and then they left me alone.

Randy came over to me once, while Michael was outside and Richard was on the phone. "Michael is scared," she said. "He asked me what was the matter with you and I said he wouldn't understand but that you'd be fine in a couple of days. You'd better tell him yourself, though. I don't think he really believed me."

"Okay. Do you understand?"

"Sure." She looked right at me, but somehow not into my eyes. "You had a miscarriage. I didn't know you wanted another kid. I'm sorry you lost it."

Now I looked away from her. "It's okay, honey. It's probably better that it wasn't born. Nature's pretty smart that way." Jesus, Beth.

"I know. We learned that in Health. It was probably deformed. But you could try again." Her forehead and cheeks were red.

"No. I'm happy with you two guys. Thanks for trying to make Michael feel better."

"I was just getting him off my back."

Another thing I could never tell her: remember that baby, Randy? I didn't lose it. I canceled it. In all the world, the longest list was the silences between Randy and me.

I eased myself down onto Michael's bed that night, landing a kiss on his neck before he squirmed away. He smelled of his Hulk soap. "Did I scare you, coming home sick on Friday?"

"Yeah. Daddy said to stay away and leave you alone and let you feel better, and Randy wouldn't tell me what it was."

"Well, I'm okay now."

"You missed my game." He was sleepy. It was all old news.

"Catch you next time. Did you win?"

"We creamed 'em. Three to two." He burrowed into his pillow, away from me. I watched him, lying suddenly still in his heap of twisted bedding. After a while I left him there.

34.

I felt okay Monday, but with the League luncheon over and Laura's food in the house, there was nothing pressing I had to do, and I thought I felt an echo of the old panic inflating between my ribs. Reaction to the trauma, I thought, and I prescribed for myself: one more day in bed.

I was all settled in, music in my hand, clean and calm, smelling powder and tasting toothpaste, when the phone rang. Gideon.

"This is Daniel Block. How are you feeling?"

Now you ask. Where were you last Friday? You missed it, Danny Boy. Someone else pulled up my covers. "Fine. How nice of you to call."

"I would have called over the weekend, but I didn't know—"

"He thinks it was a miscarriage. In fact, I told him it happened in your office. I hope you don't mind."

". . . Yes. That's okay. How did it go on Friday?"

"You were right: they were kind and efficient. Not counting the doctor. He was a storm trooper."

"Who was it?"

"Dr. Karlow."

"Louis? He's a nice guy."

"That depends on your position when you meet him."

"Funny. In fact, I was hoping it would be him and not his partner. *He* can be a little—well, he's a tease. It's okay with the kids and some of those women, but in your state of mind I thought you'd prefer to be treated with dignity."

No, Daniel. Wrong. I wanted him to catch his breath at the first glimpse of me. I wanted him to check our pulses in counterpoint. I wanted to leave him longing: I wanted to see the sun gleaming off that bald, tanned skull as he looked out the window to catch a last . . .

"Well, maybe you spoiled me. You have a way of making people feel . . . safe. Cared for." That's a cue, Doctor. But he didn't pick it up.

"How did you get home?"

"A . . . friend picked me up." Now go wonder about it.

"Good." Too quickly. "So. Can you come in? I'd like to check out my storm-trooper friend's work. But let's make it later in the week. Don't drive for another couple of days if you can help it. Can you take it easy?"

"I have a singing lesson in the city—"

"Wednesday, right? But you take the train?"

"Yes."

"That's okay. Just go easy on the abdominals. Uh, how's your mood? It's normal to be a little . . ."

"I'm okay."

"You don't have to be."

"What?"

"You don't have to be okay. You're entitled to be shaky, or weepy. Or angry. What are you saying to yourself—I got myself into this mess, got to buck up and take it? You didn't get yourself into it. You had help."

"I know. We learned that in Health."

"So how is your mood?"

"I could have had the baby." Where did the tears come from?

"Sure." His voice was gentle. "In your circumstances that's all you needed. Just because you're fertile and functioning doesn't mean you have to . . . topple into motherhood whenever Nature pushes."

"I know." I covered the phone and blew my nose. "I'm relieved

204

that it's over, really. I don't want to be a mother—I mean not again, not from the beginning. But that's my mood—you asked—guilty, shaky and a little panicky."

"And angry?"

"I guess so."

"Good. Just because he picked you up when it was all over—"

"He didn't pick me up. I didn't even—he didn't pick me up."

"Ah. Who took you home?"

"A friend. A neighbor."

"What are you doing now?"

"Me? Nothing."

"Can you sleep? Cry, and sleep. In that order."

"See? If Dr. Karlow had been like you, it would all have been so easy, I'd have arranged to do it every six months."

"No you wouldn't. You're not put together to unmother lightly. And if Dr. Karlow had talked to you this way on Friday, you'd have fallen apart. That wasn't the time for it. This is."

"You are a genuine White Knight."

"Me and Dr. Kildare. How's Thursday?"

"Thursday?"

"For your appointment. Speak to Sondra; she'll give you a time. Okay?"

"Okay."

Unmothered. Right.

I set the alarm for 11:30 so I could be awake and functioning for Michael at lunchtime. Laura called while he was eating his sandwich and laying out his baseball cards in packs all around the plate.

"Knew you'd be up to give Michael lunch. How're you doing?"

"Great. I'm having a lazy day. Doctor's orders."

"You saw the doctor?"

"No, he called. Not the one from the clinic. My gynecologist."

"*He* called *you*? What'd you do, forget to pay your bill?"

"No. He wanted to know how I was and to make a follow-up appointment."

"Did you call the *Guinness Book of Records* and report it?"

"He's very nice."

"I'll say. Speaking of nice, I called to make you an extraordinarily generous offer. How'd you like a pot of Laura's finest chili, guaranteed to keep 'em burping for a week?"

"I'd love it. I may never cook again." Keep those cows and goats coming. The sooner I'm knocked out of the game, the better.

"Oh, yes you will. But not until tomorrow, anyhow."

"You're a saint."

"I know. St. Laura of the Caloric. See you later, honey. You rest. Hey, you didn't buckle and tell him, did you?"

"I said it was an m-i-s-c-"

"Gotcha. Good girl."

Michael pushed the screen door open with his toe and stood there, shoving the pack of baseball cards into the pocket of his jeans. "Oh, by the way," he said, "what's a misk?"

"A misk?"

"What you said on the phone. A m-i-s-c."

Riddle: When do you know your child is gaining on you?

Answer: When spelling out secrets doesn't work anymore.

Trick answer: They're gaining on you all the time. Don't look back.

I was settling back into bed when Gideon called. "Finally reached you," he said. "I was afraid you'd left town."

"A little concert in Salzburg. What could I do? My agent said they were screaming for me."

"Patience. That'll happen, too. I called you Thursday after my meeting. I called you Friday morning and afternoon. No answer. I've missed you. What happened with Lecrief? Did you call him?"

I had to dig back under all of it: the weekend, the abortion, Randy, Jessie and The New You. When I found it, it had the dust of the ages on it, but I reconstructed the conversation for him.

"Oh great," he said. " 'You'll never make it, so when you give

206

up, come back to me and I'll let you sing in the chorus again.' Did you tell him to go to hell?"

"No, I said good-bye nicely and went to my lesson. Singing well is the best revenge."

His laugh roared through the phone at me. "You know you're marvelous?"

I was. I was funny and strong and alluring and in easy, elegant control. I had never been on that table, legs spread and crotch pried open with steel spoons. There was no Kotex between my legs. That spot was secret, warm and musky, silky and perfumed. I was lovely, all over.

"It's nice, anyway, that you think so." Alto, warm honey.

"Yes it is. Very nice. And I think it all the time . . . all the time. Do you like it, knowing there's someone who thinks of you that way?"

"Of course." Flip and easy.

"Want to have lunch Wednesday so I can tell you some more?"

"Gideon—"

"Okay. Not right now, right? Not yet. But one of these days you will. Are you thinking about it?"

"I—"

"All right. So am I. Sing, meanwhile: sing like the devil so you can put it to that jealous biddy."

"You think that's it? He's *jealous*?"

"Sure." A pause. "This is going to change the way people see you, you know. There's a certain response you expect from men. Isn't there?"

"I never thought about it. Maybe."

"Maybe." He was smiling. I could hear it. "I knew it the first time I met you, that you know what you are and you expect a man to know it, too. It's unconscious, and anyway most men don't—can't—react to it except in the kind of attention they pay to what you say, or in little acceptable gallantries. But I bet as you get further along with the singing and as your presence gets stronger, all kinds of people will be frightened by it. They'll ei-

207

ther try to minimize you—baby you, make you seem dependent —or exploit you. I don't want to do either, you know. I just want to be there when you stop being scared of it."

"I'm scared all the time."

"I know. That's how you feel before you launch. Are you scared when you sing?"

"No. When I think about singing, but not when I sing."

"You won't be scared with me, either, even if thinking about it terrifies you. Don't say a word. Just think about it."

I radiate it, coming down the steps of Mannes on a sunny day: power. Pleasure. Self, lithe and pulsing. I'm not surprised to see him there, waiting. "Brescia says I'm ready!" I tell him. "He's scheduled a concert for me at the Recital Hall."

"And what do you say? Are you ready?"

"Yes." I meet his eyes, and we're both smiling. "I'm ready."

Lunch is somewhere hushed and dim. We talk about the concert—selections, timing, the politics of press coverage—but while we talk he runs a finger along the inside of my wrist, into my open palm and back again, and the sound of our voices, soft and curling, says touch me, let me touch you. "All in Italian, I think," I say, "because the language is so fluid, it doesn't choke up the sounds. What do you think?"

"Are you ready?" he asks. "Come." He doesn't touch me as we walk out of the restaurant, but I lean toward him as though his hand were on me. He doesn't touch me in the cab, except with his voice, or in the elevator: not until we're inside the apartment. He bolts the door. I stand where I am, looking across the room to the windows, out at the river and the harbor beyond it, sparkling soundless in the silent sun. Now he takes a step, standing so close that our bodies lean in together, wanting to click tight, magnets. But he still doesn't touch me. "You're ready?" he asks. My body answers him, then I do. "Yes." Click. Waist first, then mouth to his, breasts, loins. Click. Click. Click. One of us moans. Our hands move over each other's backs, an urgent message in moving braille.

208

We undress in the bedroom, but lazily, as though we weren't drowning. The sun pours over me on its way to the river. Shirt, skirt, stockings, bra. Look, Gideon. Look at me in the sunshine. He comes to me then and, my hard electric nipples buzzing his chest, slides flat hands under my silky panties and pushes them down to my hips. I smile in the sun, easing them off, stepping out of them to follow him to the bed.

It takes us a long time to come to it, although he's hard and I am slippery wet. He's tasting my neck, the curve of my waist, the inside of my thighs. My hands are memorizing his spine, his chest, the heavy, secret balls, taut and full for me, and the hard, smooth column. His teeth are around my nipple, tongue at the tip. Suck it, Gideon. Unmother me.

When he comes into me, we move slowly, syncopated, as though we weren't drowning. I give in first, feeling the crying sound in my throat and blindly demanding his open mouth with my open mouth. I move on him, faster, but he holds me back, pulling almost out of me, then sinking back in, slowly, all the length of him. "Wait a little," he says, pushing the whisper through catching breath. "Soon." But they come over us, wave after wave, inexorable. I'm drowning, I cry to him from the hollow of my throat. I know, he answers silently; breathe me. I do and we surface, sink, surface. I raise my body to him and, one shout from him, one gasping breath from me, we ride it, it lifts us, drops us, rolls us to sandy waters where we lie tangled, finding a way to breathe air again.

"Italian is right," he says, holding me in the sunshine. "All in Italian. You'll be marvelous."

The bed was made and I was dressed and practicing when Randy came in. She looked into the living room, raised one hand in greeting, and disappeared. I had to go and find her when I was finished. She was making popcorn for Michael.

209

35.

I stayed out of the bed on Tuesday, putting the house in order, doing homework for the last session of Rosie's course, and making the calls: Laura, to thank her for the chili and to come across with all the details of the abortion. Jessie, to still my fears.

"Okay, honey, so it's over and done with," Laura said after she'd extracted it all. "You'll be in fighting form by Friday and before you know it, it'll be out of your mind. Especially because you won't have Richard reminding you of it. It won't come between you—you know, where you don't want it to. How long did the doctor say to . . . hold off?"

"Hold off? Oh, right. Six weeks."

"Seems endless, huh? Never mind, it's good if you miss each other—you know—for a little. Makes it better later. So what can I do for you? How about I come and straighten up a little, run the vacuum and like that?"

"God, no, you've done enough. I just straightened up here. It's clean enough."

"How's the chili holding up?"

"They're breathing fire and asking me how come I don't cook like that. There's enough for one more assault."

"I'll bring you some chicken stew."

Make it goat ragout and I'll turn belly up and surrender, once and for all. It was tempting: I could let her take care of us all.

She'd be happy and life would be easy; I could go on forever, healing in her bosom. But I felt an unreasoning repulsion: go away, you're not my mother. I don't think she heard it in my grateful refusals.

Jessie was brisk and chipper on the phone. "How are you, Cookie? What's up?"

"Just wanted to know how you were doing."

"Oh, great. In fact I've got one foot out the door. On my way to a meeting. Can I call you later?"

"Sure. Have fun." What meeting? Some insider's League thing? Something with Alix? Nothing I was part of, anyhow. I pushed it out of my mind and took the extra half hour to practice.

Monroe's office called while I was doing scales, open throat, one vowel sound after another.

"Mrs. Clahr? This is Valerie, Dr. Lippzer's office? He's back and he wanted to know how you were doing with your . . . problem."

"I had it removed," I said from a distance.

"You—the lump was removed?"

"No, I—it was nothing. I mean I had it checked. Tell him thanks for his concern." I was back into the scales before I realized, vaguely, that she might have been asking another question when I hung up.

It was a fluky, hot day, Wednesday. You could smell it gathering in the air, even before breakfast. Michael was standing by my bed in his last year's bathing suit when I woke up. "It's boiling out! Can I wear these under my clothes so I can go under the sprinkler when I get home?"

"Turn around."

The suit, with a yellow Superman bolt of lightning on a field of blue, didn't quite cover the cleavage of his backside, and it pulled so tight across that you could only see one tight mound.

"It's too small, honey. Anyhow, you don't wear a bathing suit to school. You can wear shorts and a T-shirt, though."

211

"T-shirt! I'm wearing my Hulk shirt! It's *boiling!*"

The Hulk shirt had skinny straps like a tank-top. It missed the top of his shorts by a hair. He jiggled on one foot before the toaster-oven, waiting for his English muffin. "Can I go in the sprinkler at lunch?"

"It's Wednesday, honey. Lunch in school today. Matter of fact, I won't be home after school for you to go under the sprinkler."

"What! That sucks! I'm not sitting here while everybody's— just forget it, that's all. Just forget it."

There was something in the set of his jaw and mouth that made me see Richard, and I let him call the Padous and ask if he could go there after school. But I drew the line at Marylynn's homemade macaroni and cheese or, heaven forbid, the from-scratch pizza. "Ask Nicky if he'd like to go to the deli with you for lunch," I said casually. "My treat."

Michael gaped at me, midword. "Alone?" he squeaked. "The deli alone?"

"Sure. You and Nicky can cross the street with the guard. I think you can handle it."

"Thanks! Hey, Nick, tell your mom we're going to the deli for lunch!"

When he left, five dollar bills folded into a tiny square in one shorts pocket and his baseball cards bulging out of the other, he was damp with the heat and the excitement. Richard was erased from around his mouth. He let me wipe his hair back from his brow, then flew out of the house. "I'll pick you up at Nicky's about five," I called, but he didn't stop to answer. He was already on his way.

212

36.

I didn't even try to look at any of the music on the train. I didn't need to, for one thing: I was prepared. I'd studied for Rosie's final exam and I'd really spent a lot of time practicing. It was the only thing I'd done all week, outside of bed. Besides, I wanted to rerun the apartment fantasy. I barricaded the seat next to me with the briefcase and put on my sunglasses. Ready. Let's see, I'm coming down the steps of Mannes . . .

But the list, my litany, jiggled across the top of the scene until I had to run it through. All right. Randy's got her lunch, sandwich is in the bag, bag's in the . . . I got to Michael and had to stop. The deli. He has his money. Hasn't he? Yes, folded small, pushed way down into the pocket. What if he loses it? He won't lose it. He'll keep touching it all morning because it's the first time. So Michael has his money. They'll cross with the guard, I made him promise. What if he wants to show off for Nicky, runs across in the middle of the block? He won't; it's the first time and I made him promise. So he has his money, they'll cross with the guard to the deli, and they'll have lunch. What if he chokes? No mommy there responsible for him. Who'll help him? I saw him, drawing frantically for air as a french fry blocked his windpipe. He's turning color, looking around desperately, unable to make a sound come out. Nicky is watching helplessly.

No one notices. Help him, Nicky, damn you. Do something! Stop. Jesus, Beth, stop. He won't choke, he never has. I'll call him, call school and make them get him to the phone, and I'll tell him to chew carefully. Okay? Okay. Okay. So he's had his lunch and he'll go back to school. Will the guard be on duty when they cross? Trucks on that street, bearing down, the kids dart out, the truck is unable to—

I closed my eyes, laid my hands palm up on my knees, breathed in forced, rhythmic quietude for a minute. Then I ran through it again, sternly blocking out all the terrors. I wound up with a Disney-neat version of their day balanced uneasily in my mind.

That's all. They're set until 5:00. Good thing I don't have six kids, I'd have to ride back and forth twice to get it all in. Now, Gideon. So I'm coming down the steps, sun warm on my back, shining off my hair and—

. . . one more kid. The little one. But I don't have him to worry about. I've already canceled him out. Nothing else can happen to—

I didn't see it happen, though, did I? I was out when they did it. So how do I know he's—Jesus, Beth, of course he's—it's—dead. How could it live, outside of me?

How do they? Randy and Michael? If I don't breathe for them? Beat their hearts?

Separate beings. They're separate beings. They do not need me to live. I can't keep them safe, even. They don't make me safe. No one can keep anyone safe. Mama, I couldn't.

I was unconscious when they did it. I couldn't have snatched it back anyway, made it live. You can't reattach them. Beached, little one, swimming helpless on life fluids out onto the ruthless sheet, gasping, sucking, clinging. Sluiced out, cut off, choking. Choked.

Do they see it, there in the muck, at three or four weeks? Can they know, see that it's dead before they—what?—flush it away? Or does it wash down, living and lost, terrified into eternity?

I had it removed. I'm having them removed, Randy and Michael and Richard. What do you call the procedure, Daniel? Abitchtion. Stop. Stop. Bethie, Beth, shh. Stop.

I never got back to Gideon and the apartment, but it was all right at Mannes. Rosie's class was lighthearted and festive, despite the exam that took most of the hour. I thought about nothing but the music, working my way slowly and with pleasure through the exam. There were ten minutes before the end of the period when everyone had finished the exam and people were sitting around on the desks, easy in the summery heat, joking with each other and Rosie.

"We should end on a musical note," she said, walking suddenly to her files and pulling out the *bel canto* book. She held it out appealingly to me. "Won't you sing for us? Do the Cherubini, for auld lang syne." She turned to the others. "Mrs. Clahr is developing her very fine voice. When we hear from her next, she'll be singing *Tosca* with Pavarotti."

"When you hear from me next, I'll be trudging through the A scales, still trying to figure out how to turn them into music," I said, but I took the music from her and sang the Cherubini.

This time I didn't fight the twists and turns and double dots. The sun shone in a shaft across me and across the book in my hands, and I thought of it, for a moment, as a ribbon of warm light going through me. I let my voice slide on the ribbon, around and over the turns and twists. It felt good, singing the little piece and seeing the pleasure in their faces. They applauded generously and then the bell rang and the leave-taking was easy.

Halfway through lunch I remembered Michael. Too late; he and Nicky were probably eating already. How could I have called him anyway, and told him to chew carefully? You can't do that to a kid.

Brescia had me jumping from the chest voice to the high velvet, up, down, up. "When you descend you must keep the velvet, only add more depth," he said.

"How?"

"How. How you got the velvet, you keep the velvet. Only there is more depth in the voice. More depth, less velvet—always a shifting balance."

We worked at it for most of the hour, me sliding around wordlessly in all directions, catching the velvet, trying to hold it, pull it smoothly down with me to the lower range, thinking I had it, riding it triumphantly, stopping in despair when he shook his head again.

"Peace," he said finally, touching me lightly on the chin with an easy fist and smiling sunnily into my eyes. "I break my own rule because I am in a hurry for you. This voice of yours teases Brescia away from his first principle: one does not make a voice by frontal assault. It will come. To you, my lady, it will all come. You're working, eh?"

I nodded.

"I hear it. So it will come. Meanwhile we will reward ourselves a little. You prepared the Caccini? So, let me hear you sing it . . . 'Amarilli mia bella.' Breathe, open the voice. A little sweet on a summer day."

The Caccini was the first song he'd given me. We'd spent weeks on vowel sounds and on the techniques of going from open voice to words. The words, even these in Italian, were a snare. They involved teeth and tongue and lips, and they made it even harder to create a series of pure sounds. I despaired of ever getting past them.

But Brescia was sitting back on the bench and waiting, as if for a pleasure, and he was still looking at me with that intimate good humor. I moved a little, into the sunshine, invoking again the ribbon of bright warmth, willing it into my voice. I breathed, eased the muscles in my jaw and throat, and sang.

Halfway into the piece I heard it come together. Without concentrating on it at all, I went down the octave from high C to middle C and the voice kept the rich velvet of the high notes. Ah God, there it is, I thought in delight, and I opened it up, reaching for everything I had. Power, richness, clarity, carving out

216

every note, evoking every phrase. I held the last note, clear and reverberating. When I let it go, I closed my eyes for a minute, feeling the ribbon slide away. When I opened them he was standing in front of me. He took my hand, looked intently at me.

"It's dangerous, what you just did," he said. "To give it all is dangerous. The hardest thing to learn when you have it in your grasp is to keep a little back. Do you understand?"

I shook my head.

"You cannot—ever—go all the way, go as far as the voice and the music together can go. There is a point, near the limit, where you must hold back, save a little. It is a line—and you will come to know it—that you cannot cross. You lose the control past that point, and the performance will suffer." He let go of my hand and walked back to the piano, gathering up music and papers. "Never try to give away that last inch. Hold it back, keep it for yourself. Anyway, you cannot give them everything. They do not hear it and you are left . . . drained. Emptied." It was quiet in the room for a minute as he pushed the stack of papers into a canvas satchel and looked around the room.

"It's a good voice," he said. "We will make it very good. When I come back, we'll work on finding the limits. Meanwhile, the arpeggios, the scales, open throat and vowel sounds, the intervals, and again the Caccini. And another song or two, let me see—"

"When you come back? Are you going away?"

"Of course. The semester ends, Brescia goes away to renew the blood."

"Where will you be?"

"Capri, for solitude. Firenze with friends. Three weeks of—"

"Three weeks? You'll be away for three weeks?"

"Yes, my little racer. You will survive three weeks without Brescia. It's good to work alone for a while. You'll see, when we return some of the knots will have untied themselves. Meanwhile you'll have three weeks without the bully, eh?" He smiled in my direction, missing me. He was gone already. The sunlight, beading through the glass, was burning my arm. I moved away, kept moving toward the door.

217

"Maybe," he said jovially, "it will be such a relief you will not wish to return."

"Maybe," I said, smiling. "Have a good vacation."

"But return anyway." He demanded my hand. I held it out. "We have work to do, bully and racer together. Till then, you will practice giving and holding back."

I didn't need you to tell me that, I thought, making my way furiously through the halls and into the blinding light. That's what I do best, giving and holding back.

I found a seat on the train, jammed the briefcase into the overhead rack, and pulled off my sunglasses, looking grimly at the window and seeing the hard lines of my face reflected in it. Anyway, Mama, I thought, that's $75 we're saving. It'll help pay for last week's outing to the unbaby doctor.

Curled up in bed that night—my other bed, my nighttime bed, the one with Richard in it—I was almost asleep when the voice pulled me back. "Bethie?"

Mama? Where? I sat up, my heart pounding at the top of my breastbone.

"Baby?" Richard. Only Richard.

"What?"

He put a hand on my arm, tentative fingers brushing at the skin. Don't. Don't. Touch. Me.

"—want another baby?"

"What did you say?"

"I'm asking you if you want to have another baby. We could, you know. We're young, you're a great mother. Be nice for the kids too, huh?"

I looked at his face until the air began to hurt my eyeballs.

"What do you think? You've been kind of . . . low, withdrawn. I don't know. Especially since the—since last Friday." Voice noise. I looked away from his damp eyes, locked myself in tight against his fingers begging my skin. "—distant, hard to . . . like when

218

your mother died . . . but when you had Randy . . . brought you out of it. . . . So I thought . . ."

You thought you'd put me in the box and sit on the lid. You thought I'd curl up in a gingham shroud and smile. "You can't afford any more children, Richard," I said. I turned over, pretending to be asleep, but it was a long time before my heart stopped pounding and I could unclench my teeth and sleep.

37.

I stripped my bed in the morning, before I got ready for the appointment with Dr. Block. Before I got into the shower, I called Bloomingdale's and ordered another set of the white Super-cales. "Can you rush them out?" I asked. "It's kind of an emergency."

"It would be better if you came for them, then," the lady answered. "I couldn't guarantee—"

"I don't get out very much," I said gently. "I'm . . . house-bound."

"Oh. I'm sorry. Well, in that case, I'll run down to loading with them myself. You might get them by tomorrow. Would that be all right?"

"That would be a godsend. You're very kind."

I can have clean sheets every day, I thought, pulling out of the driveway and heading for the parkway. These new ones I'll never put on his side. They'll be mine.

"You got to the city yesterday?" Daniel Block asked, standing by the side of the table and making conversation politely before effecting entry at my other end.

"Yes."

"You had a lesson?"

"Yes."

"I went in, too—must have come and gone on different trains. Well, let's see." He disappeared past my knees and I felt the steel spoons, then some pressure. "I went to the Ansel Adams exhibit at the South Street Seaport Museum. A genius, Adams. . . . Well, Karlow may have come on like a storm trooper, but it seems he handled you very gently. You're in great shape." The spoons released their pressure, slid out. His voice came from the other side of the room, through running water. "You can get dressed and come on into my office."

He was on the phone when I went into the office. He ended his conversation briskly. "Do you know Adams's work?" he asked me.

"The photographer?"

He nodded. "I'm an amateur photographer. I think I'm pretty fair until I see what someone like Steichen or Adams can do. That's what I do on Wednesdays, mostly. Exhibits or the galleries, or I wander around the city and take pictures. Then they sit there in the camera and cry out to me until I can get into the darkroom." He sat back in his leather chair, grinned at me. "They're miraculous shots, every one of them, until they're developed."

The goldfish caught the sun in the corner of my eye. I looked over to see how they were doing.

"Well." He cleared his throat, sitting forward. "You're in great shape, physically. Like new. Just—Karlow told you, no . . . intercourse . . . for about six weeks, and then be very careful about contraception until the menstrual pattern settles down?" He was a little pink.

"He told me."

"And how are you—otherwise? Did you cry?"

"Did I. Cried and slept, doctor's orders. Thank you—it helped. How did you know?"

"I saw you that day on the train, remember? You were dis-

221

traught. And you told me yourself that your life was . . . complicated. You don't have to be a genius to figure out that if a sensitive woman goes through an abortion alone, and if the pregnancy was the result of a . . . complex relationship, she's going to feel angry and guilty and depressed when it's over. You needed to face it, and to cry. And then to express your anger, I hope." He searched my face. I looked down, sad but contained. It's all over with my lover, my neck and shoulders and lowered eyelids said to Daniel Block.

He leaned back in the chair again. "Everyone has to have a release," he said. His voice was relaxed now. He traced the edge of his desk blotter with a finger, looking at me. "Some days when I leave the office I'm tense or depressed. I bicycle, sometimes for hours in good weather. And I take pictures. Did you ever go to—"

"I have a question," I said.

There was a tapping at the door. It was the receptionist, the grim one. "You turned off your phone," she accused him. "Dr. Meredith is trying to reach you, and Mrs. Stone is—"

"Two minutes," he said. It was an order. She retreated. I picked up my handbag and shifted forward in the chair. He put up a hand, motioning me to wait. "You had a question?"

"Oh. Yes, I did. Ridiculous, but—are you sure I'm not pregnant anymore?"

He blinked. "After all the bleeding, you have to ask?"

"Yes. I had to ask."

"The pregnancy is ended; I'm very sure. And you are, as I said, as good as new. In fact—"

"Do they see it?"

"What?"

"The . . . fetus. Can they see it, when they—I mean, how do they know it's—"

"Beth. It's—it was—a minute collection of cells. But there's no mystery about an abortion at three weeks. You destroy the environment and you force the whole apparatus out. It's gone. Over. The whole episode is as over as you want it to be." He

222

was watching me, his face stern and pink again. I smiled, stood up, held out my hand.

"I do want it to be over," I said. "All of it."

He didn't shake my hand, only held it for a minute. "Then it is," he said. "Will you believe it and relax a little?"

No it isn't, I thought, driving home. Not all of it.

38.

So it was all right when I went out that morning to see Daniel Block—a Thursday, it was—and I guess that was the last time.

When Michael left for school after lunch that day, I showered again. I ran the shower lightly and left the bathroom door open so I'd hear the phone when Gideon called. I got into bed. It was very quiet, there in the bed, and I thought about people to call. Richard's sister, Dot, to say hello. Laura. Jessie. But if I made a call I'd miss Gideon. So I lay there, drifting. I was seeing Michael the day before at Nicky Padou's, running shrieking under the sprinkler, stopping the flow with his foot, and then ducking away and letting the spray explode, laughing in hysterical triumph —when the phone rang.

"Hello. What's funny?" Gideon.

Nothing. I was just thinking about Mi—about summer coming."

"Ah. I can hear the sunshine in your voice. Where are you, anyway, when I call? You sound so . . . languid."

"In bed."

"Are you sick?"

"No. I . . . get into bed sometimes."

There was a silence while we both listened, in shock, to what I had said. I made it worse.

"I crawl in under the covers, sometimes, to sort things out.

No one knows that I do it. The world gets so noisy, and I need to turn it off. Is it a crazy thing to do?"

"Not at all. You're making a cocoon. I'd like to be in there with you, instead of out here waiting for you to break out. I could be, you know. You could be quiet with me. We could tune it all out together, all day if you want. It could be arranged."

Someone else's bed? Someone else in my bed? He had it all mixed up. There couldn't be anyone in here with me if it was going to be safe. I changed the subject, told him about the last lesson with Brescia, what he'd said about holding back. "It's true," I said. "If you give it all and people don't hear you, it could tear you apart."

"But you have to risk it. You have to go to the limits sometimes, if only to know where they are. What are you wearing?"

"When?"

"Now. In your bed."

I looked down at the white cotton gown. "A nightgown."

"What color?"

"Violet silk."

"Oh, my God. That takes care of the rest of my afternoon. When will you have mercy on this poor soul? It's cold out here alone. You're alone in your cocoon, I'm alone in the cold. . . ."

"I am on my own, actually. He's away for three weeks."

"Richard?"

"Brescia."

"Oh. *Oh*, so your Wednesdays are free."

"I feel abandoned."

"I'll be there in forty minutes to rescue you."

"No."

"Wednesday? Lunch?"

"I can't."

He sighed. "It's getting harder all the time, this rescuing-maidens-in-distress business. Just when you spot a great one, she tells you no thanks, I'll rescue myself. A hell of a note."

"You ought to find another line of work."

"Want me to?"

225

No. "Well, it isn't very promising."

"I'll hold onto my steed and my sword for another couple of weeks. You might invite me to help bust up the cocoon. Violet, eh? Silk?" He sighed again, with a smile in it. "I'll hang around out here for a while."

I had car pool the next day, so I was up and dressed when the UP man brought the sheets. I ran them through the washer and drier a few times. I was about to iron them when I thought of the smell. Mama's fresh sheets on the line. I put them through another quick cycle in the washer and while it was going I went outside. The people who'd owned the house before us had had a clothespole. Richard never got around to taking it down, and the kids used it sometimes to tie things to. I struggled with it until I got it unfurled. Then I hung the wet sheets and pillowcases on it in the sunshine. But not for today, I told myself. You don't need a cocoon. So I made a whole list of errands to do: groceries, get the left blinker on the car fixed, take Richard's shoes to the shoemaker. But when I got into the car and started down the hill to the village, it began, running through my head, at first vaguely and then so insistently that I had to pull over to the curb and run it through. The motor was running and the car jiggled raggedly under me. Randy has her lunch, I thought. Sandwich in it? Yes, tuna on whole wheat with lots of lettuce. Her health-food kick. In the knapsack? Yes. Car pool will bring her home. Wait, car pool is me. This isn't Wednesday, I'm not away from them; why am I doing my list? Jesus, Beth. I pulled away from the curb and headed toward the village, but it kept pulling at me. Randy. Forget Randy, I did her. Michael. Weather's great, he walked to school. Didn't take lunch, he's coming home. . . . Walked to school. What about the cars? Teenagers, juiced up on the hot weather. He isn't paying special attention crossing streets today; I didn't tell him to. He's walking with Evan; they're jostling each other, his baseball cards fall out of his pocket in the middle of the Willow Street intersection. He bends down to get them, the kid is driving too fast, doesn't see him—

226

I jerked the car to a stop, looked around wildly for a driveway to turn around in. Beth, it was an hour ago. He's in school, he's fine. Come on. Michael. Lunch. No lunchbag, he's coming home . . .

The car backed up, found a driveway, turned, headed back up the hill. I ran a stop sign, pulled into the side street at the Willow intersection. No one. Peace. No traffic. I got out of the car, looked up and down the silent streets again. No bodies. Shaking, I got back into the car. Jessie, I thought, and I drove blindly to her house, fending it off. Michael's fine, home for lunch, I have car pool . . .

Jessie's house was abandoned. I rang the doorbell over and over, but there was no answer. I made for home. Laura's car was not in her driveway and no one answered her door, either. Where are you, Mama, when you're suddenly not there? Where am I? The list battering my mind, I ran into my house. I was leaning against the living-room wall, warming my cold, wet hands under my armpits and rocking forward and backward when I heard the quiet. It had stopped. I'll do the errands after lunch, I thought, when I'm calm.

But after lunch I took in the sheets, ironed them, put one contour on my bed and a pillowcase on my pillow, and the big top sheet across the whole bed. I showered and powdered myself and put on the nightgown and lay carefully down.

They smelled like the summer night. Like one of Mama's summer night kisses.

It was quiet, there in the bed. I tried Jessie's number. She answered.

"I came to you for coffee this morning and you were gone. What'd you do, find your own fast man and slow carriage?"

"How long could I wait for you to come up with them? Actually, I was at a meeting."

"League?"

"No, FEMALE."

"Female?"

"Following Every Mastectomy A Life Emerges. It's a group Alix

227

and Jan started. You know—coffees, lectures, fashion shows. I told 'em they ought to make hospital visits, too, bring the fashion photos to show people what can be done, help 'em over the low spots, you know? Next thing I knew I was in charge of it. I'm running like a jackrabbit. The worst of it is I haven't seen a single interesting man. Not too many around in these circles. But it's okay. My man'll do." There was a little reminiscent grin in her voice.

"You devil. You did it."

"Well, they're not real swift, you know, men. By the time he figured out what was happening, it was happening."

"What did he say?"

"Not a whole lot. He's not a big talker, John. But he's sure been making up for lost time since then. Give me action over speeches every time." She was purring.

"Did he like the clothes?"

"Would you believe it? He loved 'em. I thought he'd faint when I came out in the bathing suit, but he made himself look, and was he relieved. You know what he said?"

"What?"

" 'You're still a piece.' Not bad at umpty-ump years, huh?"

"Not bad. You said you came out in the suit. You're still dressing in the bathroom?"

"Oh well, sure. He'll never look at me naked again, I know that. But listen, at my age the view is deteriorating anyhow. So it's another thing you do to keep them from seeing what they don't want to, right? Hey, don't we do that all our lives for them? My mother, she should rest in peace, used to say, 'What they don't see not only wouldn't hurt them, it's half the marriage.' Anyhow, I now have a whole wardrobe of nightgowns and everyone's happy. Especially Alix and Jan—I'm their best customer."

"You spend a lot of time there, I guess." Without me.

"Yeah, well it beats the League; I never left one of those meetings looking any better. How *is* the League these days?"

"I don't know. I'm a dropout. I've been systematically dropping out of everything, but now I'm wondering—"

"Good for you, Toots. Let 'em waste someone else's time. Well, listen, it's good talking to you—I'm off to the hospital now. Can't you see it? An aging candy striper with a rubber boob and a heart of gold."

"Jessie? Listen, I—" I dropped out of everything and I'm having the rest removed and it's too quiet in here, but the noise is terrible out there, I wanted to say. Stay with me, I wanted to whisper. Sing to me, Jessie. "I'm glad you're rehabilitated," I said. "In spite of everything, I always thought you were redeemable."

"There's hope for the worst of us."

She was gone. I couldn't keep her.

It was about time, anyway, for me to pick the kids up at the junior high. By the time I'd dressed and made the bed, I was almost late. I filled my lungs with air and vocalized all the way there, pushing the speed limit. It probably looked strange but it worked: it was quiet inside my head.

They piled into the car, giggling, complaining, jostling for space. Five new females. Good as new, Daniel had said. Compared to what?

"—bowling this Saturday, wanna come? We go to the Starlite, the one in—"

"Starlight," one sang through her nose. Junior high version of radio rock. "Sta-har bright—"

"First star," wistfully, from Allison, the plump one.

"I see tonight." Randy.

"Wish I may, wish I might—"

"Have the wish I wish tonight." All of them, grand finale. Coda of moans.

"Hey, remember that? I used to do it all the time, even when there were millions of stars." Rebecca. "I'm serious. My father, he'd hold me up to the window and there'd be all these stars, right? So he'd say, 'Which one did you see first? Wish on that one.' I believed in it, too."

"Ah, little Becky."

"My mother—"

229

"I once—"

"My mother—shut up, you guys—you know, my mother had this neat lullaby she used to sing:

> Blackbird singin' in the dead of night
> Time to spread your wings and take the sky.
> All your life
> You've been only waitin' for this moment to arise."

"That's a Beatles song. And it's not even the words—"

"I *know*. Listen, so about last year I finally heard the song—the real one, the Beatles? And I said, 'Hey, that's what you used to sing to me,' and you know what she said? She knew it was a Beatles song. *She* learned it in the sixties, can you imagine? My mother and the Beatles?"

"Well they're old—"

"Listen, listen, I once—"

"They're not so old. In the sixties they were—"

"Will you *listen*? I once—"

"Here's one my mother used to sing to me," I said. They stopped talking. I sang it sweetly, not with any volume.

> Toora loora loora
> Toora loora lie
> Toora loora loora
> Hush now don't you cry . . .

I sang it all. It was quiet. In the rearview mirror two of them looked at each other and shrugged, grinning.

"That's *nice*," Allison said.

"Yeah, really." They shifted around in their seats.

"About the bowling, what do you think? My mom can drop us off." The conversation closed around me.

"It's great weather now," I said to Randy when we got into the house. "Don't you think you girls could take your bikes to school? You don't really need the car pool unless it rains."

"Yeah, sure. We can ride. You don't have to drive."

230

39.

It wasn't that I wanted to be in the bed, really. It was too quiet in there, but that was the thing, the quiet. When I tried to go out—anywhere, even to the market—the noise was unrelenting. It came at me over and over: Randy, bike to school, lunch, bike home, what if—Michael, walking to school, home for lunch, traffic, what if—did I turn off the burners? Lock the door? Over and over, meaningless and terrifying. I'd tick it all off, it would come back, ruthless, drumming. I could sing in the car and hold it off, but I was helpless in the supermarket or on the street. Anywhere.

So I stayed in. It was all right, in the bed. I started ordering groceries by phone and having the car picked up for servicing. I even ordered Father's Day gifts over the phone, having the woman at Bloomingdale's write my messages on the cards and send them out. All from my bed. I wasn't lying still in it anymore; it was my base of operations. The radio, the phone book, memo pads and pens, my sewing box, magazines, books, nail polish paraphernalia—everything piled up around the bed. Richard wasn't on my side of it at all, these days, so I only changed the sheets twice a week.

Randy was going to the village on her own a lot now. She'd just tell me at breakfast that she was going, and she'd come

231

home by five on her bike. One night at dinner Michael said he needed a present for Evan's birthday party. "You hafta get him something good," he said. "You know what he's getting for his birthday? A TXR racing set—VOOOM!" He shot a hand out, knocking his milk over onto Randy's plate. "It's okay," Randy said, looking at Richard. She wiped it up, refilled his glass, and went on eating.

"What should we get him?" I asked.

"I dunno. A baseball mitt, maybe."

"Too expensive. What else?"

"How about a baseball bat?" Randy asked. "I can get it at Big Top."

"But I wanna pick it out."

"Come on, Mike, a *bat*? There's nothing to pick. I'll get a good one."

"What's the problem?" Richard asked me. "You can take him, can't you?" It was the first week; he didn't know yet about my staying in.

"I love to go to Big Top," Randy said. "I *want* to. I'll pick a good one, okay Mikey?"

"Okay. A regular hard one."

"Right."

But by the next week I wasn't hiding it from him. "A little vacation," I said. "A semester break."

"You're in the house all day? What do you do?"

"Well, I sing. I've been practicing a lot." I had. I stayed in bed until one of the kids came home, and then I got out of bed and practiced. I sang for a couple of hours every day. "I'm really singing better," I told him. "I have songs now, hard ones, and they're—"

"That's great. But don't you—"

"I'll sing for you. Want to hear one?"

"Yeah, sure. Maybe after dinner."

After dinner I waited for him to ask me to sing, but he disappeared into the den with the newspaper.

232

Michael spent a lot of time with Nicky Padou. They played at our house; that way I didn't have to pick him up. One day, into that second week, Marylynn came to get Nicky early. I answered the door in my nightgown, music in my hand.

"Oh," she said, "you're sick?"

"Yes, a little under the weather. Nothing contagious." I could see her calculating the effect of my microbes on her child. "A woman thing."

"Ah?" Tell Marylynn all about it. "Nothing serious?"

"No, no. Just cramps."

I followed her look around the room. Muddy sneakers on the bottom step. Baseball bats and balls on the couch. A coffee cup and a banana skin on the end table.

"Let me take Mike for dinner. Let me take both the children."

"Aren't you nice. But we're all set—I made boeuf bourguignon. A nuisance, but the kids do love it."

She wanted to peek into the pot, but I decoyed her around to the den window to see the boys running bases out in the yard. She left without seeing the hamburger defrosting on the counter.

40.

I am swinging in the dim light, swinging. There is only the silken thread holding me but I am wrapped in it, all wrapped, and swinging gently from it.

"Sleeping, Bethie?"

"No. I'm in my cocoon."

"Blackbirds don't have cocoons, they have nests."

"No."

"Sure they do." She sings: " 'Blackbird singin' in the dead of night / Time to spread your wings and take—' "

"No! No! Not that one!"

"Don't raise your voice to your mother, young lady. Don't you raise your voice to—"

"—the sky. / All your life / You've been only—"

"No! Mama!" Crying now, tears blocking my throat, pushing against the block, trying to make the sounds come out. "Not that one. Sing Toora loora, Mama, please—"

"—waitin' for this moment to—"

"DON'T SAY THAT!" Too late, it's unraveling, rolling me over and over, silken threads slipping, loosing me, I'm falling, I'm—

———

"—in Iran, the hostages enter their two hundred twenty-fourth day in captivity. The students holding them have issued—" News. Television. Bed. Richard. Night. I picked up my pillow and slid over to where he was. He was sitting up, looking at the newspaper. I lay quietly but it wasn't enough. Please, Richard. He didn't move. I took his hand and put it on my head. He scratched a little, absently.

"Run your fingers through my hair," I whispered. He laid the paper down and rolled over to face me. He put his hand on my head, ruffled my hair. Not like that. Smooth it. Smooth it back.

"Well. It's about time. Want a little petting, baby?"

I nodded. Just smooth it, Richard. Rock me a little. But his hand was on my breast, his mouth covered mine. His smell—

"—but how'll we manage? You can't—we can't really do it, right? Or is that just medical rigamarole?"

Now I was awake. "No, we really can't. He was very firm about it."

"You asked, eh? Well, it's been a long time. Maybe we could . . ." His hand snaked up under my nightgown.

"No. Richard, really, I—it's still tender. Don't." The hand stopped. To get away, I shifted in the bed, reached over for him. It was big, poking up beneath the jockey shorts. I pushed them down a little. He was out of them in a second, leaning over me. I lay still until the kiss was over, then rolled him to his side of the bed and put my hand over it.

"A hand job? Just like old times, huh doll?"

I nodded and made a smile. Then I closed my eyes and worked at it.

It took a long time. Behind my closed eyes I finished the song. Toora loora loora—

He was beginning to grunt a little. "Harder, baby. Oh, that's good. I love—"

—hush now, don't you cry—

Ah, finished. It was warm and wet on my hand. He moved to kiss me. It almost got on my leg. I moved it, but if I moved

235

too far he'd roll over and get it on my bed. I bent and kissed him instead, where he lay. He stayed there.

I changed my sheets anyway, in the morning. Then I called Jessie, early, before she could leave.

"What's up, Toots?"

"Are you in a hurry? Going out?"

"In a couple of minutes, over to the shop."

"They open this early?"

"No, not until ten, but we have this fashion show we're trying to get together for the hospitals. You can't imagine the amount of planning—well, never mind. This is your dime. What's up?"

"Nothing special. Just wanted to see how you were, thought maybe you'd come and have a cup of coffee. I'm all dropped out, and you can't sing all the time—anyway I can't—and—"

"Hey, that sounds great. Now you have time to find one for each of us. Should we all share the carriage, or is that too advanced for you?"

"You think they're worth the trouble, Jess? Men?" *I wouldn't have gone with him, Mama, if I'd known. I'd never have left you. I should have—*

"—decent substitute for butter, let alone men. So until they come up with something better. . . . Whatsamatter, honey, you down?"

"Kind of."

"How's about after lunch—no, that's no good. How's three-thirty for coffee? I'll drop in after my ap—after my visits."

I hung up, noticing that my other hand was in my hair and my face was wet. How soon is 3:30?

41.

I am with Daniel Block when they tell me that Richard is dead. I'm on the train. No, I'm in his office. In one of the examining rooms, in a hospital gown. White cotton. The receptionist comes in. She takes him aside, tells him something. Her face is sober. She looks over at me. He sends them out, her and the nurse. He comes to me, takes my hands. "I have to tell you something," he says. "Your husband's office called. He had a heart attack. He's dead, Beth."

I look up, searching his face, then down at my lap. I don't cry, but my breathing is ragged. I turn my head from him. He leaves for a minute, comes back saying, "We're alone. I sent them all home. Come. Come here." He takes off his white coat, puts it on me. He leads me into his office. We sit on the couch in the dim light. He tilts my chin up so he can see my face. "You didn't love him?"

I shake my head.

"I know."

"No one else knows. He didn't know."

"I knew it the first time I saw you. Trying to be tough, and so small and scared. I wanted to carry you home in my pocket, keep you warm." I press my arms in tight to my body. He pulls the white coat closed around me, touches gentle fingers to my

237

cheek. "I spent the whole day of your abortion in turmoil, did you know it? I had to keep myself from going over there. I wanted to be there when you woke up. I knew that other bastard wouldn't be with you."

"I never told—"

"I know." His fingers trace my cheekbones and eyebrows. He pulls me to him and in the dim light, in the quiet, he runs his hands through my long and shining hair. Over and over, rocking me and smoothing it all away.

I am with Gideon when they tell me that Richard is dead. I'm at Mannes; he's there in the hall, waiting for my lesson to end. Someone knocks on the door. Brescia slams his hand down on the piano bench: "What is it?" A woman from the office comes in, draws him aside, whispers something to him. He nods quickly several times, shoos her out. He comes to me, holding both hands out for mine. He studies me for a minute, then makes me sit on the windowseat. He paces. "You are strong?" he demands. I look at him, puzzled. "There was a call from your husband—his office." He comes up close. "Be strong, *cara*. He is dead."

"Dead? Richard?"

"The heart."

I run wildly from the room. Brescia watches me go. He is frantic, worried that I'll disappear, he'll never see me again. Abandoned.

I run to Gideon. Now I'm crying, eyes wide, tears running down my face.

"What is it?"

"Richard."

"Richard? Something happened to him?"

I nod.

"Not—he's dead?"

I nod.

"Jesus. Come, let's get out of here." In the cab he says, "You loved him, didn't you?"

"Yes." So softly that he has to lean in to hear.

"I know. Maybe no one knows as well as I do. He wasn't

238

enough for you, was he? You were too strong, and you were growing all the time, but you loved him. Listen, does anyone know?"

"No. Not yet. I have to—"

"One hour. Take one hour with me, before you face it all. Beth."

I look up at him.

"It'll be days of pain and aggravation and people. Take one hour and let me love you."

He undresses me in the sunshine. I'm quiet now, looking out at the river. "Come." He leads me to the bed. I lie back, still, looking at him. My eyelashes are stuck together and shining with the tears. My hair is tousled in short tendrils on the pillow. "My God," he says. "What you are." He kisses my eyelids, my ears, the hollow of my neck. He touches my breasts, watches the nipples harden, bathes them with his tongue. His tongue moves down, a path between my ribs, makes a circle in my belly button. It traces the crease where my thigh meets my body. He looks up at me. The sun crosses his face, slants down across his arm, lights his hand on me. "Just let it happen," he says. He parts the lips with his fingers; his tongue finds the spot, moves over it in easy, lazy waves, dips down, plunges in, returns, not so lazy now. I'm moving, someone is moaning, I'm coming in long, jackknifing waves. When I'm quiet, he holds me against the length of his body and comes into me, quiet and tender. He's very hard, but he moves easily and slowly. We rise and sink forever until it surprises me and I pull in a breath. "Gideon." "Ready?" he whispers. We come together, a long and powerful coming. He holds me against him. I'm crying again, different tears. "I love you," he says. "You're ready now."

I am alone when they tell me that Richard is dead. Do you want to see to the casket? they ask me. No, it doesn't matter about that, I say; he doesn't care how he sleeps.

239

42.

Jessie came at 4:00. I was dressed and the house was neat. I was singing when she came in.

"Was that you? No kidding? You sound like a regular opera type. Shoosh." She plunked herself down on the couch. She looked exhausted. "Too much, this heat. Beats the hell out of a lady. Who needs it, in June?" She took the iced coffee gratefully, sipped at it, and put it down. "So what's up, Cookie? What's got you down?" She touched my arm. Her face was beaded with sweat, but her hand was icy. There was a sweet smell about her —not perfume, some other sweetness. I moved away to get her a napkin, settled down at a little distance.

"Tell Jessie. Tell Mama." She smiled at the words.

"Oh I don't know. I'm just—you know how I always bitch to you about the League, the way it swallows your time and nothing ever happens but talk?"

"Sure. And you re—"

"So I dropped out. They asked me to sit on the board and I refused it."

"Great. What's bad about that? You suffering withdrawal?"

"No, I don't miss it at all. That's not it. But at the same time —you have time to listen to all this?"

"Of course. At the same time what?"

"At the same time, well you know the whole point was to make time for the thing I want to do, the singing. So my teacher told me if I was going to be a soloist, I'd have to drop out of the chorus. You know I was singing with the Philharmonia Chorale in the city?"

"Yeah, but it seems to me the more singing you do, the better—"

"His point—my teacher, Brescia's point—was that when you sing in a chorus you train yourself to think of your voice as part of a total sound. You subordinate yourself not only to the director's concept of the music, but also to the group. It's not just a different way of singing; it's a different way of thinking. That's the real problem. It's terrifying to sing alone, Jess. It's your voice alone against the silence out there. Your timing, your choices. You push against the limits of the music and your voice, and you compel them to listen and hear it. You grab control of that moment and you fill the silence."

She was leaning forward, watching my face, her forehead creased in understanding. She nodded.

"And it's so hard to think that way, like a soloist. You have no idea, Jess. So Brescia said, 'You can row below, or you can seize the bow'—that's how he talks—and I'm trying. I'm trying to seize the bow, so I quit the chorus. Dropped out of that, too. To be a solo singer."

"Right. So you're not busy enough with your family and the house and your singing? You want me to bring over my wash?"

"Really, the kids don't need as much time as they used to. They—I've discovered that when I'm not right there holding the net they land on their feet anyhow. They need me, but not to be right there, you know? They're really leaving me. I dropped the junior high car pool—that's another thing—and it really didn't matter to Randy. She gets around on her own. She even does errands for Michael."

"So here you are. You got what you want."

"I know, but I—it's stupid, but now I feel left out, and everyone's angry—" My voice slid up and I was crying, like Michael, with my face all scrunched up. She rummaged in her handbag

241

and handed me a Kleenex. She took my hand with her damp, cold one.

"Who's angry? Come on."

"Well, you should have heard Leone when I refused the board position. 'We didn't *think* you'd be interested.' "

"Oh, Leone. She probably makes love in committee. And what do you bet they never reach consensus?" We laughed. "Come on, who else is mad?"

"Oh, it's stupid to care, I know. But the chorus director, when I told him, got all cold and huffy and implied that I'd fail and come crawling back to the chorus."

"If you were running a galley, would you want your crew to go checkin' around for better work?"

"I know." I smiled and blew my nose again. "But—and there's Richard and the kids. They're confused that I'm not Supermom anymore. They don't know how to treat me. They used to sabotage my practicing, but they don't do that anymore. In fact they tippytoe around me. The other day I was vocalizing and I heard Michael come in. He went to the kitchen and I heard him say, 'Randy? I got a cut and Mommy's singing,' and *she* said, 'I'll take care of it, Mikey. Get me the Bactine and wash your hands good. Use soap.' "

"Fantastic."

"It is? I was right here, right in the house, and he went to *her*. He let her fix it, too, and didn't carry on the way he does with me."

"That's fantastic. They're growing up. Come on, your family loves you and they're proud of what you're doing. Let 'em be a little self-sufficient. So how's the singing?"

"The singing is the only thing that's good. I'm stronger all the time. Things I couldn't have dreamed of doing a few months ago—"

"See? So you're giving up the garbage and making time, and you're getting somewhere with the singing. Believe me, Cookie, there's no time to waste. None. You do what's important because one day they pull the cord on you, and that's all, kid." She stood up, using her left hand to push herself up off the couch. A wave of the sweetness choked me. The afternoon light played cruelly on the tired lines of her face.

"You all right, Jess?"

"I'm great, honey. But all these good works run against my nature. I gotta go home and kick the cat. Then I'll be fine." She stopped at the door. "You sing, Toots, and the hell with the rest of it."

When she got into the car she leaned out of the window and yelled, "Oh, and I'll be over tomorrow with my wash." Then she backed out of the driveway and was gone.

But I hadn't told her the real thing. I hadn't told her about how the less I did for the children the more I feared for them. I hadn't told her about the murderous noise of my litany of safety for them. I hadn't told her about the silent bed and its silken threads, my bed where I was Bethie, and safe. And now she had gone.

"Jessie doesn't look well," I told Richard at dinner.

"You went over there? She in bed again?"

"No, she's up and out and busy. She can hardly fit me into her schedule. But she came here today, and she—"

"You been out today?" The kids were quiet now, listening.

"No."

"Since when?"

"Since when what? Michael, eat the meatballs, not just the spaghetti. I made it because you—"

"When is the last time you left the house? I know you never got my shoes to the shoemaker, for instance. So—"

"I'll take them, Daddy." Randy. "I'll drop them off on my way to school. It's right on the way."

"Your mother has all day. She can't sing every minute. I just—"

"She sings a lot, a real lot. It sounds fabulous, too. Mrs. Linder even asked me—"

243

"Beth? Baby? Will you take my shoes? Get out a little bit?"

"Yes, Richard. Of course. It's no big deal. Randy, eat, honey. Your dinner's getting cold."

I vocalized all the way there in the car and all the way back, and in the shoe-repair shop I met Carol Green and there was no time to think. So it was all right. When the kids came home from school, the bed was remade and I was dressed and waiting for them.

"Grab a drink and a cookie and let's go."

"You're taking us out?"

"I don't wanna. Me and Evan—"

"—to Jack & Jill's. You guys need your stuff for camp."

Michael whistled once through his teeth, then grabbed me around the middle. The sound cut through my ears and I winced.

"All *right!* I need a canteen, don't I, Randy? And a knife. This year I want a knife, you said—"

"Michael, let go of her!"

He fell back, looking scared. "How come?"

"She was sick, you know that. You can't go—"

"Hey." I put a hand on her cheek, pulled him in to me. "I'm fine. I don't break. Are we going for camp stuff or not?"

I had figured it all out after the shoe-repair shop. If they were with me when I went out, I wouldn't have the litany dinning at me. I was right. But I didn't sing at all that day. There was no time.

I thought about it, sitting at dinner, working through a problem I was having with the phrasing in "Ombra mai fù," the part where—

"—and the neatest bathing suit, Daddy. Not in Jack & Jill, of course. We had to go to Bloomie's to—"

"Yeah. Randy got all the stuff. Lantern. Bathing suits. Braws. Bee-yoo-ti-ful braws."

"Michael! You got so much stuff!"

"I did not. Just a lot of crappy clothes."

244

"You got your canteen, and the mess kit Mom got you that you didn't even need, and—"

"Yeah? Well how about the knife? She didn't get me the knife and she *said*—"

"Who is *she*? The cat's mother?" Richard sounded irritated. I tuned it in. "Don't call your mother *she*. Now, what knife? Beth? Was he supposed to have some kind of knife?"

"*Yes*. From last year. She *told* me. A folding knife with two blades, and she—"

"Beth?"

"He's seven years old, Richard. You want him to have an army knife?"

"Nicky has one. Him and his father use it when they go fishing." Michael had scraped his chair around to face Richard, and he looked challengingly up at him. Richard shifted his eyes away from me. "What about the mess kit, Mike?"

"A mess kit? So what about the dumb mess kit?" He was working his mouth against the tears.

"You wanted it bad enough in the store. You made Mom—"

"That'll do, Randy." Richard, tight and menacing.

"Well he did. You should have seen, he made this huge—"

"Randy, I said—"

"—and she didn't have to take him at all. She—"

"Go to your room."

She looked at him, stunned, a flush overtaking her throat and face. She turned to me, but before I could move, she was gone, thudding up the stairs, slamming the door, then opening it again and running back downstairs. She threw the Bloomingdale's bag onto the counter. "You can return these," she shouted at him. "I don't want them. I don't want anything from you." He was out of his chair after her "—open a fresh mouth to me, you'll—" but I stood up and blocked him.

"Don't you say another word to her." I was starting to cry, too. "If you want Michael to have a knife, you buy it. And when he severs a finger or slits open an artery, you take him to the emergency room and listen to him screaming. You listen for a change."

245

I went to her. She was sprawled out on her bed, sobbing. I closed the door behind me and locked it, and I leaned over her and tugged at her until she sat up and let me hold her. I had to kneel on the bed to get her head to reach comfortably to my breast. *Don't you open your mouth to me, young lady, don't you dare raise your . . .* not anymore. No one's girl now.

I held her there and rocked her until it was quiet and we had stopped crying. She shifted away. "I'll pay for the bathing suits," I told her then. "I have some money."

"It's okay. I don't care if I have them."

"I care."

"So let him pay, then. It doesn't matter."

Yes it does, I thought, but I didn't say it to her.

"What went on down there, tonight?" Richard pulled the sheet out, flopped into bed. "I finally had to put Michael to bed myself. He was pretty upset, you know. I looked for you but you were barricaded in there with Randy. Was the door locked?"

"Yes. She was pretty upset, too, Richard. You keep sending her away, you'll look up one day and find her gone."

"Come on. She was picking on the kid."

"She was trying to make you hear her."

"What are you so mad about? You're all upset. C'mere." He pulled me to him. "I know how to calm you down."

"Did you tell him he could have the knife?"

"Never mind the knife. Just—"

"I told you, Richard, we can't." I said it very slowly so he would hear it. "I lost a baby. I'm hurting. I don't want to be touched." His hand stopped moving. He lay very still. "If you're —if you want me to, I'll do what I did the other night."

He thought about it. "You want to?"

"It's okay."

"But do you want to?"

"Sure." I kept pushing it out of my mind as I pumped away at him, the picture of that sharp little blade coming near this boneless cylinder, slicing . . . no. Yes. Slicing through. No, Jesus, no.

246

43.

.I didn't even think of going out the next day. I called in a grocery order and another to the drugstore, and then I changed the sheets and got into bed. WNCN had Mahler's Fourth on, but even so it was very quiet in the room. Jessie didn't answer her phone. Neither did Laura. Finally I dialed Richard.

Frances answered. "Why hello, Mrs. Clahr. How's every little thing?"

"Fine, Frances. How are you?"

"Busy, dear. Want to speak to the boss?"

"Yes, but tell me first, how's your niece doing in college?"

"Just a minute, dear." Muzak in one ear, Mahler in the other. "Sorry. It's a madhouse here. Can't chat now, much as I'd like to. I'll connect you, all right?"

"Hi, babe. What's up?"

"Frances is back with you? That's good. Is it permanent?"

"Nothing's permanent around here except aggravation. What's—"

"But you're doing better? You got the New Jersey bid, right?"

"How come you don't ask me these things when I'm home? I can't talk now, baby. When I get home, we'll sit down with a drink and lock the kids out and I'll tell you all about it, if you're interested. Are you?"

247

No. But it's very quiet in here. "Of course."

"I'd never have known it." A silence. I couldn't help him with it. "So. What's up? I really have to—"

"Nothing. Just wanted to say hello."

"You did? Coming out of it, eh? That's good, baby. That's great. See you tonight, huh?"

"Right."

I was reading the paper and thinking of trying to reach Jessie at The New You when Gideon called.

"How's Cho-Cho-San?"

"Think I'm ready to sing *Butterfly*?"

"I think you're ready to be one. How is it, in the cocoon?"

"Quiet."

"Still violet silk?"

"Red today."

"Silk?"

"Yes." A little smile in my voice.

"Of course. What else would it be? Where do you buy them?"

"The nightgowns?"

"Yes."

Where would you buy silk nightgowns? I cast around. "Once in a while you find one among the polyesters. I always feel a little funny, buying—"

"No you don't. You feel exactly right. You look at the other ladies buying the cotton flannels and the sensible underpants and at the tramps buying cheap black bras, and you know exactly what you are and what you ought to wear, don't you?"

"I guess so." Talk about velvet in the lower ranges. Oh, Vincent, you're missing it. Tough. You left me.

"So do I. Believe it or not, when I've fantasized about you—and I do, I'm sorry, all the time—you'll have to forgive me, but I've pictured you in a silky blue nightgown. Not a baby blue, you know, like you give your mother on Mother's Day, but a strong, deep blue. When you said violet silk you just about did me in. Did you know it?"

248

"No, I just—"

"That's it. You're just you. You know, I think about you there in that bed, and I—put your hand on your throat."

"What?"

"Take your hand and put it on your throat. Just touch it. Got it there?"

"Why—"

"Now touch your mouth." I could hear the catch in his voice. "That's two kisses." My fingers were cold on my lips. "Beth, are you sitting up?" It was almost a whisper.

"Yes."

"Lie down. Please."

"Why? Gideon—"

"You are alone in your bed. I am alone in my office. Right now I can't touch you, and you aren't ready, this minute, to come to me. Are you?"

"No."

"But this minute I want to—have I gone too far? Are you horrified?"

"I should be."

"We're both long past that, whether you know it or not. Lie down, Beth, and close your eyes." Double rest. "Does the gown open?"

It didn't. "Yes."

"Open it."

I pushed it up. Slowly, gently. He does it very gently.

"Hurry. Touch your mouth again. Hard. Another kiss. Beth?"

"What? Gideon, I—"

"Nothing's happened. I can't really touch you, there in your cocoon. Right?"

"Yes."

"Both eyelids, love." *Love. He said* . . . "Touch them both. And all the ridges in your ear. And the side of your neck."

Simon says touch your—

"Is the gown open?"

"I—"

249

"All right, you don't have to say anything. Open your hand and slide it down over a breast. Move over it. Now touch the—Beth?"

"Yes?" *I love you, Beth. I love you. You're the only—*

"You won't hang up?"

"I—"

"Touch the nipple." That's his mouth. "That's my hand." I could hear his breathing. Gideon. Could he hear mine? The nightgown was bunched up around my shoulders. I buried the mouthpiece in its white folds. More, Gideon. I arched my ear against the phone as though it were his shoulder. More.

"Take one edge of the nightgown—I can see it, the red against your skin—and pull it back over one side of you. Run your hand over the silk, over you, from your breast to . . . down your side, down to your leg and back. Up. Jesus, Beth, I wish—" It was a whisper now, urgent. "Does it feel good, being touched through the silk? Beth?"

"Gideon—"

"Now listen. Listen, love. Touch yourself. Just lightly, at—"

"Gideon, I can't do that." I was wet, all wet, and the fingers were there, just lightly. I buried the mouthpiece deeper so he wouldn't hear me. He couldn't see me, could he? Wet, and harder now—

"Then let me do it. Christ, Beth. Get on a train and come here and let me."

"I can't. Gideon, I can't." I hung up the phone, fumbling, and we finished, coming, with his mouth hard on mine and me arching up against him. Oh God, Beth, I love you. Gideon. Love.

So I had to change the sheets again, and my nightgown. The phone rang when I was about to get back into the shower. It was Gideon.

"Are you all right?"

"Yes. I'm okay."

"I'm not. I understand why you hung up, but I'm not going to apologize. In a weird way, I think it's what you wanted: long-distance loving. I understand that, too. You think it leaves you

250

untouched. But it's too late for that, Beth, for either of us. I'll tell you something—when we finally get together, we'll know just how to touch each other because we've really been lovers for weeks and weeks. Don't you think I know how you want to be made love to? Didn't I just tell you I knew? Wasn't I right?"

Almost. "I can't—"

"Can't say it? You have to. It's time, now. Anyway, you have already. There's a whole Beth that no one knows but me. Isn't there? Who else knows about the singing, the way you tell it to me? Who else knows about your cocoon? Anyone?"

"No."

"Do you know why you told me about it?"

"No. I didn't mean to."

"You told me because you know that when you come out of it —and that'll be soon, you can't hang there very much longer— you want me to be there. I want to. But I won't play this way any-more. Sitting in my office making love by phone. Listen, love. Are you listening?"

"Yes." Don't go, Gideon. Don't—

"This is my last phone call. In the next day, or week—soon— you call me. Tell me you'll see me. Any way you like, as slowly as you like. Lunch. Walks. Whatever. But face to face, in the here and now. Do you have my office number?"

"No, I don't think—"

"Write this down. Are you ready?"

I grabbed a photograph out of the drawer. Me, holding Randy's hand and carrying Michael. All of us dressed up. I wrote the num-ber under the inscription on the back, "Mother's Day, 1974. Wave to Daddy."

I heard the doorbell as I finished writing the number. I shoved the photograph back into the drawer and pushed the drawer closed.

"I have to go, Gideon. Michael's home for lunch."

"All right. Good-bye. Call me, love. Please."

I wiggled frantically into a pair of jeans and pulled on a shirt and ran to the door, thinking, Allee allee infree, now I'm It.

44.

I thought about doing it, too, sitting cool and powdered in the bed after lunch. I thought about dressing and getting on the train—I could do it on a Wednesday; Richard didn't know Brescia was away—and just appearing in his office. Tag. Now you're It again. Or picking up the phone—now, even—and saying all right, Gideon. I'm ready. When? he'll ask and I'll say, Wednesday. And we'd have from now till Wednesday, both of us, to think about how to touch each other, knowing—

But I dialed Jessie's number instead and listened to the hollow ring, over and over, pulling cold fingers through my hair. I redialed it twice. No answer. I waited five minutes, watching the clock, and tried again. Still no answer. I tried Laura.

"Hi, honey. Where ya been? Haven't seen you around. You okay?"

"Sure. I've been spring cleaning."

"Sublimating the old drives, eh? How long's it been?"

Just this morning. I was with my lover this morning. "Forever. Meanwhile, it's great for getting the house clean. Listen, Laura, have you seen Jessie?"

"Last week in the village. She's real perky, but I thought she looked a little—"

"But not today?"

"No. Why? Is it—"

"Nothing. I'm just trying to track her down. Well, thanks. I've got to run now. Take care."

"Hang in there, honey; it can't be much longer now."

Right. I pulled the phone book out of a pile of stuff on the night table, knocking over a stack of camp clothes and the name tapes I'd been sewing into them. The name tapes scattered and looked up at me from the rug: RANDY CLAHR RANDY CLAHR RANDY CL. Little billboards. I found the number of The New You.

"Hello there. This is Alix. Jan and I are out of the shop just now. Please leave your name and phone number after the chime, and we'll call you just as soon—"

Try the hospitals, then. Which one? Hello, do you have a single-breasted candy striper named Jessie in your breast-surgery department? But which hospital?

That was when Leone called.

"How have you been?" she asked. "I haven't seen you since the luncheon. By the way, I don't know how many people said to me what a smashing job you did. And the feedback on that *man*. Now all we have to do is live up to it next year. Well, you don't have to worry about that, lucky you. How's your singing going?"

"Well, it's hard. I don't know if I'll ever be any good. But I really feel I have to give it a shot." That's right, Beth. Grovel a little. I found "hospitals" in the Yellow Pages. It was a long column.

"Well of course you'll be good. You'll be a star; we're counting on you. Look, I'll tell you why I called. I know you must be terribly upset, but I had to barge in and ask, because I know how close you are, you were so adorable and supportive to her at the luncheon when the rest of us just—well, but I told you then, that's how it went with my sister-in-law, too, poor soul." She stopped. The phone book closed. I lost my place.

RANDY CLAHR RANDY

"Ask me what?"

"Well, you know, how did it go this morning? I mean, I guess it can't be good, more surgery this soon, but do they think—"

253

"Jessie?"

She paused. Was she counting beats? "Well *yes*. I mean, if you don't want—"

"What do you mean, more surgery?"

"You didn't know? Or—I mean, it's okay, it's no secret. John told Jerry on the—"

"Please, Leone." I'll be good. I won't raise my voice. Only tell me, this time. Please. "Jessie had more surgery? When? Where?"

She told me all of it and I wrote it down inside the front cover of the phone book. "Sloan-Kettering. Op 6/14." Today, that was. "Other brst—and uterus?"

"Oh, I just feel terrible. I had no idea you didn't know. I can hear in your voice how—look, shall I come over?"

Why? You're not my mother. You're not even Jessie. "No. Thanks, Leone. I think I'd rather—"

"I understand. We'll talk when you're—listen, maybe we'll visit her together. Not that it's easy. It's like living it all over again with my sister-in-law, but—"

I must have said something polite. I must have hung up. Anyway, when Randy came in I wasn't still holding the phone. I sent her downstairs because I needed quiet to figure it out. This was Friday. I'd seen her . . . Wednesday? She was okay then. No, God, the strain in her face, the sweet smell. But she didn't tell me. Did she know? Sure. But she never told me. Like—

I heard them screaming downstairs and running, banging doors and squealing. I got up then and dressed and went downstairs. A mother should see to her children.

Randy came screaming around a corner as I walked into the dining room. I put out my hands. She stopped, threw herself into my arms. She was sweaty and breathing hard. "Save me!" she cried. I can't. "He's going to drag me to the corner! Save me! I don't want to look!" She hid behind me, giggling wildly, as Michael burst through the kitchen door after her. He stopped when he saw us and came at us slowly, stomping one bent leg and then the other, arms out and fingers curved to seize. "You will look at the Monster of Death," he chanted. He fought his glee to make a fierce face. "You will look—" he darted around me, almost grabbed her. She screamed and ran up the stairs. I caught him around the waist before he could follow her. He squirmed wildly. "Lemme go! She'll get away! She has to look at the M—" I put one hand over his mouth, held tighter around his middle with the other. In a few seconds he subsided, giggling sporadically behind my hand.

"If I let go, will you be still?" He nodded. I let go, keeping a hand poised to grab him. "Now what's all this?"

"He tried to drag me up the block to look at some grossifying thing." Randy, grinning and gasping, sprawled out on the top step, looking triumphantly down at Michael. "You jerk."

"Baby. Wouldn't even look at a mouse. A little teeny mousie," he squeaked. "Eeuw. Don't let the monster get me!"

"Shut up." She got up. "Sorry for the noise," she said to me. "He's your kid." She went into the bathroom and closed the door.

"Come on," I said to him. "You're filthy." I stood him in front of the kitchen sink and washed the sweat off his face with a wet paper towel. I was working on the hands when he said, "You wanna see it?"

"See what? You'll have to change your shirt. This is soaked."

"The *mouse*. You wanna hear?" He wiggled out of the shirt and stood balling it up in his hands. I smoothed his hair down. The skin on his chest was smooth and perfect. I could see the orderly line of ribs on each side.

"You saw a mouse?"

"*Yes*. In the street, up in front of Dawsons's. See, I was walking home from school and I saw it and at first I thought it was sleeping, 'cause it was lying like this—" Down he went on the kitchen floor, lying in a C, paws arched under his chin, knees tucked toward his belly, an innocent, mousy smile on his face. He opened his eyes. "Then I saw he was mushed on the other side. There were a couple of guts coming out. That was gross. But on the *first* side he was just a mouse." He sat up. "You wanna come and see it?"

"I've seen it."

255

"You saw it already?"

He came into focus. "No, honey. Not this one. But I've seen dead things. You do have to look closely, sometimes, to see that they're . . . mushed."

"How come you're crying?" His face was all wrinkled up, peering into mine. "You didn't even see it."

"Listen, Michael, I want you to change your shirt and go outside to play. Don't touch the mouse, okay?"

"Can I take Evan to see it?"

"Yes, but don't touch it. Promise." I cupped my hand under his chin and made him look at me. "Promise?"

"*Okay.*"

I went upstairs and knocked on the bathroom door. "Randy? I'm going to take a shower. You're in charge. Don't go anywhere. Stick around for Michael."

"But you're right—"

"Stay here, Randy. You're in charge."

I made the bed first, with a set of sheets that had been dried on the line. I took a long time and got it right. Corners lined up, bottom sheet very taut. Hospital corners on the top sheet, the top edge folded down straight. Pillow fluffed evenly into the pillowcase. The softest white nightgown was clean. That was lucky.

I took all the stuff off the night table and put it away. That took a little while, especially because I had to keep brushing the pictures out of my mind before I could get on with it. They were only pictures then. Snap. Richard and me naked on the bed, before the phone rang. Me with my hand on him there in Bermuda, and Mama lying trapped in blackness on the uneven tufts. Snap. Me, in my own bed, naked, holding the phone and Gideon's voice moving my hand down my own body, silky over my breasts and the knife slicing at Jessie, the breast falling away. Snap.

The room wasn't ready yet. I had to put all of Richard's things away. The newspaper. The magazines, his shirt from yesterday, his pajamas. His comb and brush. Out of sight. What else? The other pillow. His pillow. I put it in his closet and closed the door. All right. So then I took the rings off and put them away, and I clipped my nails and cleaned my ears and brushed my teeth and by the time I got into the shower, it wasn't just pictures—I had to sing to shut out the noise, but I couldn't sing, I couldn't make the sound come out. Sing, Beth. No. Michael. . . . Michael. All right. Michael was up the street. He had a dry shirt on, I washed him off so he was clean; but he wouldn't touch the mouse, would he? No, he promised. Door was open? Yes. He could come back in. Randy. Randy was home. In charge. Me on the bed with Richard. I wouldn't have gone, Mama, if I'd known I would never have let him touch me. The mouse is just a mouse, on the first side. Jessie. Guts coming out, but smiling on the first side. Jessie? Because of his hands, my hand, on me? Throat, breasts, silky over my thighs and up again. Touch yourself, Beth, just lightly. He wouldn't, would he? Touch the mouse? No. Randy is in charge. Jessie. I wouldn't have done it, Jessie, if I had known. But you didn't say, you only showed me the one side, Mama, the mouse side. Who will you be now, without breasts? New You. No. Dead. No, Jesus. Blackbird. No. Sing, Beth. I can't, Mama, he said Don't raise your voice, young lady. Then why did you beach the baby, little airless fish, if you weren't going to sing? Sing, damn you. Sing.

I dried off carefully and dried my hair, and powdered myself everywhere with the baby powder. I put on the nightgown. The noise came at me and came at me and my throat was locked but it was all right. I was on my way to being safe. Do it right, this time. Quiet. Alone. Still and safe.

I turned off the phone.

I lay down carefully. Nightgown smooth under me. I raised the sheet up over my own self and let it drift down over me. Sheet straight under me, flat over me. No wrinkles. Now don't move. This time, don't move. Do it right.

But there was Randy. Darker outside, and she stood by the side of my bed. "Daddy's on the phone."

"What does he want?"

She gestured at the phone, bewildered. I shook my head. "See

257

what he wants. Not here, downstairs." No time, and she was back. "He says he'll take the six-oh-four. I told him you were in bed, and he said he'd get home by himself." She was still standing there. "Aren't you going to practice your singing?"

"Not just now, honey."

She went away, but then there was Richard. Dark out now. I saw him just in time. "Don't touch my bed, Richard. Don't touch me or the bed. Please."

"You sick?"

No, I'm in my cocoon. Get away. "No, but I need to be alone and quiet for a while. I need the room to myself. Please, Richard, just for a while."

"You telling me you want me out?"

"I just need to be alone for a while."

"To think?"

"No, not to think."

"What about the kids? What about dinner?"

"Pizza. Or Laura will feed you. Or you can throw something together."

He left, and after a while the room was quiet again. But he came back and he had them with him. They were clean and brushed, and he had a suitcase. He opened drawers and doors and put things into the suitcase. Then he snapped it shut. "We're going out to my sister's, Beth. We'll be there when you—if you want us. There's gas in the Chevy. I'm taking the Olds. We'll wait to hear from you. Beth?" His voice cracked. "At Dot's, did you hear?"

"I heard. Have a nice time. Randy?" They had turned to go, but she was still there, by the bed. "Randy, don't be scared, honey. I'm not going to die or anything. I just really need to be quiet for a little while. Okay?"

"I could stay. You might need—"

"Let's go, Randy. I told you, she's not sick. She just wants a little peace and quiet. Right, Beth? Tell her."

"Right. That's right. Bye, troops. Tell Aunt Dot I said hello."

258

After they left, the noise was in the room, and his smell, so while I waited I switched on the phone and called Daniel Block.

"Feeling better? You ought to be bouncing around by now. In fact, I've been thinking—"

"Can you give me some information? I don't know who else to ask."

"Of course. What's the problem?"

I told him about Jessie. "And now it's only a couple of months later and she's had another mastectomy, and maybe the uterus, too."

"Mm. And you want to know—?"

"Will she—does it mean . . ."

"Who's the doctor?"

I told him.

"Tough. He's good, and very conservative. Not a mad slicer by any means. If he went in . . . I don't know, Beth, but—she's a good friend of yours?"

"Yes."

"Start saying good-bye. She may be lucky, but—inside yourself, you know, start saying good-bye."

"It's not what I do best."

"I don't imagine it is. But—"

"In fact, when people are away from me, I even think I can— you won't laugh?"

"No."

"It's ridiculous, I know it, but I think I have to keep them safe by keeping them in my mind. Then when they—something happens—I think that—"

"—it's your fault?"

"Yes. I mean, I *know*—"

"Do your kids exist separately from you? Do they go to school, make ashtrays, say funny things, get into trouble? Do their bodies grow without your making it happen?"

Randy, breasts under the T-shirt, tossing back her long hair. Michael, perfect skin over rows of precise arches of ribs.

259

"Yes. But I did stop one from . . . becoming."

"So life will punish you and abort the other two unless you breathe for them?"

He punished me for being away with Richard. And for my lip. For raising my voice. He buried Mama without me.

"Beth? Do you really think that? And if you'd concentrated enough on your friend, the cancer would have melted away?"

"No. I know it wouldn't. I'm not crazy, just—"

"Just tied to people. And so used to having them tied to you that you lost track of the limits of your power over each other. All of us wish we could keep the people we love safe. And that someone could keep us safe. Look, I'm a doctor. Don't you think I wish I could keep it all from happening? I'll tell you what I know, Beth. It's random and senseless. You do what you can, but it's out of your hands in the end. And that's how it is."

That's how it is.

You can raise your voice now.

45.

I switched the phone off. It was quiet now and I laid my head on the pillow and sang to my own self, Toora loora. I smoothed my own hair, smoothed it, smoothed it, and sang toora loora out loud all the way through. One last time. I smiled. And then it was quiet for a very long time.

46.

The sunshine unrolled me when it was time. It pulled at my arm and the side of my face and rolled me out. I stood up and went to the window, still rolling, bare and dizzy in the sunlight.

After a while I switched the phone back on and went downstairs, ravenous for breakfast. I was devouring a pile of scrambled eggs when the phone rang.

"Hello? Is this Mrs. Clahr?"

"This is Beth Clahr."

"Good morning, Mrs. Clahr. My name is Kathy Something. I am a representative of Liberty Foods, and we—"

"What day is this, Kathy?"

"The seventeenth, I believe."

I checked the calendar. Monday. Jesus.

"—to offer you our unique service. What we do, Mrs. Clahr, is deliver to your home each month your selection of fresh and frozen foods and premium meats, cut to your order and packaged for the freezer. We have a complete selection of frozen and packaged goods, and an extensive dairy line as well. Our representative, Mrs. Clahr, would be happy to—"

I almost did it. It sounded so easy. Never to go out to the supermarket. Never to bear it all home from the market. But then I thought, What about all the stuff I used to look at even if I didn't buy it? The Pyrex custard cups and the flowers and the canned pâté, and the raspberries. If Liberty brings all the groceries, I might never see a raspberry again. So I thanked her and said no.

Monday. I'd better go and get the kids, they belong in school. I'd better call Dot and ask her to get them ready.

But I wandered into the bathroom instead and tried out my voice. It was croaky. Didn't use it for two, no, three days. Can't do that again, I told myself in the mirror, knowing that I wouldn't. Then I looked around. What am I doing in here? I can sing anywhere.

So I sang in the living room, in my nightgown in the sun. I had to work up to it, and I didn't even try the songs. But at the end of an hour I had it back: my voice, clear and strong. Then I was hungry again. I found a pear in the fruit basket on the kitchen table. It was warm from the sun, and more liquid than solid. I wiped the juice off my chin and found the number of Sloan-Kettering and rang Jessie's room.

She answered the phone herself. "How are you?" I asked. Gone.

"I'm a goner, Toots." It hung in the air.

"Are you sure?"

"Yeah, but I'll tell you this, I'm sure as hell going out kicking and screaming and snorting and whooping. None of this sweet martyr stuff for me, sliding out under the door. They want me, let 'em come and drag me out by the heels. Right?"

"Right. What I can't figure out is why would They want you?"

"Damned if I know. I've been lying here planning my—what's the opposite of a debut? Whatever, it's going to be an extravaganza. Will you sing me out, Cookie? You owe me one, you know. You never did come up with that fella."

"Jessie." I relaxed my vocal cords, made the words come out easy. "I'll sing you out. What hymn? Not that it'll help."

" 'There'll Be a Hot Time in the Old Town Tonight,' I thought. Or 'Roll Me Over in the Clover.' That'd be suitable . . . you know, discreet and tasteful but to the point. Say, speaking of fast living, how're you making out in your spare time? Did

263

you find us each a fella? You may have to use 'em both, is the only thing. How slow *is* that carriage?"

"I don't know how much spare time I'll have, actually. My singing teacher comes back Wednesday, and the summer session starts. I think I'm going to go into a full-time voice program."

"Well, it doesn't hold a candle to foolin' around, but then as far as I know, foolin' around never got anyone to the Met. Not to sing, anyhow. Hey, is that voice stuff going to cut into my time?" A hollow sound now, and lost. "I'll be home next week, me and the White Tornado. You going to have time to sit with the corpse?"

"I'll be around so much you'll be sick of me."

"Maybe you'll sing for me. Kill two birds with one stone."

"I'll sing to you every day. Every day. Give 'em hell, Jess."

"Are you kidding? They'll remember me here for years. Bye, Toots."

So will I, Jess. It's all I can do to save you, and I will damn well remember you for all my years. A promise.

11:30. Too late to get the kids to school anyway. I called Dot. Randy answered the phone.

"How are you?" she asked me. She sounded polite and formal.

"I'm fine. I had a wonderful rest. I'm good as new—better. How are you guys?"

"Okay. Michael fell off Tommy's bike. It was too big for him, but he had to ride it."

"Is he hurt?"

"Don't *panic*. He just got a cut. And Tommy's mad at him because he dented the fender. Are you coming to get us?"

"I have something I have to do in the city. Then I'll take the train out there and meet you and Daddy and we'll all have dinner somewhere and come home. Where's Daddy?"

"He took the day off. He and Aunt Dot went out to get Tommy's bike fixed and then we're going shopping for stuff for me. Should he call you?"

"No. Tell him I'm fine, and I'm going to Mannes to change my schedule for next semester. I'll meet you at Aunt Dot's at five o'clock. Okay?"

"Sure. See you."

"Rand?"

"Yeah?"

"I can't wait to see you."

"Are you—never mind."

"What?"

"It's just—are you okay to go to the city? Out?"

"Yes, I'm okay to go out. I had a semester break and it's over, and now I'm up and ready to go. Better than new, I told you."

"Michael missed you. He was afraid you'd never come for us."

"But—"

"But I told him you just needed some sack time and then it would be like always."

"It may not be just like always. I've decided to go to school full time next year, and after a couple of years of that I may have to travel sometimes, to sing."

"We can come with you. In your private jet."

"Sure. Or anyway, I'll send you a cute boy from London."

"I'd rather pick out my own."

Right. "We'll work it out. Five o'clock. I love you, Miranda."

"Love you too. Sing good."

"Well."

"Good."

"Bye."

"Bye."

I showered and dressed. Almost time to leave, if I was going to make the train. I made the bed in a hurry, then looked around the room. I went and got Richard's pillow out of the closet. He lives here. Can't expect him to sleep on the couch while he lives here.

I started out of the room, then went back and rooted around

265

among the photos in the night table drawer until I found the one with Gideon's number on the back. I stuck it into my pocketbook and closed the drawer on the others.

The car was at a stoplight halfway to the station when I looked at my hands on the wheel and realized I hadn't put the rings back on. Well, too late to go back. Then, gliding down the hill and around the corner to the station, I heard the quiet. I held my breath and listened. Nothing. See, Randy? I came out.

N.